# Carroll Multz

# The Devil's Scribe

D1604424

# Other titles by Carroll Multz

**The Chameleon**- The Chameleon is an undercover cop and master of deception. As he lives and works in the world of illusion, he neglects the real world and the family that finally gives up on him. When he realizes what he has sacrificed, he is determined not to blow his second chance at love and happiness. Meanwhile, he continues to try and solve the execution-style slaying of his father, a former FBI agent. His hopes begin to fade when he discovers the woman he loves is connected to an underworld kingpin. As everything unravels and he is plunged deeper into danger and darkness he also learns this man is perhaps the very person responsible for his father's death. The Chameleon must play the role of a lifetime so he can finally step out of the shadows.

**License to Convict**- Morrey Dexter wasn't used to losing. As a district attorney in Paraiso County, Colorado, Morrey owned the courtroom. He was dauntless in his quest to seek justice, committed to his sense of fairness, and vigilant in his role as a protector of the community. But, when a surprising verdict shakes his faith in the system, he begins to see that things are not as simple as they appear. Can Morrey use his license to convict to preserve the things he holds sacred?

**Deadly Deception**- Everywhere he looks, Harvard grad and former golden boy Drew Quinlin from the district attorney's office sees Joy's piercing turquoise eyes. He tries to end their affair and things spin wildly out of control. There is a horrible accident and Joy is dead. Now Drew Quinlin is drawn into the biggest case of his career, defending the person charged with her death--her husband. Will winning an acquittal appease his tortured conscience or will judgment come before he can atone for his crime?

**Justice Denied**- Max has come home to help. His father, Jamie Cooper, a devoted dad and faithful employee is accused of stealing $30,000 from the bank for which he worked. He hires a defense team and fights to clear his name, but will that be enough to battle the combined strength of the town's powerful chief of police, a man who has held a grudge against the Cooper family for years?

**Shades of Innocence** - The years come and pass in a flurry, much like the seasonal snows of Paris. What was no longer is in the lives of Crimson and Jade Ziang, identical twins, whose respective destinies were forged long before their births. The outward manifestation of the inevitable and unavoidable is that of the yin-yang, an ancient Chinese symbol sacred to their ancestors, which was tattooed to their right ankles at birth in order to tell the two apart. Their tattoos are not their only distinguishing features. Their inner souls are as different as day and night. One bespeaks selflessness; the other selfishness. When Jade flees the family after high school graduation, Crimson and older brother, Indigo, are left to maintain family unity and to try to mitigate her parents' heartbreak at her desertion. Thirty years later, the three siblings must play their preordained parts in a tragedy that leaves the reader asking, "Do we shape our destiny or does our destiny shape us?" Follow the intriguing tale as it unfolds in Carroll Multz's new novel, Shades of Innocence, and be prepared for its many twists and turns and especially its riveting and unexpected conclusion.

# The Devil's Scribe

## A Novel

**BRASS FROG BOOKWORKS™**
Independent Publishers
Grand Junction, Co

# CARROLL MULTZ

Published by BRASS FROG BOOKWORKS™ Independent Publishers
2695 Patterson Rd. Unit 2-#168 | Grand Junction, CO 81506
909-239-0344 or 970-434-9361 | www.BrassFrogBookworks.com

Brass Frog Bookworks is dedicated to excellence and integrity in the publishing industry. The company was founded on the belief in the power of language and the spiritual nature of human creativity.
*"In the beginning was the Word…"* John 1:1
Book design copyright © 2013 by Brass Frog Bookworks™
All rights reserved.
Cover & Interior Design: JL Leon
www.ClickCreativeMedia.com

Inquiries should be addressed to:
Carroll Multz
859 Quail Run Dr.
Grand Junction, CO 81505

Printed in the United States of America | First Printing 2013
Library of Congress Control Number:    2013947551
ISBN: 978-0-9857191-4-2
1.    Fiction/Legal   2.   Fiction/Suspense   3.   Fiction/Romance
Set in Garamond 11pt

# DEDICATION

*This book is dedicated to my journalism students past, present, and future, and to journalists everywhere. May their quest to enlighten and inspire never be deterred.*

# CARROLL MULTZ

## ACKNOWLEDGEMENTS

This novel about the media in general, and journalists in particular, is a composite of knowledge and insight gleaned through wearing the hats of a producer and host of a weekly television program, co-host of a television series, co-host of a radio talk show, co-host of a radio series, guest editorial writer for a newspaper and contributing author for various publications. To Channel 3 Cablevision, KJCT TV – Channel 8, KREX Radio, KPIK Radio, *The Gazette Telegraph* and *The Daily Sentinel*, I am most grateful for having had the opportunity.

To the following members of the media and journalists, who provided the impetus and inspiration for this novel, I bow: Richard Kirby, Hal Oyler, Paul Unwin, Don Teets, George James, George Orbanek, Jay Seaton, Laurena Davis, Bob Silbernagel, Gary Harmon, George Vahsholtz, Bob Sweeney, Ellen Miller and Mike Moran.

My perspective would not be what it is had it not been for my journalism law and ethics students at Colorado Mesa University, from whom I learned so much these past twenty-two years. I am grateful to them and a friend and fellow professor in the mass communication department at CMU, Byron Evers, who con- scripted me to teach the course, lo, those many years ago.

# THE DEVIL'S SCRIBE

For preparation and review of the manuscript, I am indebted to the following: my daughters Elizabeth Knudsen and Natalie Lowery, Dr. Arline Burnell, Jeanine Linster, Amber Burnell and Judy Blevins.

And last but not least, to my publisher Brass Frog Bookworks, I share the curtain call. Thank you, Patti Hoff and Jan Weeks.

# CARROLL MULTZ

## TABLE OF CONTENTS

# THE DEVIL'S SCRIBE

*The pen is mightier than the sword.*

*Baron Lytton*

## INTRODUCTION

A journalist must wield the power of the pen wisely, for it can be as lethal as a sword, spear, bullet, or bomb–depending on how it is used. It is a power that, if abused, can have disastrous and irreversible consequences. The pen has toppled governments, exposed corruption, brought leaders to their knees, and has solved crimes and thwarted criminals. Unfortunately, from time to time, there is unintended collateral damage–damage that cannot be rectified by an apology or a retraction. Sometimes it is not possible to put Humpty Dumpty back together again. Distorting the truth is not something ethical journalists do wittingly.

With every great power comes great responsibility. He who has power over another has power over the other's life, whether it is physical, mental or emotional. And sometimes, the stroke of the pen means death.

# PROLOGUE

On Thursday, May twentieth, Sister Mary Catherine rushed anxiously down the long tiled corridor to the large corner room at the far end. She knocked frantically on the solid oak door. There was no response. She knocked again, only this time more assertively. Still no response. Not wanting to awaken the other sisters, she hastily retreated to her station at the front of the building. Her trembling fingers dialed extension one twenty-eight, the quarters of Sister Agnes Cecelia, the Mother Superior of St. Vincent de Paul Orphanage. She let the telephone ring long enough to arouse even the most ardent sleeper. No answer. Mother Superior was not in her room.

It was past midnight and past curfew. Sister Catherine felt panic roiling in the pit of her stomach as she raced to the chapel at the other end of the building. She hesitated at the entrance and crossed herself, trying to calm her pounding heart. There in the Lady of Sorrows Chapel, she found Sister Agnes Cecelia kneeling in prayer, an onyx rosary between her fingers. As a novice, Sister Catherine was hesitant to interrupt Mother Superior, especially in the middle the night, and while she was saying the rosary. Tonight she was left with no other choice.

"Mother," Sister Catherine blurted, "someone has left a baby at our front door."

A pale, bespectacled woman in her early sixties stopped praying and looked up. "A what?" she asked, certain she had heard incorrectly.

"A baby," Sister Catherine insisted, clasping her hands nervously over her mouth. "Alive and wrapped in a fluffy white blanket."

Mother pulled herself to her feet and straightened the folds of her black habit. "A baby," she repeated doubtfully. "Show me."

The two nuns hurried to the front entrance, their habits billowing behind them like two ships sailing into port.

"I assume you did not leave the baby alone on the front stoop," Mother said gruffly.

"Of course not! After I received the telephone call instructing me to look outside, I promptly went out and confirmed the call was not a prank. I brought the precious little bundle into the office and put it in one of the leather chairs." She pointed to the overstuffed chair that had been pushed against the wall to keep the child from falling.

"What's the gender of our surprise package, or is that a surprise as well?" Mother asked brusquely.

"Well, since it was not wrapped in a blue or a pink blanket, I don't know for sure."

Mother's eyebrows formed a stern arch and she stared at Sister Catherine for a moment, not the least bit amused by the reply. Just then the baby stirred and started to cry. Sister Catherine lifted the baby into her arms and finally succeeded in quieting its wails, at least for the moment.

"Mother, whoever left this little one with us also left a bag of supplies. There is a bottle and extra formula."

Mother fumbled through the diaper bag and found the bottle. She handed it to Sister Catherine, who placed the nipple between the baby's eager lips. It wasn't until then they discovered the child had a cleft palate. Once the baby was fed, soothed, and changed, it was determined that the baby deposited on the front steps of St. Vincent de Paul Orphanage that quiet moonlit night was a girl.

Suddenly overcome by a feeling of exhaustion, Mother Cecelia dropped into a chair and sighed, her face pinched into a frown. "You must tell me everything."

Sister Catherine adjusted the sleeping infant in the crook of her arm, unexpectedly feeling protective. "I was working at my desk when the phone rang. The caller was a man with a young-sounding voice. It was clear he was nervous, but insistent that I go to the front entrance and look outside, as something important had been left there. I told him I would only go if he waited on the line. He must have gotten scared or suspected the call was being traced because that is when he blurted out that it was a five-day-old baby out on the doorstep."

Mother Cecelia shook her head and clucked her tongue. "Dear me–"

"Of course I dropped the phone and rushed outside, realizing then the call was *not* a hoax. I discovered this poor little foundling and a diaper bag filled with formula and supplies." She dabbed at moistness filling her eyes with the edge of her sleeve. "I'm sure the caller was a relative, perhaps the father. Of course that is my own conjecture." She hung her head.

Sister Catherine was having a difficult time stifling her emotions. *Who would do such a thing?*

Mother Cecelia patted the girl's shoulder reassuringly. "We cannot judge whoever left this child on our doorstep. We will pray for that miserable soul and seek God's will for this one." She sighed and studied the floor for a moment. "Perhaps she was abandoned because of her imperfection."

"What a cruel thing to do," Sister

Catherine murmured, tears threatening to flood her cheeks.

"We can't judge what we don't fully know or understand," Mother Cecelia reminded her. "I'm sure there is a rational basis for the parents' decision. This is not the first time this sort of thing has happened, and no doubt, will not be the last. All we know is that God has brought her to us. Whatever the reason is for abandoning this child, it was a merciful one, when you consider alternatives."

"I suppose you're right," Sister Catherine admitted, not wanting to think of an innocent child being aborted.

Mother pressed her lips together thoughtfully as she picked up the diaper bag and sorted through it, hoping to find something that would give them more information. There were bottles, formula, diapers, ointment and a few articles of clothing, but at the very bottom was an envelope containing fifty crisp $100 bills. Nothing more.

"Oh, my…" Sister Catherine's eyes widened.

Mother Cecelia frowned at the money, letting the bills flutter into her lap. She cast a pitying glance at the sleeping infant and thought a moment before she finally spoke. "The baby will be placed in our orphanage," she decided. "First thing tomorrow morning we will have our attorney, Murray Kingman, start the paperwork. If this matter should somehow leak to the press, caring for this infant will send a powerful statement affirming the Catholic Church's stance against abortion. The birth and relinquishment of this innocent child is definitely a welcomed alternative."

Sister Catherine let out a sigh of relief, and pulled the child closer to her chest.

"She will need a name," mused Mother Cecelia.

Sister Catherine suddenly brightened. "Since she was left here with us on May twentieth, the feast of St. Bernardine of Siena, how about naming her Bernadine Siena?"

A smile tugged at the corners of the older woman's mouth. "I'm sure in this instance, St. Bernardine would not object to the feminizing of his name. She will be called Bernadine Catherine Siena."

The younger sister smiled and gently stroked the newborn's cheek with her finger.

While St. Vincent de Paul Orphanage pondered the future of Bernadine Catherine Siena, her parents pondered her fate.

Between sobs, the mother blurted, "My doctor is not God, you know! How could you do such a thing?"

The father pulled the mother close and lovingly wrapped his arms around her. "We had no choice. We have two doctors telling us that it is in the best interests of both you and the baby that we give her up for adoption."

"With all the medication, I can't think straight. The consent form I signed I felt was coerced. I don't want to give up my baby!" The mother then buried her head in her hands and sobbed uncontrollably.

"There, there," the father said as he tried to soothe his wife. "We are only doing this to preserve and enhance the quality of life for both you and the baby."

"To take away a mother from her child and a child away from her mother hardly enhances the quality of life for either." Hanging her head and clinging to the pink identification bracelet that had been placed on her newborn shortly after the baby's birth, the mother went to be alone.

# CHAPTER 1

## THE PULITZER PRIZE

**Thirty-six years later**

Nadine had always been behind the proscenium. She never felt the need to be in the spotlight, content to fade into the background. Now, Bernadine Catherine Siena would return to Columbia University, her *alma mater,* and be center stage–the main highlight of the event. She was being presented with the prestigious Pulitzer Prize for distinguished achievement in investigative journalism, one of the highest awards a journalist could claim. Though she had not started out as the head of her class, she certainly was there now.

Sister Catherine, now Mother Superior Catherine, had been by her side every step of the way, as a surrogate mother, sister, cheerleader and coach. Even during childhood Mother Catherine had been there to love and care for her through numerous surgeries to correct her cleft palate. She had taken the little abandoned ugly duckling through every challenge and watched her blossom into the beautiful woman she had become: a tall, trim, attractive brunette with penetrating dark eyes, olive complexion, fine features and a broad, ingratiating smile. Nadine fiercely loved Mother Catherine and cherished the special bond they shared. There was no one more fitting to be with her for this amazing experience.

The Pulitzer Prize was not something Nadine had sought or even dreamt of receiving. When she attended Columbia, she admired the exploits of Joseph Pulitzer and his furious circulation battle between his publication, *The New York World,* and William Randolph Hurst, a second generation publishing magnate that used yellow journalism to influence public opinion through his primary publication, *The San Francisco Examiner.* Pulitzer did not succumb to the tactics of yellow journalism. Instead, he became a crusader known for holding the rich and the powerful accountable, and as a champion of the First Amendment. He was the quintessential investigative journalist. It was his work that initially piqued her interest in journalism and what shaped her belief in the concept that the welfare of all basic human rights was dependent upon freedom of expression and, of course, freedom of the press. Today she would be able to share that belief with the world.

Groups of well-dressed people threaded their way across the meticulously manicured campus of the Columbia University and made their way toward the steps of the Low Library. The building rises majestically from the landscape amidst the broad canopies of mature trees, trimmed grass, fountains, statues and artfully placed flower beds, bursting with color. The neo-classical architecture was reminiscent of Rome's ancient Pantheon with its high, granite domed roof and fluted marble columns. That impression was punctuated by the striking bronze busts of Zeus and Apollo that flank the entrance.

Guests were guided to the entrance between thick velvet ropes. Inside, light streamed through the high windows of the rotunda. Crystal sparkled atop elaborately set tables draped with wine-colored linen. Waiters in immaculate white coats scurried from table to table, filling pitchers in final preparation for the prestigious luncheon. Docents escorted guests to their seats while the chamber orchestra played softly in the background. Nadine smiled and thanked the docent as he led them to a table near the stage. She looked around nervously as she and Mother Catherine were seated and began chatting with other guests. The auditorium filled quickly and the background music was replaced with the tinkling of glasses and silverware and the din of conversation.

There was a brief electronic squeal when the emcee turned on the microphone. Immediately, as if on cue, the clamor of the crowd subsided, and every head pivoted toward the stage. The guests were greeted by the emcee. Then he introduced the first speaker. The award ceremony had commenced. Mother Catherine reached over and squeezed Nadine's hand.

The presenter was Dr. Phillip Newell, Dean of the School of Journalism and one of Nadine's former professors. After outlining the six reporting categories, and presenting the prizes in the first, he announced that the second award category would be for a distinguished example of investigative newspaper reporting by an individual.

"This award," he emphasized, smiling out at the crowd, "was based on the relevance of the topic, the quality and depth of research, resourcefulness, and writing excellence."

As her name was called and echoed through the auditorium, despite knowing she was a recipient, Nadine found herself hesitant, almost paralyzed for a moment. There was a vague sensation of her legs carrying her forward, but everything around her blurred and seemed to move in slow motion as she made her way to the podium. Her ears only caught bits and pieces of Dr. Newell's presentation.

"We are extremely honored" he continued, "to bestow this most prestigious Pulitzer award in the investigative reporting category to Nadine Siena, a reporter for the *Candela Daily Mirror.*"

His speech was interrupted by a round of applause while Nadine stood wide eyed and trembling at the edge of the stage.

"Ms. Siena sacrificed her own safety and well-being to uncover and document the mental, physical and sexual abuse taking place in a mental health facility in Pembrooke, Kansas. What she discovered was more far reaching than what she or anyone could have imagined. Her story has blown the lid off abuses happening all over the country and has already initiated legislation advocating for the protection and rights of the mentally ill in no less than a dozen states. Ms. Siena's poignant story titled 'Seeking Asylum' was chronicled in a ten-part, front-page series. This series was subsequently picked up by news outlets across the country, and led to other investigations. We are pleased to be given the opportunity to announce to Ms. Siena that the Head of House for Simon & Schuster is a guest today. He has come to this celebration specifically to meet with Ms. Siena, as his company has expressed an interest in producing this amazing story as a book."

The audience applauded as Dr. Newell turned and looked at Nadine and smiled. For a moment she couldn't breathe. *A book?* Her thoughts were spinning. The idea of doing a book had not even once come to mind. Suddenly she was cued to come to the podium. Nadine swallowed her nerves and crossed the stage. She stood next to Dr. Newell.

"It is now my privilege to present this official certificate, together with a check for $10,000, to Nadine Siena of the *Candela Daily Mirror*, winner of this year's Pulitzer Prize for excellence in investigative reporting."

They shook hands as she accepted the prize. In that same moment she was suddenly blinded by a wave of flashbulbs lighting up all over the room. She could only stand there, crimson rising in her cheeks, as the audience rose to its feet in a long round of applause. Dr. Newell nodded toward the podium, then took his seat on the other side of the stage.

Nadine adjusted the mic and cleared her throat. "Dr. Newell, members of the Pulitzer Board, ladies and gentlemen, fellow recipients," she began. "The mentally ill are among the most vulnerable of all populations. They are, and have been over the years, largely forgotten. Two years ago one hundred and twenty-three patients died under suspicious circumstances while institutionalized in a facility that was supposed to be caring for them. No one had answers for what happened to these fragile souls. No one seemed to care. That was the impetus for starting my investigation–trying to be the voice of the voiceless.

"The nightmare of the 'treatments' given to psychiatric patients in general, such as insulin shock treatment, electroconvulsive therapy, psychotropic drugs and lobotomy, pales in comparison to the ongoing conditions in which patients were forced to live, confined in what amounts to cages, locked in rooms for hours on end and not provided with adequate food and water. I saw these confinements with my own eyes. Even little children, after being drugged into numbness, were left to wallow in their own excrement. I reviewed that data of seventy-one studies conducted by fourteen countries over a period of ten years dealing with reports of violence against mentally ill patients around the world. No, ladies and gentlemen, the problem is not confined to Pembrooke alone. Pembrooke is only one small example of what is happening on a broad scale. It is an epidemic that carries with it a long, dark history. But this was only the beginning.

"Then there was the graveyard. You see, in addition to the many tortures and indignities suffered by the mentally ill, violence and sexual abuse by their caretakers, is rampant. There have been countless pregnancies as a result. This was one of the darkest secrets to be brought to light. The pregnancies are hidden, babies are delivered, their spines clipped and their discarded bodies buried for many years in the vacant acreage just north of the Pembrooke facility. There are other secrets buried there. These are women of all ages who became pregnant and perished as a result of attempted abortion. They, too, rest in the forgotten field with the children. The silence of that place is filled with their pain and anguish.

"I was struck by the fact that nothing grows in that field, almost like a testament to the secret it holds. The bones of the innocent have not yet been completely exhumed, so we don't have an actual number of victims yet. What has happened to the human heart that it is capable of dealing such cruel misery in what we like to believe is a civilized nation like the United States?" She paused as her eyes scanned the audience and a slight quaver of emotion formed in her voice. "I dedicate this award to them, to the mentally ill who have, until now, had no voice.

"Joseph Pulitzer, the pioneer for whom this award was named, was every bit a journalist and more. He didn't merely gather, write, publish and disseminate the news. As a crusader, he helped create the news. The role of guardian was and is something Joseph Pulitzer and others like ourselves who seek to emulate him consider most sacred. Ours is a position of trust and confidence, and the legacy of Joseph Pulitzer shall

forever serve as reminder to all of us in this most noble
of all professions.

"I now know what Baron Lytton meant when
he said, 'The pen is mightier than the sword.' We have
it within our power to bring about needed change. We
can no longer sit idly by and watch bad things happen
to people incapable of helping themselves. Everyone
should be held accountable for their actions. And, if it
is left to the press to make sure that that happens, then
so be it. I thank the Pulitzer Board for recognizing my
work, for honoring me with this award, but most of all
for providing a voice for those incapable of speaking for
themselves."

The audience rose to its feet and offered a
rousing applause, clearly touched by her words. Mother
Catherine made her way to the front of the auditorium
and threw her arms around Nadine's shoulders as she
exited the stage. She couldn't believe she was hugging
the Pulitzer Prize winner who thirty-six years before was
no larger than a loaf of bread—a castaway.

When Nadine introduced Mother Catherine to
Dr. Newell after the ceremony, it became apparent that
somehow Mother Catherine had been involved in the
nomination process leading to the awarding of the
Pulitzer. The tipoff was Dr. Newell's greeting as they
shook hands.

"Well, we finally meet after all the telephone

calls."

Mother Catherine cast a furtive glance toward Nadine and then shrugged absently. All Nadine could do was smile and roll her eyes. Surely it was divine providence that she had been placed in the hands of Mother Catherine or, more aptly that Mother Catherine had been placed in her life. There had been many times while growing up when she wondered about her biological parents and why they had abandoned her. Today, none of that mattered. Behind it all Nadine felt certain there was a divine plan for her life–a grand scheme. Though she could not see it clearly, she wondered where it would lead her.

# CHAPTER 2

## THE EMPIRE STATE

Blaring car horns and the rumble of traffic reverberated off the tall buildings as Nadine emerged from the hotel. The doorman smiled and hailed a cab, holding the car door for her with a white-gloved hand as she climbed inside.

"Where to?" asked the cabbie in a dull tone, glancing back at her in the rear view mirror.

"Trump Tower. Midtown West, please."

He nodded and flipped on the meter, then jammed his foot on the accelerator, forcing his way into the line of traffic. Nadine held her breath as the endless procession of cars behind them hit their brakes in unison with an angry screeching sound and a cacophony of blasting horns and epithets.

"You crazy bastard! Get off the road!" *Honk! Honk!*

The cabbie paid no attention to the commotion as he rocked the steering wheel and zigzagged through the midday traffic, Nadine tried to calm the nerves fluttering in waves at the pit of her stomach. She had agreed to have lunch with Ronald Morgenstein, the Head of House for Simon and Schuster. They had arranged to meet at Jean Georges, an upscale restaurant known for its excellent French cuisine. Nadine knew she was being offered a book deal. *Hopefully I can make it through this lunch without doing something completely lame.*

The cab pulled over in front of the Trump Tower and came to an abrupt stop. The driver glanced over his shoulder and frowned at Nadine as she rummaged through her wallet for money to pay the fare. He impatiently tapped his left thumb against the steering wheel, waiting. Nadine paid him and climbed out onto the sidewalk, barely closing the door before the cab lurched back into the flow of traffic. She tugged on her blazer and smoothed her hair before she went inside.

Ronald Morgenstein was a large-framed man with a friendly smile. His dark tailored suit impeccably fit his frame, and his thick mane of graying hair was perfectly styled. He stood up and extended his hand as the maître d' ushered Nadine across the elegant dining room to the table. Morgenstein's affable manner was disarming and Nadine relaxed a bit as she sat down.

After a delicious lunch and a two-hour meeting, Nadine accepted his offer. Of course the contract would need to be drawn up and timelines established, but she accepted the arrangement.

Morgenstein sipped the last of his wine and

dabbed his mouth with his napkin. "Look, Ms. Siena"

"Please, call me Nadine."

"Nadine, I know you are new to the game and this must all be terribly overwhelming, but for your verbal acceptance of our offer today, I will give you my personal assurance, and that of Simon & Schuster, that we will match *any* deals the other houses may pitch before our contract is executed. I know you will likely get calls from Random House, McGraw Hill, and perhaps one or more of the smaller houses. We all know each other's business. Hell, we're all in the same town.

"I also think you should find a good literary attorney to help handle all of this for you. It will be worth it in the long run." He smiled. "You are going to be in this game for as long as you want to be."

"I accept your offer, Mr. Morgenstein," she repeated.

"Good! We are so pleased to have you aboard. Here is my card. Give me a call on the twentieth around ten in the morning. That should give you time to hire an attorney and get your feet on the ground."

"That's perfect." She could barely contain her euphoria.

"Oh, and if you need help finding a good attorney, you can call my secretary and she can provide some referrals."

Morgenstein gestured to the waiter, who

discreetly brought him the bill.

"Would you please have my driver meet us out front?"

The waiter nodded politely. "Of course, Mr. Morgenstein."

"Nadine, why don't you let me drop you off at your hotel?"

She started to protest.

"No trouble," he assured her, and ushered her toward the door.

Nadine's head was still spinning when she returned to the hotel where she had arranged to meet Mother Catherine who spent all morning shopping. There was so much to talk about. They collected their luggage and waited out front where the doorman hailed a cab for them. There was still a little time for some sightseeing before they headed for the airport.

Even though it was fast, noisy, crowded and rude, Nadine had always loved the hustle and bustle of New York City. It was the first city where she learned people could be alone together. It wasn't anything like Pembrooke, where everyone knew everyone else. On the streets of New York City, people seemed preoccupied and seemed to look past each other, as if to avoid eye contact at all cost. She learned early that a friendly greeting to a stranger in New York ended in a scowl, or a query about how much she charged for her "services." It was here she learned the true purpose of a car horn, and the importance of certain words and gestures used as a backup.

Nadine didn't have time to familiarize Mother Catherine with every local haunt, although they did visit the Empire State Building and Times Square. Perhaps in the future she could bring Mother Catherine back to visit the Statue of Liberty and see a Broadway show. For Mother Catherine, her first trip to New York City would have been a dismal failure had she not experienced firsthand the sacred magnificence of St. Patrick's Cathedral. They marveled at the beauty of the vaulted ceilings, the magnificent statues and ornate friezes. The two of them took time to kneel in prayer and light a candle before they left. Nadine couldn't help but remember Mother Catherine telling her since childhood to trust God because nothing was impossible with Him. Today confirmed it.

The taxi ride to John F. Kennedy International Airport was somewhat of a spiritual experience for Mother Catherine. She said a full rosary and several heartfelt acts of contrition as the taxi lurched and zigzagged its way through the busy streets of New York City. The driver spent every minute of the ride hunched over the wheel like a madman, either pounding on the horn or shrieking obscenities out the window. Each time he would glance in the rear view mirror as if he had forgotten one of his passengers was a nun.

Meanwhile, Mother Catherine spent most of the ride with her eyes closed and completely overcome by fear. She linked her arm though Nadine's and gripped her hand. When the cab finally screeched to a halt in front of the airport terminal, her legs were shaking so hard she had to hold onto the edges of the door and drag herself out of the car.

The taxi driver was praised and appropriately rewarded by Mother Catherine—mainly for delivering them to the airport alive. Her prayer of thanksgiving was audible to all as she exited the cab. She would have knelt down and kissed the concrete if no one had been looking.

"Want to go to the stock car motocross next weekend, Mother?" Nadine asked in jest.

"Not until after I have gone to confession," Mother Catherine quipped. "Maybe bungee jumping or paragliding, but no more cross-country jaunts with a Yellow Cab kamikaze."

Even Nadine had to admit to herself that she might need to breach her suitcase and retrieve a clean pair of underpants before boarding the plane.

The two of them made their way through the

slow-moving check-in line, and then plodded toward the clogged security area. Both women were relieved to finally arrive at the gate where they would board their flight. By the time they sat down, their bags seemed ten pounds heavier and both of them were eager to get home. Nadine stopped at a nearby shop and bought hot coffees and scones. Mother accepted the refreshment graciously. They sipped coffee and chatted as they waited for the boarding call.

The announcement crackled over the loudspeaker about thirty minutes later. Like a line of penguins, the passengers stumped down the gangway and squeezed through the narrow aisle of the aircraft, stopping every few steps as someone took their seat or jammed luggage into the overhead bin. Mercifully, Nadine and Mother Catherine finally slid into their seats. Nadine fastened her seatbelt and glance out the porthole at the distant skyline far beyond the terminal. She leaned back and sighed. Suddenly, everything they had done over the past three days seemed completely surreal. She looked over at Mother in the adjacent seat. The older woman was already deeply engrossed in an inspirational booklet she had purchased at a bookstore, oblivious to the passengers still jostling past her shoulder. This whole experience had been amazing, but it felt good to be going home. The thought of home created a sense of serenity and peace, like snuggling under a soft blanket. It was a feeling she had not experienced in quite some time. As the plane prepared for takeoff she leaned back and closed her eyes. Scenes of the award event and her meeting with Mr. Morgenstein replayed in her mind like a video on an endless loop. For her, winning the Pulitzer was a sort of mandate to continue to uphold the standard of journalism that won her the award.

Before the aircraft reached cruising altitude, Nadine's chin dropped to her shoulder as she succumbed to exhaustion and fell fast asleep. Images of her life tumbled across her mind like snippets of movie trailers, random scenes that were strangely out of sequence. First a giggling five-year-old Nadine emerged from hiding in the folds of Sister Catherine's billowing habit. The ring of laughter and the warmth of Sister Catherine hugging her small shoulders felt reassuring. But in an instant, she was torn from the comfort of that moment and instantly transported to the killing field of Pembrooke, dry and lifeless as the bones of the dead. The wind scoured and clawed the surface of the field as if trying to unearth its secrets. Pale specters lifted from the ground, extending their ghostly hands in a plea. Somehow she could hear the distant anguished cries of those who had been buried and forgotten. In a flash the scene changed and Nadine watched herself cross the stage to accept the Pulitzer Prize only to discover her entire mouth had disappeared. The audience sat wide-eyed and startled as panic and gloom darkened her countenance.

Nadine woke with a jerk as the plane passed through some turbulence. She bolted upright and gawked around, tracing her lips with her fingers as if to reassure herself her face was normal. Her dream phantoms dissipated and secreted back to their hiding places as she regained her senses.

Mother Catherine chuckled and patted her arm. "You were dreaming."

"More like having a nightmare," Nadine replied as she settled back in the seat.

Mother Catherine peered over her glasses that rested comfortably on the bridge of her nose. There was gentleness in her eyes. "You used to have nightmares when you were very young," she commented wistfully.

"And you were always there to soothe me," reminded Nadine, placing her hand on Mother Catherine's.

"When I was a girl," Mother Catherine reminisced, "I used to get very nervous before playing the organ for Sunday church. For months, the night before every service I would have this terrible dream that I would either forget my sheet music or that the notes would disappear just as I started to play." She pumped the arch of her eyebrows impishly and leaned toward Nadine. "That's why I know how to play so many pieces of music from memory."

"I've never forgotten my sheet music," Nadine said, "but I do remember having to debate a constitutional issue in front of my journalism class at Columbia and being totally unprepared. I was feeling cocky and didn't even make notes. Ironically, it was in one of Dr. Newell's classes. A fellow classmate, Kevin Orchard, a name I will *never* forget, literally took me to the cleaners. The assignment was to debate the First Amendment right of a free press versus the Sixth Amendment right to a fair trial. Now *that* was a nightmare!"

"Speaking of Dr. Newell," Mother Catherine interjected, "I didn't realize until he was introduced at the awards luncheon that he had been a Supreme Court Justice prior to becoming a professor. When we visited, I was curious about the career switch and asked what gave him the greatest satisfaction, being a justice on the state's highest court, or teaching mass media law and ethics."

"Great question. What was his response?"

"He said serving as an appellate judge was constraining and he could only make decisions within the confines of the law. He could interpret but couldn't create."

"I was always curious about his background.

Somehow being a professor seems like a step down."

"Dr. Newell says it is an honor to teach young journalists, to demonstrate the double-edged power of the pen, and hopefully inspire a new generation of ethical journalists in the field. Now *that* could have some far-reaching effects." Mother's eyes widened as she remembered the gift Dr. Newell had given her. She rummaged through her bag and retrieved his latest book. "Here, you might like to read this."

Nadine turned the book over in her hands and cocked her mouth to one side. "Hmm. *The Power of the Pen*. That sounds very much like a Dr. Newell title. I still greatly admire him and his philosophies on First Amendment rights." She read his bio out loud. "The power of the pen is mighty, and can become a perilous instrument in the hands of the unscrupulous." Nadine put the book in her lap and thought for a moment. "What do you think about that?"

"About what, my dear?"

"What we talked about earlier regarding First Amendment rights. Do you think that the First Amendment should be given preference over rights that are in conflict?"

"Example?"

"Well, in the college debate with Kevin Orchard, I took the side of the journalist and argued— although poorly—that the First Amendment guarantees freedom of expression and freedom of the press, that if it is in conflict with other constitutional guarantees, it should be the one to prevail. Kevin argued the side of an accused under the Sixth Amendment which guarantees a fair trial. He expressed the Sixth should trump the First. I rebutted that the public has the right to be informed and that journalists should be allowed to report on both pretrial as well as trial matters. Kevin postulated that publishing inflammatory material that would otherwise be inadmissible at trial would torpedo a fair trial and taint the minds of jurors who had been exposed to the print and/or electronic media."

"Child, I think constitutional values are like people and should be treated equally. To tilt the scales in favor of one right or entitlement over another is like the grocer who has his thumb on the scales as he weighs your tomatoes. My father used to call it 'stacking the deck.'"

"That's the problem with my profession. As a journalist I'm called on to constantly balance the equities, to reconcile conflicting rights. Sometimes, everything seems to be on a collision course. I ran into that issue head on while doing my story on the Pembrooke Asylum. Look at what has happened as a result. We have positive new legislation that will protect patients, brutal medical treatments can no longer be practiced, standards in mental health facilities are being established and there will be more oversight. On the other hand, family secrets have been pulled into the light of day, Pembrooke facility was closed, jobs were lost and the patients transported elsewhere. Mental health providers everywhere are being scrutinized, doctors' and other healthcare workers' reputations and livelihoods ended because of the scandal. Criminal charges may be brought as the deaths are investigated. So many ripples in the pond…" She sighed and studied her hands. "For every action, there is an equal and opposite reaction. By informing the public, you inevitably invade someone's privacy. By advancing the good of the community as a whole, individual rights sometimes fall by the wayside. We don't even know yet how this will all play out in the court system."

"In the convent, we call it a trade-off when you trade one right for another. By giving to one you take from another. In the workplace, when one is excused because of illness, another is usually required to do double duty. Sometimes, it is the lesser of evils. When you add to one side, you have to subtract from the other and vice versa. It's seldom a win-win situation."

"That's the way I often perceive my conundrum as a journalist. At least I have learned that not everything is black and white, and I've learned to recognize gray." She shrugged absently. "You can see why I lost my debate to Kevin Orchard. Apparently, I'm not much of an advocate."

Mother Catherine was amused. "If the United States Supreme Court Justices can't all agree, how can we? There are persuasive arguments both ways."

"I guess that is a good reason to have a darn good attorney on the team." Nadine laughed.

"Speaking of attorneys, isn't Charles Adkins on retainer at the *Candela Daily Mirror*?"

"He is, Mother, but he is not always available. My friend, Christopher Gould, is always begging me to go to lunch with him and when I do he enjoys tutoring me on the law. I refer to him as my guardian angel since he is always looking out for me."

"He's been after you ever since his divorce. I assume the divorce is the reason you never dated him. He is a most handsome man, don't you think?" She cocked her head and peered at Nadine searching for a hint of reaction.

Nadine's forehead creased with a look of dismay. "We've remained good friends by just that— being *friends*. Besides, he's not the man of my dreams and it doesn't appear that I will find such a man anytime soon—and maybe never."

The lively conversation was interrupted by the pilot's voice as it blared over the loudspeaker advising passengers to prepare for landing. Their flight from New York had been quite a late departure, but it had allowed them time to do some sightseeing before leaving. Nadine and Mother had talked, read and napped during the flight, making the trip feel like no time at all. Nadine peered out the window as the plane dipped its nose for the descent. Below, she could see the lights of Coronado Airport situated on the outskirts of Pembrooke.

Nadine loved the Great Plains of rural Kansas. There was something exhilarating about the vast expanse of landscape that spread like a finely woven carpet all the way to the distant horizon. What could compare to the perfume of fresh-cut grain or how the fields turned golden and glistening just before harvest? She smiled as she settled back into her seat and tugged on her seatbelt. Just then the wheels of the Boeing 727 screeched as they made contact with the runway, jostling the passengers in their seats. The engines roared as they labored to slow the plane. She could see the terminal as they taxied toward the gate. The Empire State was fine, but the Sunflower State was better because it was *home*.

# CHAPTER 3

## A HERO'S WELCOME

The *Candela Daily Mirror* promised to have someone at the airport to pick up Nadine and Mother, but even at this late hour, when they deplaned they encountered a crowd of a hundred or more people waiting anxiously to greet her amidst fanfare reserved for celebrities. Thornton Marimon, the editor of the *Daily Mirror* stood there, accompanied by a fellow reporter and one of the newspaper's photographers.

While exchanging hugs and warm greetings, he handed Nadine the previous day's edition of the paper with the lead story headline *LOCAL REPORTER RECEIVES PULITZER PRIZE* over a quarter page colored photograph of Nadine receiving the award. Below it was a wordy write-up, including a verbatim recital of her acceptance speech.

Nadine stared at the front page, her eyes wide. "Wow! I've written a lot of headlines, but this is the first time that I *am* the headline."

Chuckles rippled through the crowd. Before

long, the television crews from the local channels were filming and shoving microphones in Nadine's face. Three of the local radio stations had positioned recorders in front of Nadine and aggressively made sure they captured her every word. Even the rival newspaper, the *Coronado Globe Telegraph*, had a reporter and photographer on the scene. Nadine was unaccustomed to such VIP treatment.

# CHAPTER 4

## A SCANDAL REVEALED

O n a hot, muggy Friday in July, the combines were busy cutting wide swaths in the landscape as they harvested the golden grain fields of Coronado County. Nadine was sitting in her office finishing up a story when the phone rang. The anonymous call was from a youngish sounding man who claimed he had information about someone supplying prescription drugs to teenagers. Nadine listened quietly, giving herself time to consider the call for a moment and decide if it was worthy of pursuit, or just another crackpot. The voice sounded nervous but insistent. He asked to meet with her so they could talk.

"Why don't you just make an appointment and come in to my office?"

"Are you kidding me?" The voice was now incredulous. "I'm putting myself at risk by even making this call." The man hesitated and relented a bit. "I won't come to your office, but I'll meet you half way. There is a coffee shop in the Holly-Mayfair Hotel in downtown Pembrooke. It's not far from the newspaper office. We can meet there, but only if you come alone. Will you meet with me there?"

Nadine considered for a moment, then agreed to the meeting. At 2:30 p.m. sharp, Nadine entered the coffee shop and sat at a table in the extreme northeast corner of the room. She had no sooner ordered a limeade when a smartly dressed young man, who appeared to be in his early twenties, entered the coffee shop. He said something to the hostess, then headed directly towards the table where Nadine was seated. He stood there for a moment, looking around and fidgeting nervously, then introduced himself as Corey Samuelson.

Nadine stuck out her hand. "Corey Samuelson, I'm Nadine Siena. Won't you sit down?"

He cleared his throat and sat where he could see the entrance. The waitress approached the table with a pleasant smile. He pointed at the drink sitting in front of Nadine. "One of those, please."

The waitress returned with a tall limeade with lime wedge perched on the rim of the glass. He dropped it into the glass and poked it with his straw.

"Will there be anything else?"

"No, thank you."

The waitress smiled and retreated.

"I hope I didn't alarm you by having you meet me away from your office and away from the prying eyes of the public," he said.

"It's not as unusual as you think," Nadine responded. "But I am naturally curious. What is it you have to tell me?" She crossed her arms on the table in front of her and peered at Corey.

"I am a good friend of Megan Hopkins and accepted an invitation to spend the Fourth of July weekend with her and her family. When I returned home to San Mateo the end of last week, I was troubled by some things that happened at the Hopkins' residence while I was here. By the way, neither Megan nor her family knows I am back in town. That is the reason for this clandestine meeting."

"I know Dr. Maynard Hopkins. In fact, Hopkins Pharmacy is where I have been doing business for years."

Corey fiddled with the wedge of lime and rotated the glass between his palms. "First let me explain that I am engaged to Megan and we attend Stanford University together. This is the third summer that I have been invited to Pembrooke. I love Megan and think the world of her family. I would never do anything to hurt them. That makes what I want to tell you even harder. I could lose the woman with whom I want to spend the rest of my life." He sighed and shook his head. "I'm not sure I'm doing the right thing by being here—"

"Forgive me for interrupting," Nadine said as she took a long sip. "Before you say anything, keep in mind I am not a priest, a lawyer or a doctor and you are not my client or patient. What I am trying to make sure you understand is that there is no privileged communication between us. I am not bound, legally or ethically, to keep confidential what you tell me. Is that clear?"

"I do understand," he assured her. "When I was here in July, your name and picture were all over the headlines. Everyone was still buzzing with excitement about the good news of 'local girl makes good.' I read the article about you winning the Pulitzer Prize because of your investigative reporting. As far as I can tell, you are considered one of the few trustworthy reporters in the business. You uncovered a scandal that rocked the county and you were not at all bashful about taking on the powers that be. I have something that is equally as scandalous in its own way."

Nadine sensed his sincerity. It was something in his eyes and she was impressed by his courage. He came across as a level-headed young man. "Corey, are you sure this information isn't something you need to divulge to law enforcement authorities instead of a reporter?

He lifted his hands in a helpless gesture. "I'm sure. Maybe I am only seeing ghosts. It's just that I lost one of my best friends back in high school because I was too loyal to blow the whistle when I should have.

At the senior picnic, he OD'd and might still be alive today if I had turned him in." An anguished look crossed his face. "I think about it every day and feel responsible for his death. I won't make that mistake again." He stared at his hands and blinked back tears.

"Anyway," Corey continued, "I need to get this off my chest to someone I feel is trustworthy. On top of that, you know the ropes and won't rush to judgment. If this isn't handled properly, I might lose my fiancée and ruin innocent lives–including my own–in the process. My conscience is gnawing at me to do something, so here I am."

"And if I don't promise to keep your identity confidential, then what? Kansas does not have a reporter's shield law. What that means, Corey, is that here in Kansas there is no law protecting journalists from forced disclosure of confidential sources of information."

His eyebrows arched in surprise. "I guess I just assumed that all journalists were protected, no matter what."

"Don't get me wrong. There are states with shield laws. Kansas just doesn't happen to be one of them."

Corey drained the remainder of his limeade and considered what Nadine had just told him. After a moment his expression changed and Nadine knew the emotional struggle had ended. "Your promise of confidentiality is good enough for me, Ms. Siena. I don't believe you would breach it even if you were compelled by a court to do so."

"How can you be so sure? Should I be subpoenaed to testify in court, I would only have two choices. Divulge your identity or stand mute. In that case I could be held in contempt, fined, or even thrown in the county slammer for some indeterminate period of time. Not only that, it would also be subjecting my newspaper to liability. How do you *know* you can trust me if I make such a promise?"

Corey's eyes met hers. "*Will* you promise me, Ms. Siena?"

Corey's sincerity shattered her defenses. "All right," she agreed. "Just so we are clear, I am promising not to divulge the *source* of my information, *not* the information itself."

"Fair enough." Corey smiled for the first time and extended his hand to Nadine. "We have a deal."

Nadine pulled a digital recorder out of her bag and set it on the table. "With your permission, I am going to record this as well as take written notes." She flipped open a note pad, then checked to make sure the light on the recorder was green. "Go ahead, Corey. I'm all ears."

"I arrived at the Hopkins' residence on July

third," he began, "somewhere around 2:30 p.m. Dr. Hopkins had not yet returned from work and was not due until dinner time. My arrival was a couple of hours earlier than originally expected. Megan and her mother had not yet done their Fourth of July grocery shopping. They left together to go to the store, and I decided to take a shower. I was just getting ready to get in the shower when the telephone rang. Thinking it might be Megan and wanting to 'earn my keep,' I answered. The voice on the other end said something like 'Maynard, this is Edmund. I'm glad I caught you in because I'm in a hurry. I just wrote some heavy-duty prescriptions that will need to be filled *today*. I tried to call you at the pharmacy, but they said you were out. I didn't want anyone but you to process them. Call me and we will arrange for these patients to get their meds. Remember, we have a long weekend in front of us and don't want them to take their prescription business elsewhere. Sorry, but I have to run. I have a patient waiting.' He then hung up."

"The only physician I know in this area with that first name is Dr. Edmund Simms, a local D.O."

"That's who it turned out to be. I actually met him in person the following Sunday when he showed up at the Hopkins' house. It was unusually early when he arrived. At about 7:30 a.m., I heard loud voices in the downstairs family room, which was right next to the

42

room where I was staying. I threw on my robe and went out to see what all the commotion was about. Just as I walked into the room, I saw Dr. Hopkins handing a bundle of money to a man who was subsequently introduced to me as Dr. Edmund Simms. Both seemed perturbed by my appearance. Dr. Hopkins' face turned absolutely white when I came in. Later, he apologized and said he forgot I was staying downstairs. Dr. Simms glared at Dr. Hopkins and stuffed the wad of cash into a bank bag and left."

Nadine was scribbling furiously. "Then what?"

"More strange things happened over that weekend that made me suspicious and suspect that maybe Dr. Hopkins was involved in some type of dispensing scheme. For instance, a young man came to the door and interrupted breakfast early on the morning of the fourth. Dr. Hopkins acted flustered and left abruptly saying he had to run down to the pharmacy to fill an emergency prescription. He said it was for his gardener's mother. Megan's mother brushed it off, saying that was par for the course."

"Were there other occurrences that caused concern?"

"Just odd telephone calls that Dr. Hopkins took on his cell phone over the course of my visit. He would always leave the room and talk in private. Some of the conversations were quite lengthy. I thought it curious, with other pharmacists on duty and all, that he would personally service certain customers. It made no sense. It also struck me as odd that Dr. Hopkins seemed very intimidated by Dr. Simms. On the Sunday when I walked in on their conversation, he left to meet with Dr. Simms again later that same morning."

"Sounds like a very strange alliance," Nadine commented. "What do you make of it?"

"I think Dr. Hopkins may be giving kickbacks on the prescriptions he's filling for Dr. Simms' patients. The argument I walked in on was perhaps a disagreement about the amount paid to Dr. Simms. If I'm right, Dr. Simms is putting prescription medications into the hands of junkies, making him a common drug dealer. It would be interesting to know what types of drugs we're talking about. Filling prescriptions for the gardener's mother in the middle of the Fourth of July weekend appears to have been a ruse. Maybe someone was looking for some additional fireworks other than those shooting into the sky. At least, that's my take. And I forgot to mention, I saw the gardener pick up a sealed package from Dr. Hopkins on the preceding day."

"Those are pretty serious allegations."

Cory frowned. "The time, manner and place of the various transactions made me suspicious."

"I'll have to admit you have piqued my interest.

It is common knowledge that school kids in our community are somehow getting their hands on various prescription drugs. I think the authorities believe these drugs originated from the medicine cabinets of their parents. Through the grapevine, I learned that at the end of last school year, several students had to have their stomachs pumped in the ER. Perhaps there is a connection."

"I hope I am wrong. However, I feel better having told you about it. With your contacts and background, you will know what to do. Hopefully, I've given you enough information to launch an investigation or at least cause one to be launched."

She punched the OFF button on the recorder and put the notepad in her bag. "I'm flattered by your confidence, Corey. I definitely will present this to my editor with a recommendation that we pursue the leads you have provided and conduct an investigation in as a discreet a manner as possible. We'll see what turns up. In the interim, if you learn anything more, call me on my cell. Here is the number." She handed him a business card.

Corey gave her a contact number where he could be reached. He placed a five-dollar bill on the table and thanked her as he got up. She watched him walk out of the restaurant, wondering if there really was any substance to his story. Being intrigued was one thing, getting to the truth was quite another. Nadine wasn't sure how she would approach it just yet, but she knew she would.

# CHAPTER 5

## THE PLOT THICKENS

S hortly after receiving a degree in pharmacology and then his Ph.D., Maynard Hopkins married the daughter of a prominent local physician, Ephraim Simms. They had been high school sweethearts and he always knew Katherine would be his bride. The stars seemed aligned for the couple as their hard work was rewarded. Maynard established Hopkins Pharmacy, which had been one of the most successful pharmacies in Pembrooke for the past twenty years. His business was ideally located across the street from Coronado State College and within two blocks of St. Boniface Hospital. Hopkins was well known and respected in the community. He had been involved in numerous philanthropic community projects, sat on numerous boards and committees and served as president of the Pembrooke Chamber of Commerce.

If there was a name in the community whose reputation was beyond reproach, it was the Hopkins name. Katherine's family was also well respected. Her father, Dr. Ephraim Simms, had helped establish the college and brought in millions of dollars in endowments for programs and expansion. It was no surprise when Katherine's brother, Edmund, carried on the family tradition and became a doctor.

As Nadine Siena sat at her desk poring over family histories, the possibility of any of these people being involved in criminal activity seemed absolutely impossible. Still, Corey's story had been convincing, as was his sincerity. He was risking a lot to come forward with nothing obvious to gain by doing so. Still, something tugged at the back of her mind. She pulled open the bottom drawer of her filing cabinet where she kept old notes, articles and other bits of information she had collected over the years. After rummaging through a half dozen folders she found what she was looking for.

In the past dozen years, there had been eighteen teenage suicides. While suicides happened on occasion, this was an extraordinary number for Pembrooke and the surrounding area. There had been an outcry from the community, but sadly, no answers for the tragedies. The families had folded up their grief and tried to move on as best as they could.

Nadine pulled an assortment of clippings and articles from the folder and began to line them up on the desk in front her. She had collected a lot of information over the years. In fact, collecting information was almost an obsession. As the number of suicides and other teen deaths grew, Nadine meticulously saved articles, photos and other bits of information, trying to make some sense of what was happening—to make sure these youngsters were remembered. It bothered her that there were no answers to what was happening—that they had been filed away and seemingly forgotten. Now, the grainy images of young faces smiled up at her from the fading newsprint. A wave of sorrow washed over her. All of these bright young lives with all their potential were lost. She felt the weight of their tragedy. Their memories were revived only when a new child was added to the list of casualties, or when family members periodically demonstrated in front of City Hall asking for answers.

But there was nothing extraordinary about these two prominent families that even hinted at scandal. They appeared to be perfectly normal. She scratched a note on her desk calendar to remind herself to check all of their community and business connections. Right now there just weren't any dots to connect, or if there were, she couldn't see them. The frustration of what seemed an impossible situation made her irritable and she began going over the articles and obits again. At least it was a place to start. She began to read each one and arranged them in the order of their deaths: Terri Strohm, 17; William Castle, 15; Donnie Gallager, 19; Susan

Corcoran, 16… She jotted down notes as she went through each one, hoping to find a connection. Finding nothing, she threw down her pencil and massaged her temples. It was time to call in a couple of favors. She needed to see both the coroner's and toxicology reports on these cases. Nadine had developed a rapport over the years with various officials and experts, including the county coroner/medical examiner, toxicologist and pathologist. She picked up the phone and dialed the familiar number. A woman's voice answered on the third ring.

"Coroner's office."

"Hi, Melanie. This is Nadine Siena at the *Daily Mirror*. I am working on a story related to the increase in teen suicides over the last few years in Coronado County and I'd like to review toxicology reports for the eighteen youths that were listed as suicides over the past 12 years. Would Drs. Pendleton or Percival be available?"

"No, but if you will email the list of names I'll see what I can do."

"Mel, you are a *gem*. I will get those to you right away."

"No problem. Talk to you soon."

Nadine scanned her note page onto the computer and emailed it to the ME. While she was waiting to hear back she would contact the Pembrooke Police Department and see what she could dig up there.

The conference room at the Pembrooke Police Department seemed more like a jail cell than a meeting room. It was a stark, windowless cubicle, austere and dreary. The worn furnishings consisted of an oblong oak table bearing the scars from years of abuse. Six straight-backed chairs were positioned two on each side and one on each end. The far wall was lined from floor to ceiling with sectional bookcases with glass fronts. The brass plate on the top of one of the shelf sections read *The Globe-Wernicke Co., Standard C-11 Unit, made in Cincinnati.* The books housed there contained various outdated police manuals and a leather-bound set of the first 199 volumes of the *Pacific Reporter,* which contained the decisions of the Supreme Courts of twelve states, including Kansas.

As Nadine was examining volume one, copyrighted in 1884, Detectives Lance Perriman and Leland Frey entered the dimly lit room, each carrying a stack of file folders, which they immediately deposited on the end of the table closest to the door.

"Sorry we kept you waiting," Leland said. "We had a time retrieving the files you requested."

"Doesn't look like your library is current," Nadine commented, stifling a smile as she replaced volume one and closed the glass door. "Also looks like the room could use a good dusting."

"We don't use the dungeon very often," Lance replied with a shrug. "Since it is adjacent to the stored files and saves trudging up and down the narrow stairs, we thought you wouldn't mind."

"We have a similar room at the *Daily Mirror,* only we call it the morgue. And, no, I don't mind." She smiled.

"You have asked us to pull case files involving teens and drugs," Leland said. "That's a pretty tall order. However, we managed to pull about sixty that fit the bill."

"Those are just for the past five years," Lance added.

"Perfect," Nadine responded. "As I told Leland on the telephone, the public voice is getting louder. Some members of our community consider this to be the result of a drug epidemic among teenagers. People want answers."

"We have DEA agents working on the problem as we speak and have had for some time now." He hesitated. "But, that's, uh, that's off the record."

Nadine nodded. "Of course."

"Trying to find whistleblowers and insiders with something more than just hearsay is like trying to find another Hope Diamond." Looking straight at Nadine,

Leland added, "Well-intentioned individuals go to the police and the press with tips every day. Most of the tips we get go either nowhere or around in circles. Perhaps by combining our leads, we can make some inroads on this thing."

"Perhaps," Nadine responded hopefully as Leland handed her a file marked "Susan Cochran." As she examined the contents, her eyes caught the name *Hopkins Pharmacy* on the label of a prescription bottle enclosed in a sealed plastic evidence bag. Her eyes also caught the name of the drug: Oxycodone. "Hmmm," she muttered.

"Onto something already?" Lance asked.

"Right now all I have is a bunch of puzzle pieces," Nadine groused while continuing to review files. "I'm hoping to find something—*anything* that looks like it belongs to the same picture."

Several minutes passed before anyone spoke. Nadine replaced the contents of the Susan Cochran file and returned it to Leland. She put her elbow on the table and cradled her chin in her palm, thinking.

"The teens are getting their drugs somewhere. A lot of the OD cases covered by the press involve prescription drugs. We know that doctors have to prescribe them and pharmacists have to fill the prescriptions. That might mean extra pills in the medicine cabinet that are easy for kids to get their hands on when looking for a cheap high, but it just doesn't seem to jibe with the big picture. I guess I just don't get it."

Lance leaned across the table and pushed some files marked CONFIDENTIAL in Nadine's direction. "Everything is speculation right now, but check these out." He gestured with his chin. "When Leland and I started going through this stuff before you got here, we discovered that of the sixty some-odd cases we pulled, many had a common denominator."

Nadine was suddenly hopeful. "What? What did you find?"

"We didn't count them yet, but a significant number of the ones where officers actually confiscated drugs when the arrests were made, and in some of the suicide cases, the prescriptions we recovered listed Dr. Edmund Simms as the prescriber and Hopkins Pharmacy as the provider." He glanced at Leland, who nodded.

She chewed her bottom lip and thought for a moment, looking at Leland, then at Lance. Her face was serious. "Have you given that information to Captain Wolsey?" she asked, suddenly realizing this was consistent with Corey's hypothesis.

Lance shrugged and cocked his mouth to one side. "No one looking at this ever saw the correlation until you called and we began examining the files." He hesitated and studied his thumbs. "As you are aware, information that we believe could compromise our investigation has been redacted from the files. Otherwise, you're privy to everything else."

"That's standard procedure," Leland hastily added.

Nadine said, "I'm familiar with the Kansas Freedom of Information Act." She jotted down some notes from the Cochran file, then pushed it aside, trying to let the new information settle into her brain.

"I have an idea," Lance said. "Why don't we divide what's left of these files between the three of us? We'll each review a stack. Then we'll compare notes and compile a summary when we're done. That will get us through the process faster and hopefully we'll see if we can find these dots Nadine hopes to connect."

Leland and Nadine agreed, so they all set to work. Lance came up with a common template for them to go by. The categories were listed across the top of his notepad: Name, Age, Drug in System, Result (Lethal or Non-Lethal), Prescribed (Yes or No), Name of Prescriber (if Yes), and, Name of Pharmacy (if Yes). After a couple of hours the wooden chairs began to torture their backs and the dingy room closed in on them. They decided to take the files up to the conference room on the main floor where there were comfortable upholstered chairs, a water fountain, vending machines and sunshine streaming in through the floor to ceiling windows. The work seemed to move much faster and the results were astounding.

Of the sixty cases reviewed, the average age of each subject was approximately 16. The drugs involved varied, but over eighty percent of the subjects had taken some form of prescription drugs. Deaths resulted in fifty-five percent of the cases, and of the fourteen medical doctors in the community, Dr. Edmund Simms prescribed over fifty percent of the drugs, and no less than sixty-eight percent had been filled at Hopkins Pharmacy.

When Nadine returned from lunch, she found a stack of pink telephone messages impaled on a spindle in the middle of her desk. In sorting through the stack, she retrieved a message from Captain Fenton Wolsey of the Pembrooke Police Department. Marci's notation on the slip read: "Important that he reach you."

"Fenton Wolsey," the raspy voice on the other end answered.

"Chief, this is Nadine Siena of the *Daily Mirror*. You had left a message for me to call. Hopefully, I'm not calling at a bad time."

"You couldn't have picked a better time to return my call. This is the first free moment I've had all day."

"When I stopped by your office earlier, I was

told you were preparing to meet with the Pembrooke City Council. Hope that meeting went well."

"Hell, does any meeting with the PCC ever go well? Begging for supplemental appropriations for the department is like two shipwrecked sailors fighting for the only life jacket in the middle of the ocean."

Nadine had to chuckle when she thought of the combatants in the battle of the budget. It was like King Kong versus three newborn kittens. "Don't tell me you're intimidated by three elderly ladies."

"I'm always intimidated by the female of the species. That is why I'm calling you. Leland and Lance tell me they were unable to answer all your questions regarding the role drugs, both illegal and legal, play in the spike in our crime rate. I guess I'm wondering where you're heading with this thing."

"Fair question," Nadine responded as she pulled her notes from her earlier meeting with Detectives Lance Perriman and Leland Frey. "The *Daily Mirror* is intrigued, if that is the proper word, with a silent killer, namely prescription drugs, that is having an adverse effect on the citizens of this community. Apparently, there is an untold story out there that needs to be told and our newspaper is in the process of gathering the data."

"It is embarrassing for the department to have an outsider point out the obvious. Hell, up to now, we have been focusing our attention on illegal drugs as the source of our problems. It has taken a newspaper reporter, like you, to cause us to think outside the square."

"Have you had a chance to examine the data Detectives Perriman and Frey and I compiled this morning while you duked it out with the commissioners?"

"Indeed I have. And I've had my staff pull all the DUIs for the past two years. Last year, approximately thirty-nine percent of the DUIs were due to excessive drug use. That's almost double over the previous year."

"Do you have any idea what percent were attributable to the use of prescription drugs?"

"Hmmm," he murmured. "Give me a minute." Nadine could hear the Chief rummage through the paperwork and an occasional "Damn, I know I have that information here somewhere."

Nadine cringed as she heard the bang of the mouthpiece as it fell to the desk. "Sorry about that," he said. After many agonizing minutes, for the chief also, Nadine surmised, he was back on the telephone. "Where consent was given to administer drug testing, twenty-six percent of those who were examined tested positive for prescription drugs."

"Any idea, Chief, as to how many crimes in our

fair city last year can be blamed on the use of prescription drugs?"

"Wish we could determine that. Unfortunately, many crimes go undetected. So, unless we catch the perpetrator, either in the act or shortly thereafter, there is no way usually to tell whether the drugs or alcohol or neither . . . or both were involved."

"Care to speculate?" Nadine asked.

"Promise you won't quote me?"

"Yes."

"Sixty to seventy percent."

The numbers spoke for themselves, but now Nadine had hit a wall. There was no way for her to get more information that would validate the illegal distribution of pharmaceuticals. Only law enforcement could obtain a search warrant, and only when probable cause made it the right time to act. They needed more evidence. Now back in her office, with notes strewn across her desk, she paced back and forth, rubbing her forehead with her palm as she tried to think. *If only I had a source connected to Hopkins Pharmacy. Maybe a whistleblower or disgruntled employee.* She stopped in her tracks as a thought struck. *Perhaps a plant. Someone Dr. Hopkins wouldn't recognize. Who could or would agree to go undercover?*

By the next afternoon Nadine received the copies she had requested of various official reports concerning teen suicides in Coronado County. She made a note on her desk calendar to make a thank-you call to the ME's office. When she made an appointment and conferred with each of them concerning their respective reports, it was clear that none of them had considered the coincidences. Now the coincidences clearly stood out. They were concerned and upset for not having recognized the obvious, and unhappy that someone from the press uncovered the oversight.

Significant from their reports was the revelation that all but two of the suicide victims were patients of Dr. Edmund Simms. Of the sixteen who were his patients, *all* were found to have sizable amounts of prescription drugs in their systems, ranging from Oxycodone to Vicodin to Dilaudid to Prozac or a combination of two or more. Of the thirty-three teens that died from a drug overdose during that same period of time, twenty-four were attributable to one or more of the aforementioned prescription drugs. The other nine deaths involved cocaine and/or methamphetamines. Of the twenty-four teens who died from drug overdose, twelve were patients of Dr. Edmund Simms.

As she left the ME's office, Nadine knew it was time to correlate her notes and present her findings to her boss, Thornton Marimon, editor of the *Daily Mirror*.

He knew she had been chasing a story, but now she had reached a dead end and didn't want to bail out without a parachute. In spite of all the digging she had done, and knowing in her gut she had a big story, the truth of the matter was that she had little more than conjecture and coincidences to show for her efforts. It was time to let the boss in on what she had been working on.

Thornton Marimon was the third generation in his family to be in the newspaper business. His grandfather, William Henry Marimon, founded the *Candela Daily Mirror* then turned it over to Thornton's father, John Kenneth Marimon. Thornton had worked at the paper since he was just a boy. When his father retired, Thornton took over. Now in his mid-fifties, he had increased circulation, increased advertising and kept pace with the technological advances in the trade through innovation and sound business decisions. It had become one of the most respected and influential newspapers in the state.

With a weight-lifter's build and steel-gray eyes, Thornton looked less like an editor of a thriving daily and more like a bouncer in an upscale night club. His looks, however, were deceiving. Though he was strong willed, determined and focused, he was also compassionate. His horn-rimmed glasses transformed his handsome face into an older version of Clark Kent.

He had a paternalistic instinct when it came to Nadine, and Nadine's trust in Thornton had never proved to be unwarranted. If there were such things as guardian angels, Nadine had two: Mother Catherine and Thornton Marimon.

She walked into his office with a thick notebook and several folders cradled in her arms and slumped into an antiquated wooden chair situated in front of his desk. He regarded her for a moment, removing his glasses and chewing on one of the stems. Thornton leaned back in his high-back leather chair and folded his arms. Noticing the consternation imprinted on Nadine's face, Thornton buzzed Marci, instructing her to hold their calls.

He looked at Nadine for a moment and replaced his glasses. "I read the summary of your conversation with your source," Thornton began, "and the statistical compilation gathered from the reports and interviews with our local officials. I think you're onto something that will rock this community."

Noticing the scale of the assortment of information crammed into Nadine's notebook and bulging file folders, Thornton said, "Judging from the jumble, we should probably sit at the conference table." Thornton nodded toward the conference table positioned under a large window that offered a view of the manicured courtyard.

"Don't mind the clutter," Thornton said as he pushed several stacks of past editions of the *Daily Mirror* to one end of the table. Nadine deposited her armload on the edge of the table, and carefully arranged the notebook and file folders in an orderly configuration. Nadine retrieved a pile of documents fastened at the top with a large binder clip and slid it in Thornton's direction. "These are copies of my latest notes pertaining to the medication scandal. Hopefully, you've had a chance to review the file I put on your desk late yesterday."

"I have it right here," Thornton replied as he picked up the file and flopped it back on the table. "I have not only read the contents but have done some research of my own."

"I hope you had better luck than I did," Nadine said. "Unfortunately, I have little to show for my efforts. Even with a reliable source, or so it appears, and my interviews with the ME and PD, I have only a thimbleful of hard facts. Not nearly enough to write a story."

"I'm not so certain," Thornton said. "I did some research on national statistics because I had a hunch those numbers would be relevant, even though I don't have anything other than what you provided me regarding the local problem. Just relating the statistical data and attributing the source of that information would, at the very least, make our readers aware of the trend in teen prescription drug abuse. What I am proposing is that we print a story but make it more generic and general in scope."

Nadine brightened. "That would be safe until we have something more definitive. I think it is pretty clear that we have doctors in collusion with pharmacies and essentially being drug dealers. Obviously, this gig is much more lucrative than the medical profession." She shook her head and put her fingers to her temples. "I guess dollar signs made them forget about the Hippocratic Oath to do no harm. It's just more than I can wrap my mind around."

"Right you are. The new oath is 'get while the getting's good' and it turns human beings into destroyers. That is the very reason for my suggestion. We can start out with some real general information to get the readers engaged. We can remind the public that other than alcohol and marijuana, prescription drugs and over-the-counter drugs are the most commonly abused substances among our teenage population. The most common over-the-counter drug appears to be dextromethorphan found in popular brand cough and cold medicines. Heck, anybody can go in and buy cough syrup.

"Good grief! If there was a way to get high on

popcorn these kids would figure out how."

Thornton shrugged. "This is a good start, but right now our hands are tied from taking the next step and doing an exposé. Let's hope the cops make some progress. Our community is very sensitive to this topic with all of the young lives that have been lost. We can even throw in some stats on the tendency to overprescribe medication. Bottom line, from the drug manufacturers on down, it is all about making a buck. Pure old-fashioned *greed*."

"In all fairness to the medical profession," Nadine said ruefully, "many of the prescription drugs that find their way into the hands of teenagers appear to have been given to them by family members, their peers or have been pilfered from the bathroom medicine cabinet."

"I think there is enough blame to go around," Thornton said, "but I don't detect a lot of concern or a concerted attempt to rectify the situation. There is too much profit to be had. Hell, except for a bunch of disclaimers in advertising, no one is accountable!"

"I agree. If we just publish the facts taken from the statistics I obtained from the police department and the county ME along with the other information you compiled from your research, I think it will be easy to make it relevant on a local level. We can nail it with national numbers and it will be a great launch piece."

Thornton nodded. "If we make no reference to doctors or pharmacists, or inference of impropriety or criminality, I think we will be on safe ground. Submit your story and I will carefully edit it. At this point, if we *don't* print a story we are contributing to the problem by not addressing it. We have a responsibility here."

Nadine gathered her notebook and folders to leave.

Thornton stopped her. "Don't you think you should consider turning the information gleaned from your source over to the authorities?" Thornton asked.

"That is a dilemma," Nadine responded. "The DA will undoubtedly take the matter before the grand jury. You know he is going to duck anything politically sensitive, especially during an election year. Without the eyewitness testimony of my confidential source, he has nothing. With it, he would probably get a search warrant to search Dr. Simms' medical clinic and Dr. Hopkins' pharmacy. If incriminating evidence is found, they get their indictment. The only problem is that I made a promise to the source that I would not divulge his name or identity."

"Ah! Now we know the gender of your source," Thornton said with a grin.

"Whoa!" Nadine threw up her hand. "Don't jump to conclusions quite so quickly. The word *his* is used generically as the word *mankind* is used to include all genders." Nadine grimaced, realizing her slip.

"If you relate what you've been told by your source, without revealing his or *her* identity, you deliver your own head on a platter. The authorities will want to know your source's identity in order to establish the conspiracy theory and to provide the nexus between Dr. Hopkins and the gardener, who you refer to in the material you provided me and who, I presume, may be the intermediary between the supplier and the teens in our community. Unless the gardener is identified or comes forward, there is no case, thus, no story."

"Or else I turn over the information, protect the source, and end up jailed until I comply. That drags you into it because both the newspaper and I would be fined several hundred dollars per day." She turned to go. "This is why we need to keep pushing for a Kansas reporter's shield law," Nadine added.

"Don't count on that happening any time soon. Unless you want to be a martyr and enjoy being locked in a bird cage of a cell, you may want to reconsider keeping your promise, or forget the story. The newspaper doesn't have a contingency legal fund, not even to pay fines involving our favorite daughter."

Nadine hesitated at the door, frowning and studying the floor.

"I know you feel boxed in on this one," he said hauling himself to his feet. His tone softened. "I don't want what happened to Judith Miller to happen to you. In case you don't remember, she was the *New York Times* reporter who was jailed back in 2005 for refusing to reveal the name of a confidential source. She spent almost a whole summer in lockup. If it wasn't for Scooter Libby, Chief of Staff to former Vice President Dick Cheney, coming forward and identifying himself as her confidential source, she would *still* be sitting in the clinker. That is a situation I wouldn't wish on anyone—especially not us."

Nadine could not bring herself to look at him. She simply nodded and hurried back to her office. It was a relief when she closed the door and sat down at her desk. It felt safe there; someplace where she could be alone and think. Her eyes scanned the bulletin board where she had pinned the photos of all the teens that had died or committed suicide because of drugs. Their faces stared at her accusingly and she had to turn away. She put her face in her hands and wept. The weight of her dilemma churned in her stomach. The story needed to come out for the good of the community and would perhaps save future lives. But she also believed deeply that promises were not made to be broken. In that moment Nadine vowed to advocate for the passing of a shield law in Kansas. But for now, she would keep her promise to Corey, regardless of the consequences.

She sniffed into a tissue as she set the folder

aside. For now, Nadine would watch and wait to see what developed. A professor once told her, "Don't risk a lot for a little." This story was far from over. For now she would work on the special assignment that had just been given to her. That would keep her busy until the drug case came together.

# CHAPTER 6

## BALANCING THE EQUITIES

The case of the pharmaceutical candy man was put on hold and the initial story prepared for print, pending Thornton's edit. Marci, who served the dual role of receptionist and administrative assistant, buzzed Nadine's office. "Thornton requests your presence in the conference room pronto."

"Requests?" Nadine asked cynically.

"Strike that," Marci replied. "Get your you-know-what in there right now!"

"Yes, Mother," Nadine replied as she gathered up her notepad and pen and headed for the newspaper's auxiliary conference room on the main floor.

Thornton smiled at Nadine as she entered and nodded toward the large oak table situated in front of the bay window overlooking the adjacent park. Two older ladies were already seated there, fidgeting. Nadine recognized them from her volunteer work with the Coronado County Community Chest, a well-known local non-profit.

"You know Edith and Hattie," said Thornton, motioning Nadine toward one of the empty chairs on his side of the table.

"Of course," Nadine said brightly as she walked toward them and extended her hand.

After shaking hands and greeting the two women, she took her seat and folded her hands on the table.

"Edith and Hattie belong to the same church I attend," Thornton began as he angled his chair facing the three women. "Last week they approached me after Sunday service to seek my advice."

"I see. And what sort of advice were you ladies looking for?" Her eyebrows arched with the question as she looked from one to the other.

Edith averted her eyes and studied the tabletop.

Thornton stared at Nadine for a brief moment then turned back to Edith. "Please tell Nadine what you told me."

Edith's hand fluttered to her neck and she tugged at her collar. "Look, we are both just volunteers, but I worked as an accountant for thirty years before retiring. One of the things I help with at CCCC is the bookkeeping and accounting. Normally that is overseen by Dot Paxton, the executive director, but Dot was away on vacation. Hattie and I were preparing the quarterly budget reports for the upcoming board meeting, and we found some—well, what we think are *irregularities*."

Nadine rested her arms on the table and leaned forward. "What kind of irregularities?" She looked at Thornton with a puzzled stare.

Edith's brow creased with thought. "To make a long story short, we found a number of reimbursement checks made out to Dot for trips we're fairly certain she never took. There were no gas or restaurant receipts, hotel bills, mileage logs—nothing to back up the reimbursements. Like me, Hattie also worked as an accountant. She was the first one to see issues that raised a red flag. I was sure it was nothing, but after really looking into it, I believe Hattie was right." She dropped her hands into her lap.

Nadine pressed her lips together and gave a vague nod. "Other than the reimbursement checks, was there anything else?"

"Yes," Hattie volunteered. "Over the past two and a half years, approximately $18,000 was paid to Vanderlay Consulting Group. There were no contracts for services on file, or any information about the company or what work it provided for the money. We decided to do some checking on the company but can't find any record of a business by that name. We tried the regular phone directory, Googled, and when that turned up nothing, we looked on the website of the Secretary of State. There is no such firm registered with the state."

Edith plodded on. "We started pulling old bank statements and cancelled checks, but the harder we tried to reconcile, the more questions we encountered."

"Then there was the issue with petty cash," Hattie reminded Edith. "It's odd that an organization like CCCC has no procedure in place that requires vouchers to be submitted for petty cash withdrawals. Sometimes the monthly petty cash withdrawals exceed a thousand dollars."

"That's right," Edith agreed. "In the past, when we asked Dot about it and suggested a voucher system, she brushed it off, saying it wasn't important because the petty cash is for incidentals such as supplies, coffee, doughnuts and such for the board meetings and visitors. We just dropped it. We think Dot may have pocketed the eighteen thousand dollars and dipped into the petty cash drawer," she added miserably.

"Do you plan to confront Dot?" Nadine asked.

"Let me answer that," Thornton said. "I suggested they gather all the evidence they have found and present it to the district attorney's office or the detectives at the police department."

Hattie lifted her hands in a helpless gesture. "We want to do the right thing, but what if there is a rational explanation and it's not what it appears?" she worried. "No matter how we might approach Dot with this, we are finished at CCCC. Dot is a sensitive person with a volatile personality. The minute we confront her, we will have made an enemy."

Edith shrugged. "We've heard stories about people who have gotten on her bad side."

"Didn't she run another charity before coming to Pembrooke?" Thorton rubbed his chin as he tried to recall. "I have only heard positive comments about her. Since she's been here, CCCC's fund-raising efforts have more than doubled." He cocked his head to one side as he looked at the two women. "Were background and reference checks conducted prior to her being hired?"

"Of course they were," Edith responded a bit defensively, "or the board wouldn't have hired her. I just don't remember the specific details."

"Neither do I," Hattie said. "All I know is she was highly recommended."

Nadine frowned. "How did these discrepancies go undetected after the annual audit?"

Edith and Hattie exchanged glances.

"If we're right, maybe Dot is much shrewder than we give her credit for," Hattie admitted.

Nadine wasn't quite sure why the *Daily Mirror* was Edith and Hattie's sounding board and why they hadn't heeded Thornton's advice to report their suspicions to the local authorities.

Edith picked at a cuticle. "Hattie and I don't want to be the ones to blow the whistle and subject ourselves to Dot's wrath. Nor do we particularly want to come off as trouble makers. Hattie has a recently divorced niece who has just moved to Pembrooke and is looking for a job. We think she would make a great executive director. If the board thinks we caused Dot's discharge, it will kill Portia's chance to succeed Dot."

*There is always an ulterior motive,* Nadine thought. Edith and Hattie weren't as benevolent as they first appeared.

After Edith and Hattie left, Nadine cocked her head and peered at Thornton. "Why is it I feel as though they want *us* to do their dirty work? It's a win-win for them. If a crime is uncovered, it was due to their praiseworthy efforts. If it proves to be an unsubstantiated claim, then it was just a press witch hunt."

"I didn't realize you were so cynical," Thornton said. "Of *course* they want us to do the dirty work, not only to get Dot fired, but to avert suspicions so as not to ruin Portia's chance to replace Dot. You know that as well as I do." He chuckled. "What happened to that investigative spirit? Maybe this is your chance to win another Pulitzer."

"It's your turn." Nadine's response mirrored his sarcasm. "Besides, you need the money so that you can pay me what I'm worth."

"The newspaper will never have that kind of money—at least not without robbing a bank."

"It's reassuring to know you recognize a truism when you see it. What's that Biblical scripture I learned when my journalism law professor was discussing libel? The truth shall set you free. Anyway, O' Swami, what do we do in the case of the fundraiser who believes charity begins at work?"

"Well, uh, how about 'God helps those who help themselves'?"

"Funny," Nadine replied. "I was trying to be serious. Publicizing an unsubstantiated allegation could be as calamitous to Dot and CCCC as publishing a provable exposé."

"It looks like we may have two hot cases with which to deal and both volatile in their own right. I guess we wait for the information and see what happens. Dot may have a totally plausible explanation and Vanderlay Consultants Group may not be a phantom or the alter ego of Dot."

"If there is merit to the allegations, we are faced with two dilemmas as I see it. The first is whether the *Daily Mirror* wants to expose it or turn it over to the authorities. The second is how much play we want to give it in light of the annual fundraising campaign about to be launched. It could torpedo the whole thing."

"Nadine, you raise some good points. There are a lot of stakeholders in this thing. Everyone who has some connection with CCCC will be affected. That includes the potential recipients who are dependent upon CCCC for funding. By the way, weren't they trying to recruit you to be the honorary campaign chair for the upcoming year?"

"They were, but since I was helping the Girl Scouts in their fundraising efforts I thought there might be a conflict of interest. I respectfully declined."

"That might have been a fortuitous decision. As for me, I am still not quite sure what I'm going to do with all the Girl Scout cookies you forced me to buy."

It was Thursday morning when Nadine arrived for her appointment with Dot at the CCCC office. She waited in the deserted lobby for about ten minutes until a pale, willowy young girl with straight blond hair entered the room. Her thin lips curved into a slight smile as she gestured to Nadine.

"I apologize for the wait. Dot will see you now."

Nadine got up and followed the young woman down a short corridor. She hesitated at the end of the hall and showed Nadine into Dot's office. Nadine smiled pleasantly and shook hands before taking a seat in front of Dot's sprawling executive desk. Dot's eyes darted around the room as she settled into her chair.

"Would you like some coffee? Water?" she offered.

Nadine threw up her hands. "Oh, no, thank you."

Dot hesitated for a moment then absently arranged the pens and stapler on her desk. "What can I do for you Ms. Siena?"

Nadine leaned forward and placed a notebook on the desk in front of her. "CCCC has been a fixture in Pembrooke for as long as I can remember. This organization has done a lot of wonderful projects in the community. I have done volunteer work here myself."

Dot's face flushed. "Yes, we manage to stay quite busy." She managed a strained laugh.

"We are troubled by some information given to the *Daily Mirror* about a company with whom this organization has done business for the last couple of years."

Dot's eyebrows arched. "What company are you referring to?"

"Vanderlay Consulting Group. Do you currently have a contact for that firm?"

Nadine watched as every hint of color drained from Dot's face. She swallowed audibly and struggled to keep her composure.

"This company has allegedly been paid thousands of dollars by CCCC," she continued. "What can you tell me about this firm?"

"I don't know who is giving you this information, but I assure you . . . ." Her face suddenly contorted in anger. "I . . . I really don't have time for this."

Nadine kept her voice even. "I'm sorry. This seems to have upset you. Did this company swindle your organization, or fail to fulfill its contract?"

"Well, no. I . . . I mean they . . . It . . . ."

"What services did they provide?"

Dot was out of her chair now. She paced back and forth in front of the window, wringing her hands. Any semblance of composure was slipping away. Her voice trembled.

"Dot," Nadine's voice was low and calm, "we know that there is no Vanderlay Consulting Group. Please tell me what happened."

The executive director whirled around toward Nadine. Her face had gone from white to crimson and was twisted into something between rage and shock. She took a step forward and for a moment Nadine thought she might physically lash out.

Dot postured like a cornered animal. "What do you mean coming in here like this?" She pounded her fists on the edge of the desk. "I have spent my whole life doing charity and philanthropic work. How *dare* you!"

"Then please sit down and tell me what happened." There was no accusation in Nadine's voice. It sounded reassuring.

Dot hesitated for a moment as she stared at Nadine, then at the floor. Nadine felt a sudden pang of pity. Dot's eyes searched the room like a drowning man looking in vain for a life preserver. Nadine sat calmly with her pen poised over her note pad.

"Please sit down and explain Vanderlay Consulting. Tell me what happened."

The façade crumbled and Dot seemed to grow smaller as she leaned on the desk. For a moment Nadine feared the woman would collapse altogether. She dropped heavily into her chair and remained silent for some minutes. Nadine waited in silence. Suddenly Dot erupted in a torrent of tears. Her shoulders convulsed as she sobbed. The receptionist opened the door and peered inside, frowning.

"Dot?"

The executive director waved her away while yanking a tissue from the box on her desk and pressing it to her nose.

"I have spent my life working for charitable organizations," she began. "My passion has always been helping women in desperate circumstances, like young girls who are pregnant with no place to turn." She stared at her hands. "Then, my own marriage fell apart. My husband is an alcoholic and he was becoming more and more abusive. When he beat my oldest daughter, I threw him out and told him if he ever came back I would file charges and have him thrown in jail. He left me and the girls, but he also left us with a mortgage and a mountain of debt of which I was unaware. He was gambling on top of everything else. How could I have not known?" She looked across at Nadine, her eyes reflecting her anguish. "I was desperate and drowning, and started taking money. No, Ms. Siena, there is no Vanderlay. I made it up." Dot's forehead dropped to the desk as she broke into fitful sobs.

Nadine sat quietly as a flurry of emotions passed through her. She couldn't help but feel sorry for this woman.

Finally Dot sat up and looked at Nadine. Her eyes were red and her face still wet with tears. She looked like a defeated soldier. She cleared her throat. "Ms. Siena, I know you are looking for a sensational story, but I *beg* you not to print this. Please, *please* for the sake of my daughters. They would be ridiculed and have to suffer humiliation because of *me*. They have suffered enough. This is a good organization, and you're right, it *has* made a difference here in Pembrooke. If this scandal gets out, people will abandon CCCC and it will be a loss to the community and the people it serves."

"Are you able to make restitution for what you have taken?"

"I think my father will help me as he did before."

"Before what?"

Again, the color drained from Dot's face as she confessed she had been terminated from her previous employment for theft of funds. Nadine shook her head in disbelief.

"I will hold the story for twenty-four hours with the condition you make immediate and full disclosure to the board. Once that has been done, we will need to speak with the board chairman."

By midafternoon, Thornton Marimon got the call he was waiting for from the CCCC board chairman, Palmer Baldwin.

"Because of the effect a scandal like this would have on the Coronado County Community Chest and its campaign efforts, not to mention the disastrous impact it would have on some of the beneficiaries, we have agreed to forego criminal prosecution in exchange for a full restitution. Dot has tendered her resignation and will immediately leave Pembrooke. In addition, she will be required to undergo a mental health evaluation and successful completion of any recommended treatment at her own cost. The attorney for CCCC is drafting an agreement as we speak. Everything is expressly conditioned on complete repayment within forty-eight hours."

"That sounds like a good timeframe to wait before making our readers aware of the situation," Thornton said reflectively.

"We're hopeful the story won't be reported at all," Baldwin said as his voice crackled.

"I can't guarantee anything beyond forty-eight hours," Thornton replied. "Whether the newspaper would continue to withhold disclosure to the public is something that would require careful consideration. After all, it is a matter of public interest."

"Our attorney has suggested that we include a clause in our agreement with Dot prohibiting her from ever working for or being affiliated with any other nonprofit."

"How about inserting a clause requiring that she make full disclosure of her embezzlements to any and all future employers?"

"That is something our attorney has also recommended be included."

"Would you mind providing the *Daily Mirror*

with a copy of the final product?"

"Not at all. I think that would be most appropriate."

Thornton hung up the phone feeling uncomfortable with the decision of withholding such a story from his readers, even on the short term. Was it the right thing to do? Embezzlement of charitable funds by the executive director of CCCC was certainly a matter of legitimate public concern and interest. It was a matter of which the public should be made aware, particularly those people who had donated resources to the organization. Nadine and Thornton discussed it later that day.

"It is not a legal issue," Thornton told Nadine. "Clearly, it is within our First Amendment right to expose Dot's wrongdoing. There are no libel issues, and it is not an invasion of privacy. We certainly have a legal right to print truthful information legally obtained. And we didn't have to resort to keyhole tactics to do so. In fact, it was dropped in our laps.

"The only issue is whether it is the right thing to do."

Nadine got up and patted her boss's shoulder as she prepared to leave for the evening. She appreciated the fact that this was a struggle because it proved that he had the heart of a true journalist. Most of the time, in the rush to sell publications, a lot of publishers would already have the story splattered across the pages. To hell with who was hurt or who benefited. Just feed the public a sensational story. Get ratings, sell papers. Yet these were the types of hard decisions conscientious journalists and publishers had to make every day: weighing the public's right to be informed, the impact on stakeholders, and those trying to dodge the bullet to protect their own backsides. Trying to manage conflicting interests that always seem to be on a collision course was a balancing act. The right answer wasn't always easy, and nowadays, as long as it sold papers, few people really cared.

Whatever path they took, Thornton and Nadine knew there would be the inevitable detractors. However, both for now could rest in the assurance that they had done the right thing and there would be no turning back.

# CHAPTER 7

## CONVICTED BY CONJECTURE

A huge crash of thunder jarred Nadine from her concentration and made her jump. Three days of non-stop rain continued to pelt the streets and trace rivulets down the panes of her office windows. It was damp, gray and cold. Miserable. It was a good day to be home curled up with a warm drink and a good book. Although that was a tempting thought, the *Candela Daily Mirror* had barely closed the files on the CCCC scandal, and she was trying to spend some time working on the ongoing drug story and on her book outline. The phone jangled irritatingly from the corner of her desk. She frowned at the thing, wishing she could will it into silence. Relenting, she answered.

"This is Nadine."

"Nadine, this is Marci. There is a Charlotte Tilnen here to see you."

Nadine frowned. She could tell the receptionist was cupping her hand over the phone and whispering into the receiver. That meant trouble.

"Ms. Tilnen is upset and says she will only talk

to you." Was that desperation in Marci's voice? Not a good sign.

Nadine sighed. "Send her in." *How long could it take?* A minute later, Marci was showing the woman into Nadine's office. The receptionist gave Nadine a vague nod and raised her eyebrows as she shut the door behind her.

The woman removed her soggy jacket and draped it over the coat rack. They shook hands. Nadine motioned Charlotte Tilnen to a chair situated in front of her desk. Nadine sat in the chair next to her. It made things a little less formal than gazing across her desk.

"How may I help you, Ms. Tilnen?"

"Please, call me Charlotte." The woman's voice was tight as she fumbled in her purse for a tissue. She was a tall angular woman, perhaps in her early forties.

"All right, Charlotte." Nadine folded her arms and, elevating one, cradled her chin on her thumb.

Almost as an afterthought, Charlotte fished through her purse again and brought out her cell phone. She touched the display and slid her finger across the screen. A photograph appeared and she shoved it toward Nadine. "This is my daughter, Meg."

Nadine peered at the image of a smiling, beautiful teenage girl. Long blond hair fell over her shoulders, soft curls framing her heart-shaped face, hazel eyes and dimpled cheeks. The girl was dressed in a cheerleading uniform. Her short skirt revealed shapely, athletic legs, and the sweater accentuated her ample breasts and small waist. She held pom-poms against her well-formed hips.

Nadine handed the photo back. She gazed over at the woman and waited for her to speak.

"Meg is fifteen and a sophomore."

"She's a beautiful girl. You must be proud of her."

The woman studied her lap and twisted the tissue between her fingers.

As Nadine waited for Charlotte to relate the heart of the matter, she speculated as to why this distraught mother might be there. Had Meg become pregnant with a child of an older boy, a neighbor, a relative or a minister? Had Meg become involved in drugs or a crime spree? What had happened that would cause Charlotte to involve the *Daily Mirror*?

Finally, Charlotte sniffed into her tissue and continued. "I hesitate to tell you this," Charlotte confessed, "but when I discovered Meg had forgotten her cell phone when she left for school a couple of weeks ago, I—I intercepted a text message from one of her friends. It—it involved Meg and one of her male teachers." She shook her head miserably and began to sob. "I have no one else to turn to. Even Meg's father won't listen to me."

Nadine attempted to console Charlotte by placing her hand on Charlotte's shoulder. However, Charlotte abruptly pushed Nadine's hand aside and pulled away. "I don't need sympathy or pity. I just need help."

*You're not going to get my sympathy or help if you continue to act like that!* Nadine wanted to say but thought the better of it.

Almost as quickly as the tears started they stopped. "You might have heard of Torrington Moore. He is the boys' head basketball coach at Claxton High School. The kids call him Mr. T. Last year he coached the team to their first-ever state championship. He also teaches math. Anyway, Meg is one of his algebra students and she consistently gets straight A's in his class.

"So what is the issue with Mr. Moore?"

"He is tall, not bad looking and all the girls at Claxton seem to have a crush on him."

Nadine's face creased into a frown. "And it sounds like he is doing a good job."

Charlotte's eyes narrowed. There was a slight twitch in her jaw. "If you ask me, he's one conceited, arrogant bastard! None of the parents can stand him. Ironically, only the high school principal is paid a higher salary. Unbelievable!"

"I take it Mr. T is not on your Christmas card

list." A crooked smile creased her lips.

Charlotte flushed. "You may find this amusing, Ms. Siena, but to me it is no laughing matter."

Nadine held up her hands. "I wasn't trying to offend you or be cavalier. Please, just tell me what is on your mind."

"It all started between Meg's freshman and sophomore years. Meg attended a school-sponsored summer camp that utilized the CHS facilities. Torrington Moore was there and Meg came back from the camp starry eyed over him. When she made the cheerleading squad at the beginning of her sophomore year, she and her squad practiced in an auxiliary gym adjacent to where the boys' basketball team trained. It was inevitable then that Meg's and Mr. Moore's paths would cross on a more frequent basis." She handed Nadine a folded slip of paper. "This is the text message I intercepted."

Nadine unfolded the paper and read: *I saw the way you and Coach Moore looked at each other during practice break. The hug looked like more than a hello. Erica tells me you two have a 'thing.' How come you have never said anything to me? I thought I was your best friend. Jen.*

After reading the text message, Nadine pressed her lips together and handed it back to Charlotte. It was then that Charlotte unleashed her wrath. Nadine was glad the doors to her office were closed and only hoped

Charlotte's shrill voice was stifled enough not to alarm those within hearing distance.

Charlotte was still wild eyed after Nadine's polite pleas for restraint were reluctantly heeded. However, it was not until after her extensive list of descriptive expletives had been exhausted on Mr. T. The acronym for Forced Under Carnal Knowledge dominated the remainder of Charlotte's discussion.

"I know this is upsetting" Nadine said, attempting to calm Charlotte. "May I get you some water?"

Charlotte calmed down somewhat but irritation was still reflected in the tone of her voice. "Yes. Thank you."

There was a gurgling sound as Nadine filled a plastic glass from the water cooler and set it in front of Charlotte, who took a sip from the glass and set it on the desk as she resumed her story.

"I was disappointed in Meg. To this day, she has refused to press charges against Moore, or to even admit that it was he who robbed her of her virginity." Her voice started to escalate again and she shook her finger at Nadine. "Sexual assault on a minor by a person in a position of trust is an aggravated offense under the laws of our state. Perverts like Torrington Moore need to be taught a lesson and locked away for the rest of their lives to rot in prison!"

When Nadine didn't respond, Charlotte's mouth folded into a snarl. "You don't seem to be at all moved by any of this!" She jumped to her feet. "Unless something is done—and done soon—there will be other victims whose lives will be turned upside down like Meg's."

"I can understand your consternation," Nadine managed to reply. "But isn't this something you should take up with the school authorities and the police?"

Charlotte rolled her eyes and pursed her lips in disgust. "The first thing I did, after confronting Meg with the text message, was to haul her stubborn ass, along with the incriminating text message, to the principal's office at Claxton High. A lot of good *that* did! I had to threaten a lawsuit just to get in to see the high and mighty bitch, Lillian Townley. She has outlived her tenure at CHS and I have delivered a letter to the school board demanding her resignation."

"Was she not willing to listen?"

"Lillian has the backbone of a jellyfish. She's afraid of her own shadow. When I demanded that Moore be fired, she hemmed and hawed and said Meg would first need to be interviewed, outside of my presence, by both her and the assistant principal and be examined by the school's psychologist." She dug her teeth into her bottom lip and glared at Nadine. "You don't want to know what I told her. The audacity of that woman! She also said, before any action could be taken, she would need to talk to the school's attorney. And can you imagine? She would talk with the perpetrator himself. Can you believe she would take the word of a pedophile over that of a student?"

"But, I understood you to say that Meg denied any impropriety or wrongdoing on either her part or on Mr. Moore's part. Did I misunderstand?"

Charlotte stared at her, open mouthed and incredulous, her palms extended like a plea. "Why wouldn't she? Obviously, Meg is afraid of reprisal and embarrassment. We don't know the extent of Moore's threats and intimidation. She may even be brainwashed. Meg is still just a child trying to survive in an adult world. She is no match for a corrupt system where all the cards are stacked against her."

Mustering up courage, Nadine finally asked, "Charlotte, what is it you want our newspaper to do?"

"Isn't it clear by now?" Charlotte snapped. "To allow a teacher to interact inappropriately with the students at Claxton is to place all our youth at risk. Allowing it sends the message that the school authorities are condoning such conduct." She grabbed her purse and slung it over her shoulder. "I'm disappointed that *you*, of all people, don't feel some sense of urgency to do something."

Nadine was on her feet now, looking squarely at Charlotte Tilnen. "First of all, if your accusations are true, this is indeed a serious matter. However, a person is innocent until proven guilty. We are not in the business of ruining reputations on hearsay. Just as with the school authorities, the newspaper would need to conduct its own investigation and make its own determination before printing any story to ensure it would be fair and accurate."

"If sexual assault on a student by a teacher is not newsworthy, Ms. Siena, then *nothing* is and we should shut down all the news outlets." Charlotte's visible parts had turned crimson as she prepared to leave. She jabbed a long boney index finger toward Nadine. "Today, you squandered the opportunity to take advantage of a scoop. If the *Candela Daily Mirror* is not interested in printing the story, I know the *Coronado Globe Telegraph* would be more than anxious to do so. By doubting me, you have labeled me a liar. Maybe some of your other subscribers wouldn't be offended by the insult, but I am not one of them. Consider my subscription *cancelled*."

Charlotte grabbed her coat from the coat rack, making it teeter and sending a spray of water droplets across the office. The door slammed and Nadine dropped into the chair behind her desk, shaking her head. *Another day in the wild and wonderful world of journalism.* Outside, a clap of thunder rattled the windows. It was indeed a gloomy day.

The next morning Nadine sat with a huge mug of hot coffee and her face buried in the early edition of the *Coronado Globe Telegraph*. "Oh my God," she sputtered into her cup.

There on the front page was the oversized headline, *Sexual Misconduct Allegations in Local School – Is Your Child Safe?* Nadine tossed the paper aside and picked up the phone. She checked with the local law enforcement agencies to see if any reports of an investigation had been released to the press. She had already determined from the courts that no charges had been filed.

In a tightknit community like Pembrooke, the *Globe* article caused quite a stir. It wasn't long before Torrington Moore was placed on administrative leave due to public outcry, and the scathing letters began to pour in to both newspapers. Some of the letters criticized the *Candela Daily Mirror* for refusing to print the story and keeping the public informed. Charlotte's letter accused the *Daily Mirror* of a blatant cover-up and urged a community boycott of the newspaper. The fallout began shortly after. Almost overnight more than one hundred readers cancelled their subscriptions.

However, Nadine and Thornton were prepared to weather the storm. They would not sell their souls to the devil or compromise the ethical standards that had made the *Daily Mirror* the leading newspaper in the region, even if it adversely affected the pocketbook. And it wasn't only subscribers that defected; several of the newspaper's regular advertisers also followed suit, while others threatened to do the same.

With his name smeared all over the headlines, Torrington's fall from prominence was predictable. A teacher accused of having committed sexual indiscretions with his female student was not an everyday occurrence in Pembrooke and not something a God-fearing, and law-abiding community could or would tolerate. And Torrington's suspension with pay was evoking heavy criticism from the taxpayers who were footing the bill. No one was surprised when public pressure prompted Torrington to be fired. He immediately made arrangements to move his family out of the area to protect them from the negative press.

Charlotte watched every step of the process, hoping to see Torrington dragged through the mire of public disgrace. She had done everything in her power to make that happen, to make him pay. When the grand jury failed to indict, Charlotte was madder than ever.

It was Friday afternoon when the local news broadcast showed Torrington Moore coming down the steps of the courthouse shielded by his attorney. Like a pack of hungry jackals, the waiting reporters rushed toward him. Before they could get to him, he was pushed into the back seat of a waiting sedan. The door had barely closed when it sped away. In unison, the reporters turned toward the attorney, surrounding him and clamoring for a statement.

When Torrington's car had faded from sight, the attorney gave the press a brief statement. "Mr. Moore has not been charged with any crimes, nor will he be. He has fully cooperated with the police and the district attorney's office and as far as we are concerned, the matter is closed." With that he left, ignoring the questions the reporters shouted at his back.

Charlotte glared at the television screen, her hands balled into to tight fists. Rage rose in the back of her throat. There was no way she would just let this thing drop. *I'll show these bastards! I haven't even started yet.* She immediately started making calls and writing letters demanding the impeachment of the district attorney for what she called a blatant *whitewash*. She called for an investigation by the state's attorney general and suggested that in the interim the district attorney be replaced.

The *Daily Mirror* had been reticent to print anything other than the fact that Moore was being investigated and the investigation timeline. The publication was not about to get into unsubstantiated claims of sexual improprieties. When it was all over, the *Globe* failed to print the exculpatory facts that reinforced the grand jury's decision. Not only did it refuse to indict, but issued a no-true bill, indicating that evidence was insufficient to warrant prosecution. Nadine and the *Daily Mirror* felt it was their duty to report the facts. Nadine's story dominated the front page.

## POPULAR COACH VINDICATED – CASE UNRAVELS

*Was it just a hoax that brought down a popular Claxton High School coach and teacher, or is he a sexual predator? That is the question that the citizens in Pembrooke have been asking themselves ever since Charlotte Tilnen broke the story that appeared on the front page of the* Coronado Globe Telegraph *several weeks ago, alleging that her daughter had been sexually assaulted by Torrington Moore.*

*The* Candela Daily Mirror *was criticized for not printing unsubstantiated allegations. Subscribers and advertisers alike voiced their dissatisfaction. The* Daily Mirror *has published only the facts until the results of a full and complete investigation were concluded. That has happened today. According to a* statement issued today by District Attorney Horace Henderson, Charlotte Tilnen filed a complaint with his office alleging that her daughter had been sexually assaulted by Torrington Moore. Moore is a teacher and the head basketball coach at Claxton High School.

In his official statement, the district attorney said, "As a result of Ms. Tilnen's allegations, our office, in conjunction with the Pembrooke Police Department, lauched a full-scale investigation into the claims. Over seventy-five interviews were conducted with other teachers and staff, past employers and both current and former students of Mr. Moore. Over twenty-five witnesses appearred before the Coronado grand jury and testified."

The Daily Mirror *personally interviewed the alleged victim in the presence of her mother several times. She categorically denied any improprieties on the part of Mr. Moore.* The Daily Mirror *also interviewed Mr. Moore. Not only were his statements consistent with the statements of other witnesses, he passed not one, but two polygraphs, one administered by the Kansas Bureau of Investigation and the other by the Pembrooke Police Department.*

The statement from the district attorney concluded by saying, "The allegations against Mr. Moore are unfounded. Even the so-called victim refutes the claims. Under the laws of our state, more than mere suspicion is required before prosecution is warranted, as demonstrated by the grand jury's finding."

The Daily Mirror *has learned that Torrington Moore*

*and his family have listed their home for sale and have left Pembrooke. Their new location was not disclosed. Mr. Moore's privacy is respected and* The Daily Mirror *has made no attempt to contact him during this difficult time.*

Even though Nadine's story had a hint of an editorial, she left those honors for Thornton. The caption for Thornton's editorial read: *Convicted by Conjecture.* The lead-in to the editorial, as with Nadine's article, started with a question: *How do you prove that you are innocent of that with which you've been falsely accused?*

*Being wrongfully tried and convicted in the court of public opinion because of the press is as egregious as wrongfully being tried and convicted in a court of law. Although Claxton High School math teacher and boys' head basketball coach was accused of having a sexual encounter with one of his students, the only evidence was the mother's suspicion. Even the alleged victim refuted the allegation. If that is not proof enough of Torrington Moore's innocence, then the readers need be reminded of his having taken and passed polygraphs administered by local law enforcement authorities and his otherwise impeccable reputation.*

*Coach Moore's name and reputation have been irretrievably tarnished by the improvident rush to condemnation by an untrusting mother, by the exposition of an imprudent press, and by a group of vigilantes bent upon delivering this man's head on a platter. This is a lesson for our entire community as any one of us could be caught up in a similar snare through no fault of our own.*

*Once that question mark is raised, and once a professional reputation has been damaged, it can never be restored. It is a mark one must bear. This is particularly true for someone like Torrington Moore, who has been forced by false accusations, innuendo and unwarranted assumptions to leave his profession and his home—not only for now, but perhaps forever!*

# CHAPTER 8

## KEEPING A PROMISE

It was a cold, snowy Friday in December. Nadine was preparing to leave work a little early so she could drop off some Christmas presents at St. Vincent de Paul Orphanage. It would give her time for a quick visit with Mother Catherine. Just as Nadine was on her way out the door, her cell phone rang. She shuffled her packages into her other arm and answered. It was Corey Samuelson.

"I just got a letter from Megan," he began. "She included a clipping from last Monday's paper about the discovery of Trevor Watts' body. The article said he was found in a snow bank by an abandoned building in the old part of town, and that he had been shot execution style. I almost keeled over when I saw the guy's photo."

"Did you know him?"

"Remember me telling you about the special trip Megan's father made on the morning of July fourth? He went to his pharmacy to fill a prescription for his gardener's mother, or so he said. Well, it was the same kid–the gardener–who picked up the sealed package the previous day."

"So what are you saying?"

"The photograph of the guy that was murdered–this Trevor guy–*was* Dr. Hopkins' gardener! That's why Megan sent me the article."

"Are you absolutely positive?" Nadine drummed her fingers against her lips, thinking.

"Of course I am." His voice went up an octave. "I not only saw him at Megan's house when I was there, I talked to him."

Nadine paused as she processed what Cory had said.

"By the way, have you had time to do any investigation?"

"We did some background on Dr. Hopkins. Not a lot, but enough to know that he's legitimate. Something that you may not be aware of is that Megan's mother is Dr. Edmund Simms' sister."

Nadine sighed as she hit *end call* on her cell. She dumped her packages haphazardly on the edge of her desk and hit the buzzer on her office phone. The intercom made an annoying sound.

"What's up, Nadine?" came Thornton's hollow greeting.

"What I have to tell you can't wait," Nadine said.

"Well, what are you waiting for?"

"I'll be right there!"

Thornton stood as she entered. "You haven't been recruited by our competitor, have you?" He motioned for her to be seated.

"Heavens, no," she said as she sat and crossed her legs. "Something that might astound you is that I know, or think I know, who killed Trevor Watts."

"You've been talking to your source again."

"Just hung up with my source. We now have a name for Dr. Hopkins' gardener."

"Don't tell me Trevor Watts was Dr. Hopkins' gardener at the time he was killed?"

"Your pen name wouldn't be Sherlock Holmes?"

"You gave away the answer long before you asked the question. You would make a poor quiz show hostess. Who would want Dr. Hopkins' gardener killed and why?"

"The 'why' is easy. Trevor Watts had become a liability."

Thornton interrupted. "The 'who' is also easy. Both Dr. Hopkins and Dr. Simms had a motive, one that would have justified Trevor Watts' elimination."

"How did you know?"

"Elementary, my dear Watson."

Both chuckled. However, their comic relief was

short lived. It was Thornton who burst the bubble. "Do you realize that the knowledge you have gleaned from your source places you in a compromising situation?"

"I don't have personal knowledge," Nadine said smugly. "It is my source who has personal knowledge."

"Precisely," Thornton said as he peered over his glasses.

"That look tells me you would not like to be wearing my shoes."

"By not telling me who your source is, you have insulated me from being held in contempt in the event I'm called before a grand jury. But you, if you're called and refuse to reveal the name of your source, can be incarcerated and both you and the newspaper fined."

"The authorities don't know what I know."

"Knowing you, not alerting the authorities to avoid further atrocities is not something you can live with very long. Once you go to the authorities, they will not be content with what you were told, but they will want your source."

"I guess I better get my bags packed. Ever since I decided to become a journalist, I knew that such a day would come. Can you do without me for thirty days?"

"Thirty days maybe, but not much more." In jest, Thornton added. "Remember that counts against your vacation time and maybe even against sick leave."

"What if it's longer than thirty days?" Nadine asked reflecting her true concern.

*Then you will be eligible for retirement benefits,* Thornton started to say but thought better of it. Instead he said, "Thirty days would probably be on the conservative side. I'll call our attorney, Charles Atkins, and see if he can meet with us first thing Monday morning. Think about your fate before you make any rash decisions."

Nadine nodded. Legality and ethics had taken up opposite corners of the ring and were preparing to battle it out in her mind and heart.

Despite the hazardous road conditions, Charles Atkins appeared at the newspaper office promptly at nine a.m. the Monday of Christmas week. An older version of Brad Pitt, his step, demeanor and appearance belied his sixty-two years. Only his wisdom and sage advice exposed his true age.

Thornton and Nadine were waiting for him. He had been part of the newspaper family for as long as Thornton had been editor. Charlie had kept the newspaper out of harm's way on an *ad hoc* basis to begin with and was utilized extensively and effectively the last dozen years, so much so that he was placed on retainer.

That proved to be an ideal arrangement, especially for the newspaper which, with the passing of each day, was relying on him more and more. His reputation as a hard fighter and tenacious trial attorney made his representation all the more coveted.

Charlie poured a cup of steaming hot coffee and held it in his hands to warm them.

"I brewed that to drink, not to hold," Thornton said.

"Somebody must not have paid the heat bill," Charlie said. "I'm going to start spending my winters in Siberia. It's warmer."

"Why don't you move back to Tampa where you can bask in the sun and play backgammon all day?" Thornton suggested.

"My odds are better here. I can make more off you in one round of golf than I can lying around and playing Old Maid with the snow birds all winter long."

"Oh, wait until summer. I've been practicing my putting on my living room carpet and will beat you at the strength of your game. Maybe we'll up the ante."

"What, and watch you cry as you hand over your weekly allowance? You have a difficult time parting with a quarter."

"Ahem. Gentlemen," Nadine interrupted, "I am facing captivity in the county Bastille and yet the two of you are embroiled in self-aggrandizement, self-pity and unseemly invectiveness. Ain't you two got no couth nor consideration for anyone else?"

"A thousand pardons, my lady," Charlie said as he bowed to Nadine.

"A heck of a way to treat a Pulitzer Prize winner," Thornton said as he watched Charlie and Nadine hug.

"Charlie, I explained the situation to you over the telephone Friday," Thornton began. "Our hands have been tied for over four months now. There wasn't enough to write about or turn over to the authorities until the death of Dr. Hopkins' gardener, or alleged gardener, Trevor Watts. Nadine's source provides the nexus between Drs. Hopkins and Simms and now possibly between them and the deceased gardener. Without the source, everything is speculation and hearsay. You indicated on Friday that the source's information might give the authorities enough to get a search warrant."

"Of course, we don't know what the authorities, whether the DEA or the locals, have been working on," Charlie said as he fidgeted with his cup. "They might have infiltrated the ring and are ready to pounce and don't need the cooperation of the source. We just don't know. Trying to uncover the supplier of the prescription drugs that somehow are finding their way into the hands of the school kids is not a recent phenomenon. It has been going on now for several years. It makes sense that Trevor Watts was the intermediary. He could have been snuffed by a disgruntled dealer or user, by a competitor or even by the supplier. Maybe Trevor was becoming a liability or thought to be an informant. Drug dealers tend to be paranoid. Trevor must have known too much. Somebody wanted him dead."

"Maybe Trevor was putting the squeeze on the supplier, wanting a bigger share of the profits," Nadine speculated. "Or, in attempting to obtain a concession, he threatened to blow the whistle or flexed his muscles by threatening to obtain his inventory from another supplier."

"All possibilities," Charlie agreed. "Regardless, I think your confidential source is the missing link. If the authorities had the ammunition, they would have acted on it long before now. There have been a lot of drug-related deaths and Trevor, it appears, is only the latest. In my mind, if you provide the needed information but withhold the source, they will put pressure on you. If you don't divulge the name of the informant voluntarily, they will attempt to require you to do so under the threat of contempt of court. Without a shield law in Kansas, there is nothing I can do to help you, especially if you are called to testify before the grand jury. And, that's usually the way investigations of this nature are handled. That subpoena power is awesome unless you plead the Fifth. Even if Kansas *had* a state shield law, the feds don't. That means you could be called before a federal grand jury, if a violation of a federal law is involved, so even a state shield law, if it had one, would not protect you."

"Do you have any idea how long Nadine would be jailed if she were found to be in contempt?"

"Thornton, your guess is as good as mine. Theoretically, it would be until she complies. Realistically, I think it could be anywhere from one or two to six months."

Turning to Nadine, Charlie asked, "You're fairly certain, I take it, that your source won't release you from your guarantee of confidentiality. Is that what I'm hearing?"

"That's my take," Nadine responded as she searched her mind. "He is jeopardizing a lot by just coming forward. He is compromised by his relationship with certain family members and doesn't want to cause a chasm that would be impossible to ever cross. He has already taken the grand leap of faith in merely contacting me. I just can't envision the time when he would recant or relieve me of my assurance."

"Why not anonymously inform the authorities about the connection between the gardener and the co-conspirators?" Charlie asked. "That way, you provide them with the same information you would be providing in person. All that you are really doing in either event is withholding the identity of your informant or source. That way, they don't know about any informant and you avoid sticking your neck out and waiting for the blade to drop."

"Your metaphor is making me nervous," Nadine said as she shivered and folded her arms across her chest. "I always thought the guillotine was an inhuman way of exacting society's pound of flesh. Maybe it is better than being burned at the stake. In either event, you make a good point. This would be a way to refute the old adage, 'You can't have your cake and eat it, too!'"

"Now, Nadine, you understand why Charlie makes the big bucks," Thornton said. "Anonymously, we could make the authorities aware that Trevor Watts was Dr. Hopkins' gardener. That, in the past, he has been observed picking up packages at Dr. Hopkins' residence and at the Hopkins Pharmacy after closing and/or on holidays. That Dr. Hopkins and Dr. Simms appear to have some type of business relationship or unholy alliance. And that somehow the local teens have been getting high on prescription drugs from some inexplicable source."

"Isn't that pretty much what you would reveal without blowing your source's cover?" Charlie asked

Nadine.

"That probably would be the extent," Nadine responded.

"By reporting it in person, you risk saying too much, not to mention inviting incarceration. By making the anonymous disclosures deliberately obtuse, you won't be fingering your source directly or indirectly through inadvertent and ill-advised clues."

"I know you may not believe this," Nadine said, shaking her head and pressing her lips firm, "but I was prepared to give up my freedom for whatever time it took to protect my confidential source."

"But now you don't have to," Thornton said. "Now, all we have to do is find a foolproof way of alerting the authorities without having to feed you to the lions."

"Leave that up to me," Charlie said as he rose and donned his winter apparel. "I have a cousin who lives in Wichita. By the way, Nadine, I admire you for your stand and for your lobbying efforts before the Kansas legislature in support of a state reporter's shield law. If you had opted to identify your source, I would probably be defending you down the road for a breach of contract action brought by your source, assuming he was smart enough to hire an attorney."

Within short order, the *Daily Mirror* was responding to calls from the major wire services and both the print and electronic media in Wichita and cities from around the state. It was not long before the bordering states of Colorado, Nebraska, Missouri and Oklahoma were getting into the act. In a community known for its teenage drug problem, it was big news when a local pharmacist and physician, particularly when they were brothers-in-law, were being investigated in the death of a suspected drug dealer who happened to be the pharmacist's gardener.

Thornton and Nadine knew that Charlie could launch a rocket, but they never dreamt he would drop a hydrogen bomb. "His cousin in Wichita must be a power broker of no little significance and a guy you want on your side," Thornton said to Nadine.

It was obvious that all hell had broken loose. A monster had escaped. The mere fact that a local physician and pharmacist were being investigated was enough to organize a lynch mob as far as the rednecks were concerned. No need to spend the taxpayers' hard-earned money on a trial. Not here! Drs. Hopkins and Simms had made some enemies along the way, and their detractors were out buying the rope and looking for a stout tree branch over which to sling it.

Then the story came in on the wire service.

## PROBE CONTINUES INTO PEMBROOKE YOUTH'S MURDER

The ongoing investigation into the brutal murder of eighteen-year-old Trevor Watts, the gardener employed by a local pharmacist, has led authorities in Pembrooke, Kansas, to look more closely at the pharmacist, Dr. Maynard Hopkins and his brother-in-law, Dr. Edmund Simms. The body of Trevor Watts was discovered in the early morning hours of December 14 in a remote area on the outskirts of Pembrooke.

The county corner and chief medical examiner, Dr. Morris Pendleton, attributed the cause of death to multiple gunshot wounds to the head. Police reports describe the death as an execution style killing. The toxicology report indicates that at the time of his death, Trevor Watts had traces of Oxycontin, Vicodin and Demerol—all prescription drugs—present in his system.

In a community where several teen deaths have been thought to be linked to the use of both illegal and prescription drugs, the public is clamoring for action. Marianne Towner, the mother of a teenager whose death was caused by an overdose of prescription drugs at the end of the previous school year, stated, "Drugs in Coronado County are being distributed to teens on *school grounds with impunity." She added that she and other parents are disappointed with a lack of concern and action by local authorities. Both the Coronado Sheriff's Department and Pembrooke Police Department have declined comment.*

After the story hit the wire service, both Coronado County newspapers printed the story. The front page headlines in the *Globe* read: *DOCTOR AND PHARMACIST TARGET OF DRUG INVESTIGATION.* The headline in the *Daily Mirror* was more conservative. *LOCAL DRUG PROBLEM IN NATIONAL NEWS.* The electronic media, not to be outdone, made the exposé breaking news. The alleged nexus between Trevor Watts' death, his physician and his pharmacist was reported on all the national networks and provided dialogue for both local and national commentators.

The local media were notified that the Coronado County Sheriff's Department and the Pembrooke Police Department would be issuing a joint press release at the county courthouse. Apparently, the telephones of both agencies were ringing off the hook with inquiries.

Thornton and Nadine were among the media representatives at the Coronado County Courthouse that frigid January morning. When they arrived, the room was abuzz about the drug scandal that had rocked their small community and made national news. Many of the media were from areas outside Coronado County.

"I don't recognize half the journalists here," Thornton commented.

"Nor do I," Nadine responded. "The rumor mills obviously have generated a lot of interest."

"I'm glad we arrived when we did. I had to move some of the mics and tape recorders at the front of the podium to find room for ours."

"I've never seen so many television cameras in one place at the same time," Nadine said as the two jockeyed for a clear view of the podium.

The commissioner's room hushed as Sheriff Ignacio Rovera, flanked by representatives of the Pembrooke Police Department and local prosecutor's office strolled to the podium. Pulling a prepared script from his breast pocket and, unfolding it, Sheriff Rovera read, "Much of what the wire service reported is true. However, contrary to public perception, the law enforcement agencies in the county, with the assistance of state and federal agencies, have been involved in an ongoing investigation involving the use of both legal and illegal drugs in Coronado County. The reason why our agencies have declined comment to the electronic and print media is to avoid compromising our investigation."

The room erupted with questions. The first Sheriff Rovera fielded was from a reporter employed by the *Globe*. "The wire service story reports the death of Trevor Watts as an execution-style killing. It that a fair characterization?"

"That appears to be a fair characterization," Sheriff Rovera replied. "Our county coroner and chief medical examiner, Dr. Morris Pendleton, has attributed the cause of death to multiple gunshot wounds to the head, all at close range."

"Apparently, Mr. Watts had traces of various prescription drugs in his system at the time of his death. Is that true?" the same reporter asked.

"According to the toxicology report."

Thornton then asked, "The wire service story infers that there is a connection between Trevor Watts' death and a local physician and pharmacist. Could you elaborate?"

"Let me have Carlos Ortega of the District Attorney's Office answer that."

Carlos stepped to the podium and, clearing his throat, said, "All we can tell you at this time, is that at the time of his death, Trevor Watts was employed by Hopkins Pharmacy and did gardening and odd jobs for Dr. Maynard Hopkins at his residence. And some of the prescription bottles Trevor Watts' mother provided law enforcement authorities after his death had labels bearing the names of Hopkins Pharmacy and Dr. Edmund Simms as the prescribing physician."

Another reporter, who neither Thornton nor Nadine knew, asked, "Are Drs. Hopkins and Simms related?"

Sheriff Rovera responded, "The two are related by marriage. Dr. Hopkins is married to Dr. Simms' sister."

Sheriff Rovera then announced, "That is the extent of our question-and-answer period."

Despite the persistence of the media, Sheriff Rovera was whisked away, in the company of his deputies, without incident and without providing additional commentary.

Within minutes after the broadcast of Sheriff Rovera's statement on one of the local television stations, District Attorney Horace Henderson was on the telephone.

"Rovera's residence," the sheriff's wife said as she answered the kitchen extension.

"Morella, this is Horace Henderson. I just watched the five o'clock newscast on Channel 8. Did you catch it?"

"I watched it on Channel 5 with Igi. He said he was nervous but I didn't detect it."

"He did a very credible job!"

"He's watching television in the family room with the grandkids. Let me put him on the other extension."

Henderson could hear Morella yell that the DA was on the phone. As Ignacio's booming voice answered, Henderson could hear the click of the kitchen extension and television noise in the background.

Before Henderson could say anything, Ignacio said, "Hold on. Let me turn that damn thing down."

Within a few seconds, Ignacio came back on the line.

"You'd better update your Screen Actors' Guild card," Henderson said.

"My what?" Ignacio blared.

"Your SAG card."

Ignacio's telephone voice was so loud Henderson had to hold the receiver away from his ear. "Your performance was magnificent. Your life after the

S.O. awaits you."

"Couldn't have done it without you, my friend. All I did is read what you prepared."

"Two attorneys who represent the good doctors have left messages for me to call them back. I didn't get out of court until after five."

"I can tell you what they have to say. I spoke with both of them. Courtland Wiggins, of course, is representing Simms. He told me to get ready to defend a libel suit. Rebecca Lindsay then called and said virtually the same thing. She said she was representing Hopkins."

"Didn't take long to hire counsel," Henderson said.

Ignacio cleared his throat. "Both are smart enough to know they have been on law enforcements radar screen for some time now. If they were clever enough to eliminate an eyewitness, they are certainly clever enough to have a contingency plan in place."

"They haven't been on law enforcement's radar screen very long."

"No, but they had to realize that there would be a day when the numerous coincidences would be questioned and the dots got connected."

"Up till now, they have done a pretty good job of covering their tracks."

While the DA and sheriff spoke on the telephone, a meeting was being arranged between Drs. Hopkins and Simms.

"Did you catch the newscast on Chanel 8?" Dr. Hopkins asked anxiously.

"How could I not?" Dr. Simms responded.

"Katherine has locked herself in the bathroom and threatened divorce," Dr. Hopkins groaned.

"My sister has always been high strung. She'll get over it. Let's meet for coffee."

Dr. Hopkins knew that the invitation to coffee was code for what he really meant. *Let's meet at Grandpa Simms' old homestead.* "What are the roads like?" he asked. "The high country always gets double what we get in town."

"The elevation is not that much different," Dr. Simms responded. "We should have no difficulty."

"That road is usually the last to be plowed."

"I'll check with the state patrol. Unless you hear from me within the next ten minutes, you'll know the road is passable."

"It'll take me at least that long to get ready."

As Dr. Hopkins left the main highway and traveled on the snowpack of the narrow winding road framed on each side by plowed snow accumulation, he second guessed their decision to meet at the old homestead. While his Land Rover fishtailed and spun wildly on the turns, he thought of all the risks he and his brother-in-law had taken over the years in defying nature and the law.

Rounding a curve less than a mile from the turnoff to the homestead, he caught sight of Dr. Simms' SUV. It was parked and sat idling in the freshly plowed drive in front of the country store. As he pulled beside the SUV, Simms stepped out of his vehicle and walked towards the Land Rover. He was carrying what appeared to be a cassette case.

Simms motioned for Hopkins to stay put and hopped into the passenger side of the Land Rover brushing the snow off his jacket as he did so. "It's too slippery to attempt the drive up the lane to the old homestead." As he glared at Hopkins, he said, "What I've got to say, I can say here and now."

"What's the problem? Why are you so upset?"

"*Upset?* You damn right I am. It's obvious there's a whistleblower in our midst and it *ain't* me."

Hopkins mouth formed a tight line. "What are you trying to say?" he asked, trying to keep an even tone.

Simms stiffened and jabbed his index finger deep into Hopkins' chest. "I'm saying the only one who could have tipped the authorities is *you*!"

Hopkins knocked the offending digit aside and rubbed his chest. "Hey, you're hurting me,"

"Just answer the question. Are you trading your head on the platter for mine?"

"You think I blabbed to the authorities? There's no way I would do that. Besides, I would be signing my own death warrant by doing so."

"I hope you're not that stupid. You're into this thing up to your neck. If I go down, you go down with me."

"Why would you think I would do such a thing?" Hopkins asked as his voice quivered.

"I don't think you would. But I'm holding my insurance policy *guaranteeing* you won't." He held up a cassette and tapped it against Simms' nose. "I have recorded our conversations of Let's Make a Deal and there is enough ammunition on these tapes to hang you. This is just a copy. The digital recorder I have been carrying is hidden in a safe place."

Dr. Hopkins grimaced as he thought about what the cassette contained. Although he had had run-ins with his brother-in-law before, they never had been this intense. "Calm down," Hopkins pleaded. "I would never burn my own brother-in-law. Besides, by betraying you, I would be giving myself up as well."

Simms' glare softened. He jammed the cassette into his pocket and leaned back against the seat. He became reflective. "I'm . . . sorry, Maynard. With all the media attention and the authorities breathing down my neck, I overacted. I hope there are no hard feelings. We need each other." With that, he extended his right hand as a symbol of peace. The two then shook hands to ratify their solidarity.

"I thought our problems were over with Trevor out of the picture," Hopkins said as he wiped his brow with the back of his hand.

"Not quite," Dr. Simms responded. "The one we hired to silence Trevor is still alive and well. And, to compound matters, he is a sheriff's deputy."

"Are you saying Damon Rodden can't be trusted?"

"He can turn in a minute."

"You're not suggesting . . .?"

"Everyone is expendable—especially those who become a liability."

Hopkins felt cold shivers run down his spine and it wasn't just because of the winter freeze.

# CHAPTER 9

## REPORTING THE NEWS

"You read our article," Thornton said as Charlie Atkins stormed into his office with the previous day's edition of the *Daily Mirror* rolled up in his hand.

"Me and everyone else in the county," Charlie said.

"Let me get Nadine in here," Thornton said as he dialed her extension. "Charlie's here," he told her.

When Nadine entered, she could see fire in Charlie's eyes. "Didn't like the article, I see," Nadine said.

Nadine and Thornton braced for the scolding they knew was coming.

"The newspaper is hanging out there not by what the article said but by what it didn't say," Charlie said sternly. "The inference that is held dangling is that two brothers-in-law, one a physician and the other a pharmacist, are somehow involved in an illegal scheme to provide teens with prescription drugs and are tied into an unsolved murder of the pharmacist's gardener.

And, unfortunately, our jurisdiction does not recognize the wire service defense."

"We're sorry, Charlie," Thornton said. "We really should have contacted you."

Nadine nodded. "The story was pressing news and we were up against an unrealistic deadline. I guess we were relying on the wire service defense."

"Wasn't the story old news?" Thornton asked. "The article didn't say anything other than what was reported by our competitor and what the world already knew."

Charlie just shook his head. "To reprint or repeat libelous material, whether from the wire service, or from another news outlet, or someone on the street corner, is still libel under the republication doctrine. To publish a defamatory statement about someone that is false and results in someone suffering some injury or damage, such as the tarnishing of the reputation of a physician or pharmacist, is actionable libel. A physician's or pharmacist's reputation is his stock in trade. His reputation is everything. Ruin it and you have ruined his livelihood. His loss theoretically should be compensated for by the wrongdoer. Here, the media, including the good old *Candela Daily Mirror*, its editor and anyone else responsible for the libel is answerable."

"Personally, I thought the article was rather innocuous," Nadine said. "Isn't it the job of the press to report truthful information and let the readers draw their own conclusions? Thornton deliberately refrained from writing an editorial so as not to sway public opinion one way or the other. Everything in the article itself is truthful and balanced, is it not?"

"I have to agree with Nadine," Thornton said. "It was within my prerogative to write an editorial. That is my job, but I refrained from the temptation so as not to exacerbate the situation. The newspaper made no effort to do anything other than to report truthful information lawfully obtained. What we reported was a matter of grave public interest and concern, something that the public had the right to know. We didn't distort the news, we merely reported it."

"And," Nadine added, "the press release issued by Sheriff Ignacio Rovera says everything our article said and much more. I think the inferences to be drawn from his statements are far more incriminating than the wire story. Anything the press receives from an official government report or statement, as long as it is fairly and accurately quoted, immunizes the press from libel even if it contains false information. Isn't that what is called a qualified privilege or the privilege of the reporter? At least, that's what I learned at Columbia."

"They taught you well, Nadine," Charlie said somewhat subdued. "Sheriff Rovera issued an official statement in a public forum on a matter of public concern and printing it verbatim is as fair, accurate and complete as it can be. You were within your right to print it."

"I take it," Thornton said, "if we were hanging out on the wire service story, Sheriff Rovera's official statement rescued us."

"As a figure of speech it did," Charlie admitted. "However, I think it would behoove you to verify the statement attributed to Marianne Towner for yourselves. The last I knew, she was still working at Emory Jewelers."

"She is," Nadine said. "I was just in there last week to drop off a gold chain that needed repair. We covered the story, as you might have remembered, when her daughter Dixie was found dead the morning following a slumber party. The toxicologist reported finding a lethal amount of mixed prescription drugs in her system, including the antidepressants Prozac and Cymbalta. Apparently, each of the half dozen or so high school senior girls brought a bottle of pills from home and each poured the contents into a large bowl. Before bedtime, each took a handful and each subsequently went into orbit. Although several were hospitalized the following day, only Dixie failed to survive."

"It's a deadly game," Charlie mused, "much like playing Russian roulette except with prescriptions, there is a dangerous cartridge in every chamber."

"You might try to get a follow-up from Marianne," Thornton suggested to Nadine. "It might be interesting to get her read on the latest. Maybe her disdain extends to one or both of the brother-in-law doctors. She might just give you an earful."

"I know from the wire service story she does not have a special place in her heart for local law enforcement," Nadine responded. "It's possible she has information that she has not divulged that could advance the conspiracy theory. Even if it is hearsay, Dixie might have said something about Trevor Watts that could prove useful. They would have been about the same age."

When Nadine picked up her repaired gold chain from Emory Jewelers, she pulled Marianne Towner aside. "I assume you read the article in Monday's edition of the *Daily Mirror*."

"I did, and had intended to call you," Marianne responded. "When I received the telephone call from the wire service, I just spoke my mind. Hopefully, you don't think I was trying to bypass your newspaper."

"Not at all," Nadine said. "Our editor thought it deserved a follow-up, especially since I was on my way over here anyway."

Marianne ushered Nadine to the storeroom, "It's a lot more private back here," she said as she pulled the curtain tight behind her.

"Dixie's dad and I have been critical of our local authorities for quite some time and have not been afraid to voice our opinion. Perhaps I should have spoken to you sooner."

"Now is as good a time as any," Nadine said as she pulled out a notepad and pen from her purse. "Mind if I take notes?"

"Go right ahead. Where do you want me to start?"

"Tell me what you know about Trevor Watts."

"When Dixie was just a freshman, she had come home from the dance a little tipsy. Dixie's father and I thought Dixie might have been drinking but it turned out she and her friends had purchased pills from an eighth-grade boy by the name of Trevor Watts. The next day, however, Dixie recanted her story and said she didn't remember where she got the pills."

Marianne paused momentarily and dabbed at her eyes with a tissue. "We were so blinded we didn't recognize the signs. We discovered that Dixie was raiding the family prescription cabinet and from time to time we would find strange bottles with strange pills stashed in the bottom of her closet. When Dixie was a junior, she dated Trevor Watts for a short period."

Tears again swelled in Marianne's eyes. "After Dixie and Trevor were caught in a compromising position in the rec room, half stoned, her father and I forbade Dixie from seeing Trevor again. However, we suspected Dixie was still seeing Trevor but couldn't prove it. In fact, the pills Dixie took to the slumber party just before her death we suspect were provided by Trevor. I had intercepted a message from Dixie's cell phone the previous day from him, trying to set up a rendezvous."

Less than a week after the official statement of Sheriff Rovera appeared in the *Daily Mirror* and the *Globe*, both newspapers were sued in separate suits by Drs. Hopkins and Simms.

"Charlie's on the phone. Says he received your fax," Marci announced.

"Thanks," Thornton replied. "Please let Nadine know Charlie's on the phone."

"Charlie, I've got you on the speaker phone. Nadine will be joining us. In fact, she's walking in the door as we speak."

"Hi, Charlie," Nadine greeted as she entered Thornton's office.

"Hi, you two," Charlie replied. "I can't believe you subjected the good doctors to public disgrace, dishonor, humiliation, scorn, contempt, aversion and ridicule as they claim in their petitions. Shame on the *Daily Mirror* for ruining their reputation."

"We didn't defame them," Thornton said. "They defamed themselves. Shame on them."

"All we did was expose their improprieties," Nadine added.

"Obviously, they're claiming the statements in the press were false and that the debasement by the press has irreparably affected their careers." Charlie paused and then added, "Because the acts of the *Daily Mirror* were willful and wanton, in their eyes, that entitles them not only to actual damages in the amount of ten million dollars but an additional thirty million dollars as punishment."

"Should we write out a check now?" Thornton asked mockingly.

"Remember," Charlie replied, "each of the defamed doctors is asking for forty million. Does the *Daily Mirror* have eighty million in its checking account?"

"If both the *Globe* and the *Daily Mirror* fork over eighty million dollars," Nadine said, "that would be enough to allow them to retire."

"With at least a quarter going to their attorneys," Charlie said with a smirk, "that will only leave them with a hundred and twenty million."

"Almost like winning the lottery," Nadine commented.

"Speaking of the lottery," Charlie said in a scolding voice, "wasn't it me who said your newspaper was gambling by printing the articles in the first place?"

"Are you saying you told us so?" Thornton chided.

"Listen," Charlie interrupted, "I have to run to a hearing but can stop by your office afterwards and we can go over the petitions together."

"We'll be here all day," Thornton advised.

It was now almost noon as Nadine and Thornton sat around Thornton's conference table sipping Marci's fresh brew and sampling her sugar cookies.

"Not into cookies today?" Charlie asked as the cookies on Thornton's napkin remained virtually intact.

"Lost my appetite after being served with the lawsuits," Thornton said with a scowl. "Good thing I'm the major shareholder or otherwise I'd be looking for a new job."

"Your newspaper is not the only news outlet that has been sued by the brothers-in-law," Charlie said.

"Apparently, the electronic media has also been made the brunt of their wrath, as several local channels have been served with identical petitions."

"A lot of consolation," Thornton replied as he pushed his coffee cup aside and bit the edge of his bottom lip.

"With everyone in the mix," Charlie said, "you'd be sharing the liability with a host of other outlets. Besides, the newspaper's liability insurance policy will cover most, if not all, of any shared damage award."

"Looks like our liability insurance will only cover part of it," Thornton said as he slid the policy across the table in Charlie's direction. "Who would have thought ten million would not be more than ample. Guess we should have upped the coverage to keep pace with inflation and the ridiculous jury awards."

Charlie held the policy in his hand and removing his glasses, said, "Granted, the jury awards have spiraled, but libel plaintiffs have not fared well the past decade or two in having verdicts returned in their favor. Libel suits are filed not necessarily to recover huge awards or make the plaintiffs rich but to silence their critics. Such suits are classified as frivolous actions.

While Charlie paused to take a gulp of his coffee, Nadine asked, "Would you consider the case here a frivolous action?"

Setting his cup down on the saucer somewhat clumsily and wiping his mouth with the back of his hand, Charlie responded. "Setting vanity aside, I have come to the legal conclusion that your newspaper has done nothing wrong. Although the first article is somewhat problematic, the second one was the press release provided by the Coronado County Sheriff's Office. The article merely reflects the content of a statement issued by a government official at a public forum involving a matter of public interest and concern. Since it is a verbatim transcript of what was said, it clearly was a fair and accurate account. That, of course, is all that is required. No worry there. In fact, if the *Daily Mirror* had fairly and accurately summarized the statement and everything else being equal, you would probably still have been okay.

"The first article did cause me to pause, and quite frankly I was troubled more about not being contacted before its publication than by the publication itself. I know you have faith in the integrity of the content in the stories coming off the wire service. However, at least in our jurisdiction, you are really rolling the dice by blindly publishing stories the contents of which you haven't verified. The republication makes you just as liable as the originator.

"That having been said, let me answer your question as precisely as possible. Since everything in the

135

first article is truthful and the second article is privileged, for the plaintiffs to pursue their claims will only evoke the ire of the court. Whether the actions were brought to harass or punish the *Daily Mirror,* or to serve as a soapbox from which to proclaim their innocence, I don't know. But to pursue a frivolous suit beyond this point is to invite the sanctions I mentioned. They cannot possibly prevail and to pursue it further is a waste of everyone's time and money. Hopefully, the court will see it that way."

Both Thornton and Nadine nodded. Thornton then had Marci bring in a copy of the fax he had sent to the insurance carrier and gave it to Charlie.

Charlie read the fax and set it on the table. "Have you heard back from CIC in response to the fax?"

"Not yet," Thornton responded. "But as you can see, we did fax them copies of the complaints and, in accordance with your instructions, demanded that they provide coverage and representation."

"Now all you have to do," Charlie said, "is wait for a reply. In the interim, I'll be on standby, should you need me."

As Charlie donned his topcoat and was preparing to leave, Marci buzzed Thornton's office with news that the fax reply from the newspaper's insurance carrier had arrived. "Bring it in," Thornton ordered.

Within less than a minute, the three were poring over the fax.

"Looks like Collier Insurance Company of North Carolina has admitted coverage up to ten million dollars and has agreed to provide representation," Charlie said. Turning to Thornton, he added, "They've authorized you to hire local counsel."

"You know who that'll be," Thornton responded, smiling at Charlie. "The fax says I am to have you call Cedric Sloan of CIC and verify."

Let's get him on the phone," Charlie said removing his topcoat and placing it over the back of his chair. "Looks like there is a telephone number on the bottom of the fax."

After Charlie hung up the phone, he said, "It looks like I'm officially aboard and will be defending the *Daily Mirror* in the libel action."

Thornton shook Charlie's hand and said, "Welcome aboard!" Nadine did the same.

Before Charlie left, Nadine asked, "Does either Thornton, as the newspaper's editor, or I, as the author of the so-called offending articles, have to seek the services of an attorney?"

Charlie shook his head. "Since neither of you are named defendants or parties to the lawsuit, you need not worry about being represented."

Nadine's sigh of relief was more audible than

Thornton's.

The *Daily Mirror* had thirty days to file answers to the two complaints. In preparation of the answers, which would be essentially the same in both cases, Charlie reviewed the petitions with Thornton and Nadine.

"The petitions allege that the *Daily Mirror* printed the so-called offending articles. That is true and something we can admit to. The allegation that the information contained in the articles was false, of course, will be denied."

"Isn't falsity the real issue as to both articles?" Thornton asked.

"Absolutely," Charlie replied, "but keep in mind that truthfulness is always a complete defense. That is a defense we will assert with regard to both articles."

"What about the wire service defense? Will we assert it even though it is not recognized in Kansas?" Nadine asked.

"Receiving material from a reputable news-gathering service and not being aware of its falsity should be a recognized defense," Charlie replied. "Even though it is not recognized in our state, we will still include it as a defense. What do we have to lose?"

"Only our credibility," Thornton responded.

Ignoring Thornton's comment, Charlie continued, "We can invoke the qualified privilege defense as to the second article. What is obtained from a public official as part of an official release is immune from the libel claim as long as it's accurately reported."

Thornton leaned back in his chair and propped his feet on the edge of the conference table. "Sounds as though the *Daily Mirror* has nothing to be worried about. Now I can sleep better tonight."

"The first article appears to be the most problematic," Nadine mused.

"Not necessarily," Charlie responded. "The statements made by Sheriff Rovera at the press conference along with those of the assistant prosecutor validated all the information contained in the wire service report."

"Knowing that, I, too, will sleep better tonight," Nadine said and mimicking Thornton leaned back in her chair and looked for a place to prop her feet.

"I dare you!" Thornton said as Nadine eyed the edge of the conference table nearest her.

"Me, too!" Charlie echoed as the three laughed for the first time in a very long time.

# CHAPTER 10

## DEFENDING A LIBEL SUIT

Courtland Wiggins and Rebecca Lindsay were well known and well respected members of the Coronado County Bar. Both had extensive trial experience. Courtland had been a local prosecutor for a number of years. Originally from California, he was eloquent, quick thinking and hardworking. His Main Street office was lit up long before the locals' alarm clocks rang, and the streets were long deserted by the time he left for home. With a deep booming voice and a sturdy frame, he commanded attention. He was Dr. Simms' attorney.

A third generation Coronadoite, whose father was a retired trial court judge, Rebecca had been a federal prosecutor in Oklahoma City for over a dozen years prior to her admission to the Kansas bar, and her unusual good looks and reserved manner were deceiving, especially to the unwary. Back in Oklahoma, her nickname was TNT. She was indeed dynamite, as her success rate would confirm. Those who had been on the other side would attest to the maxim: *It's not the size of the dog in the fight, but the size of the fight in the dog.* She would be representing Dr. Hopkins.

Although Charlie recognized that natural ability coupled with training and experience were keys to a trial attorney's success, he also recognized that preparation was the most important ingredient. Early in his career, in an important case, Charlie had slain the giant of all giant trial attorneys because the Goliath had underestimated his adversary and was unprepared.

"Give me a well-prepared neophyte to an unprepared superstar any day," Charlie would often say, quoting from his father who was a well-known trial attorney from the state of Washington.

Usually, they met at the *Daily Mirror*. Today, they were meeting in Charlie's Main Street office, a replica of law offices of old. The antiquated leather law books that adorned the better part of Charlie's modest library, Nadine and Thornton correctly surmised, had originally belonged to Charlie's father.

"These books must be worth a fortune," Thornton said as Charlie entered carrying a file box containing an assortment of documents, research and notes pertaining to the two libel actions.

"Other than the Kansas statutes, I use the law

library at the courthouse. These that you see have only sentimental value. There really is no market for outdated law books, even those that are leather bound. It would probably cost me more to have them hauled away than I would get from any sale."

"If you ever decide to give them away, Charlie, call me," Nadine said.

"What would you do with them?" Charlie asked.

"Decorate my office with them so I can look important, too," Nadine replied.

"I heard that," Charlie said.

They all laughed.

"We're not here to make fun of my office," Charlie said as he feigned annoyance. "Let's talk about discovery."

"Why the big fanfare about the discovery phase?" Thornton asked.

"Easy answer," Charlie replied. "Trial preparation is everything. The key to preparation is anticipation and the key to anticipation is pretrial discovery."

"I assume you'll be taking the depositions of both plaintiffs," Thornton said.

"Depositions are my discovery weapon of choice as they are with most trial attorneys. The persons deposed answer questions under oath that pin down their testimony at trial. If their answers are inconsistent with their testimony at trial, they can be impeached by those statements. Also, knowing in advance what a witness will later testify to avoids surprise at trial."

"No trial by ambush, eh, Charlie?" Thornton said.

"Right you are," Charlie replied. "Witnesses at a deposition are not usually as well prepared as they are at trial. It's amazing how many cases are won at the pretrial stage."

"I'm sure Wiggins and Lindsay will have their clients well prepared," Nadine reflected. "By the way, whose deposition do you propose be first?"

"That's easy," Charlie responded. "Usually you start with the most vulnerable."

"I take it that would be Dr. Hopkins?" Thornton speculated.

"Absolutely," Charlie responded. "He is the weak link mainly because of his past affiliation with Trevor Watts. Trevor's death leaves a lot of questions unanswered. Suspect Dr. Hopkins can provide the pieces for the puzzle."

"How do you get Dr. Hopkins to provide the answers?" Nadine asked.

"That won't be easy. As you pointed out, Dr. Hopkins will be prepped and very cagy. If I can get him flustered, there's no telling what he might say."

"Is the style of examining adverse witnesses, such as Drs. Hopkins and Simms, much different in a deposition than in a trial?" Thornton asked.

"At trial, the cross-examiner wants to direct the responses and not allow the witnesses to roam," Charlie said. "In a deposition, the questions are usually open-ended and invite elaboration and gratuitous explanation. In a deposition, the examiner is not trying to persuade but explore. In a deposition, it matters not whether the answers are favorable or unfavorable, only what they are."

It was agreed between the attorneys on both sides that Dr. Hopkins' deposition would be conducted in one of the conference rooms in the building where Rebecca Lindsay's law office was located. The Wellington Building was an old two-story stone bank building that had been remodeled into office suites and stood in the heart of the downtown area. It was only a block from Charlie's office and in walking distance to the courthouse.

When Charlie and Thornton left Charlie's office on that cool overcast April morning, the dense clouds were beginning to assert their domination with a few spurts at first and then the inevitable downpour.

Nature had validated Charlie's tactical error in giving up the home court advantage by allowing the deposition of the adverse party to be conducted in opposing counsel's own back yard. He only hoped his opting for more accommodating quarters would not come back to haunt him in other, more important respects.

The deposition was delayed while they waited for the stenographer to appear. Lydia Rosenbloom, a former court reporter for a district judge and now a freelance stenographer and in her early sixties, had called, blaming the cloudburst for her delay. When she arrived, she set up her machine and a backup tape recorder, and then administered the obligatory oath to tell the truth to Dr. Maynard Hopkins.

Seated with his attorney opposite Charlie and Thornton, Dr. Hopkins, in his neatly pressed dark suit, starched white shirt and paisley tie, seemed very self-assured and maybe even a bit arrogant.

It was obvious he had distain for Charlie from the moment he was asked his name, address and occupation. When he was asked if he was the plaintiff in the case, he responded, "You know that I am."

After several more such answers to Charlie's questions, his attorney passed him a note. Immediately, his demeanor changed. Charlie surmised the note Rebecca gave him mandated an attitude adjustment. One thing an adversary never wants to do is get the opposing counsel's adrenalin pumping—especially not someone like Charlie.

"Now, Dr. Hopkins, you allege in your petition that you have been defamed by false statements in the two articles that are the subject of your suit. In regard to the first article, a copy of which I am handing you, please specify each and every false statement."

Examining the first article, Dr. Hopkins seemed flushed. "Implying that Dr. Simms and I are somehow involved in Trevor Watts' death is false and misleading," he managed to respond.

"Are you saying that Mr. Watts' death did not lead 'authorities in Pembrooke, Kansas, in the direction of a pharmacist by the name of Dr. Maynard Hopkins, and his physician brother-in-law, Dr. Edmund Simms,' as stated in the article?"

"It is the implication or inference that is to be drawn by that statement that I object to."

"Well, let's dissect the statement to which you object. It doesn't say you did anything wrong, only that authorities were led in your direction. Isn't that true?"

"That's what it says but it conveys a negative meaning and implies something much different."

"Let me go at it another way, Dr. Hopkins.

After Trevor Watts' body was discovered, didn't officers from the Coronado Sheriff's Office contact you and question you about Mr. Watts?"

"Yes."

"And, if you know, didn't they also contact Dr. Simms?"

"Dr. Simms said they did."

"Do you know why they did?"

"Dr. Simms told me that they found several prescription bottles with his name on them as the prescribing physician in Trevor's bedroom."

"Didn't the prescription bottles, if you know, also bear the name of your pharmacy?"

"Yes."

"What was the name of the pharmacy?"

"Hopkins Pharmacy."

"Is that the pharmacy you own and operate?"

"Yes."

"Was that something the sheriff's deputies discussed with you?"

"Yes."

"Did they advise you that the toxicology report indicated that prescription drugs were found in Trevor's system?"

"Yes."

Charlie was feeling like a dentist. Trying to pull information out of Dr. Hopkins was like pulling teeth.

Hopkins had been well coached. Courtland obviously instructed him to only answer the question and not volunteer any information, and Hopkins was following instructions to the tee.

"Have you ever filled prescriptions for Trevor Watts?"

"Yes."

"Were any of the prescriptions for Oxycoton, Vicodin or Demerol?"

"Not that I recall."

"At the time of his death, was Trevor Watts working for you at your pharmacy?"

"Mr. Watts did the cleaning and various odd jobs at the pharmacy."

"Did he have access to the drugs Oxycoton, Vicodin or Demerol?"

"Yes."

"Did you ever give him any?"

"No, not even with a prescription, as I recall."

"Did you ever see him take any?"

"No."

"Did you ever fill a prescription for his mother?"

"Some years ago, I may have. I really don't remember."

"Had you filled any within the past year and specifically in July of this past year?"

"No."

"Did you tell anyone in July that you had or were going to fill a prescription for Trevor's mother?"

Dr. Hopkins' eyes narrowed and, conveying contempt, he answered "No."

Charlie remembered Nadine telling him that on the morning of the Fourth of July her source told her he saw Dr. Hopkins leave for Hopkins Pharmacy with Trevor, announcing his intent to fill a prescription for Trevor's mother.

To keep Dr. Hopkins guessing as to how much he and his newspaper client knew, he asked Dr. Hopkins about his relationship with Dr. Simms.

"You and Dr. Simms are related by marriage, correct?"

"I am married to his sister."

"Do the two of you have business dealings together?"

"We own some rental properties together."

"Is that the extent of your business dealings together?"

"Yes."

"How about your professional relationship?"

"There is none."

"A lot of prescriptions your pharmacy filled were written by Dr. Simms, were they not?"

"What do you mean by 'a lot'?"

"An average of one or maybe two a day."

"Perhaps. I didn't count them."

"Aren't you required to keep track of such things?"

"Of course."

"Would you be willing to produce your records for the past twelve months so that they can be inspected without the necessity of me having to file a motion to produce or obtain a subpoena? I, of course, will also be subpoenaing Dr. Simms' records."

Dr. Hopkins turned ghastly pale and stammered, "That's something you'll have to discuss with my attorney."

Still visibly shaken, he took a gulp of water that went down the wrong tube, making him cough and choke. Charlie waited patiently so he could ask his final question.

"Dr. Hopkins, just one final question. Did you provide Dr. Simms with a portion of the profits you received on the filling of the prescriptions for Dr. Simms' patients?"

"Are you asking me if I gave him a kickback?"

"I suppose that's what you would call it."

Still not having fully recovered from the previous question or the coughing spell, Dr. Hopkins responded like a whale that had just been harpooned. For tense moments, Charlie pondered the need to administer the Heimlich maneuver but watching Dr. Hopkins progress steadily from displeasure to anguish to indignation and then to rage, Charlie gave up on the idea and was glad he was sitting on the opposite side of the table. After Dr. Hopkins blurted "No," Charlie hastened the conclusion of the deposition and announced he had no other questions. While Dr. Hopkins glared at Charlie, Charlie gathered up his file and headed for the exit.

"If looks could kill . . ." Thornton whispered to Charlie as the two walked out into the fresh air.

By noon the following day, Courtland and Rebecca asked to meet with Charlie. Over the intercom, Sandy announced, "Ms. Lindsay and Mr. Wiggins are here to see you."

"By all means, send them in," Charlie said as he rose from his desk and opened his office door.

"Coffee?" Charlie asked as he greeted them.

"We're all coffeed out," Courtland replied. Rebecca gestured with her hands that she also would be declining the offer.

"What can I do for the two of you?" Charlie asked as he motioned for them to be seated.

Rebecca spoke first. "Neither of our clients is

up to the emotional turmoil the lawsuits are generating. My client, particularly, feels that the lawsuits are not serving their intended purpose. Instead of extracting him, Dr. Hopkins feels imprisoned by them."

"My client feels the same way," Courtland said trying to find a comfortable spot in Charlie's shopworn chair. "All our clients wanted from the get-go was to dispel the public myth that has been propagated by the media that somehow they are or were involved in an illegal drug operation. They only want to set the record straight. Nothing more, nothing less."

Charlie was stunned. "Does that mean they are willing to dismiss their respective lawsuits?"

"Only if the *Candela Daily Mirror* prints a statement Rebecca and I have prepared. It amounts to an apology or retraction of sorts." He then handed Charlie a document that he retrieved from his valise. Charlie perched his glasses on the bridge of his nose and began to read.

*Dr. Edmund Simms and Dr. Maynard Hopkins, through their respective attorneys, Courtland Wiggins and Rebecca Lindsay, have filed motions to dismiss the pending libel suits against the local media. They have cited as their reason their desire to keep the community focused on the war on illegal drugs and not distract the public's attention away from the real enemy. "Bickering among ourselves serves no useful purpose and a community divided against itself will only destroy the advancements that have thus far been made," the attorneys reiterated in a joint statement.*

*In welcoming the dismissal, the* Candela Daily Mirror *emphasized that by their articles they in no way inferred or intended to infer that either Dr. Simms or Dr. Hopkins was guilty of any wrongdoing. "The newspaper has no evidence that either doctor has committed any criminal acts for which they should be prosecuted," Thornton Marimon, the newspaper's editor, said as part of the joint statement: "If our articles conveyed a different interpretation, for that we apologize."*

When Charlie finished reading he stroked the stubble on his chin and said, "Why not?"

"We think it is a win-win situation for everyone," Rebecca said as she looked at Charlie and then Courtland.

Courtland nodded his approval.

"I'll present your proposal to the newspaper and see what they have to say. In fact, I'll have Sandy fax the document to Thornton right now." He then summoned Sandy and, instructed that she fax it to Thornton.

"What took you so long?" Thornton chided.

"When we spoke to you an hour ago, you said you were on your way."

"My fast food was not that fast," Charlie replied. "Since I don't eat breakfast, I'm famished by lunch time."

"That fast food is not good for you, you know!" Nadine said.

"I can't win," Charlie said feigning disgust. "I hurry so as not to keep you waiting and then get chewed out in the process. Here I prolong lunch to work out a deal to save the newspaper forty million dollars."

"You're forgiven," Nadine said as Thornton nodded acquiescence. "After all, it was your deposition of Dr. Hopkins that is responsible for the first-round knockout."

"I take it you two have had time to consider the proposal. What do you think?" Charlie asked.

"I am not particularly enamored about the newspaper's proposed concession," Thornton replied. "Seems we we're not only letting them off the hook but making them heroes in the process."

"I agree with Thornton," Nadine said.

"Keep in mind," Charlie said, "the dismissal will be with prejudice, meaning it can never be resurrected as it applies to the two articles. Even if the wire service defense was an established defense that could be asserted, trading a retraction of sorts together with an apology of sorts for dismissal of a forty-million-dollar libel action, as disdainful as it seems, is a triumph."

"At least, the newspaper's balance sheet won't reflect a contingent liability of forty million dollars or keep us up all night with worry." Thornton said in an effort to convince both Nadine and himself.

"What do you think is the real reason the brothers-in-law are caving in?" Nadine asked.

"Having been present during Dr. Hopkins' deposition, I can tell you," Thornton said. "I don't think Dr. Hopkins had any idea that he and his brother-in-law would be required to turn over their accounts and records to the opposition and that they could ultimately end up in the hands of law enforcement authorities, such as the district attorney's office. The look on Dr. Hopkins' face said it all."

"Charlie, you frightened them away," Nadine said gleefully. "You big bad wolf!"

"It's fairly obvious Dr. Hopkins ran to his co-conspirator immediately after the deposition with the news that the civil action would generate all the ammo the DA would need to bring a criminal action," Charlie said. "What the DA has needed in order to obtain a search warrant has been lacking. With the discovery in the civil case, it would all be handed over on a silver platter without the DA having to lift a finger."

"What do you think the pharmacy records would show?" Thornton asked. "That seemed to be what caused Dr. Hopkins to get so upset."

"Thornton," Charlie said, "interspersed throughout the deposition there were questions hinting at insider information. Dr. Hopkins cringed when I asked about filling the prescription for Trevor's mother in July. Do you remember that? He didn't know how much we knew or who the whistleblowers were. But he knew we knew."

"The last question about the kickback, I think, is the one that pushed him over the edge," Thornton commented.

"That was just another nail in the coffin," Charlie replied. "But I think the realization that the records the pharmacy was required to keep by law were subject to being produced and inspected in the libel action was the cause of him having to send his pants to the cleaners. He knew right then that the revelation of that information would be the *coup de grâce*—the evidence that would send him and his brother-in-law away for a long, long time.

"To answer your question specifically, there is no doubt that a goodly portion of the prescriptions that were filled were written by Dr. Simms. By comparing the prescriptions that were filled by the pharmacy with the inventory and purchases from the pharmaceutical companies, you would find there would be a ton of inventory unaccounted for. It would be pretty difficult for Dr. Hopkins to attribute the shortage to shrinkage. In other words, subtracting the drugs that were sold by the pharmacy from those that were purchased by the pharmacy would equal the amount of drugs that were sold on the black market—without a prescription, of course."

"It would be interesting," Nadine said, "to find out how much cold medicine and other drugs used to cook meth were sold through Hopkins Pharmacy."

"I'm thinking," Charlie said, "that if they haven't already become involved, the IRS and the DEA would have a heyday with this one."

"Don't you rather imagine the feds are already involved and have been for quite some time?" Thornton asked.

"That would be my read," Charlie said, hoping it was true. Charlie was not enamored with the newspaper's concession, either. But for now, they would all have to live with the decision, knowing it was foolhardy to risk a lot for a little.

The detective squad at the Pembrooke Police Department had somehow heard of Dr. Hopkins'

deposition and had requested a copy. Within hours after receiving the transcript, detectives Noah Ames and Jessie Wynne were in Charlie's reception room requesting an interview.

"I can see why Hopkins folded the tent," Ames said, extending his hand.

"Thanks for seeing us," Wynne said as Charlie also shook his hand.

"Has any fruit fallen from the tree?" Charlie asked as he gestured for them to be seated in the twin leather chairs positioned in front of his desk.

"We're shaking trees, looking under rocks and checking out all leads," Ames responded as he made himself comfortable. "Most everything so far, at least for the most part, is pure speculation, supposition and hearsay."

"That is the reason," Wynne said, "we're here. We think you or someone at the *Candela Daily Mirror* might be able to provide us with the missing link— someone with firsthand knowledge, or someone who has talked with someone who has firsthand knowledge."

"What makes you think I'm able to lead you in that direction?" Charlie asked. "You know about the attorney-client privilege."

"Confidentially," Wynne responded in a hushed tone, "during the Fourth of July weekend last year, while on routine patrol in the downtown business district, a patrol officer observed two individuals who were identified as Dr. Hopkins and Trevor Watts unlock the side door of Hopkins Pharmacy, which was closed for the holiday, and go inside.

"Moments later the two emerged from the building carrying several bags of merchandise, or what appeared to be merchandise, and placed them in the trunk of a car that the officer recognized as belonging to Dr. Hopkins. What the two next did appeared to the officer to be unusual if not suspicious.

"The two dumped the contents into the vehicle's trunk and appeared to be placing items into a series of smaller bags. When the officer came up behind them and asked if everything was all right. Dr. Hopkins seemed startled and nervous. He hastily closed the trunk lid, almost slamming it on Trevor's hand. Trevor was still holding several prescription bottles, one of which fell to the ground, spilling its contents. He helped the two retrieve white tablets with what looked like crosses or plus signs imprinted on them. Even though Dr. Hopkins told the officer they were just getting rid of some old containers, the officer felt the facts indicated otherwise.

"We can't tell you much, obviously, as we don't have much and what we do have we can't share with you without compromising our investigation," Ames said as he repositioned himself in the chair. "The next best thing we have, since Trevor can't speak and Dr. Hopkins won't, is a witness who can confirm our suspicion that Dr. Hopkins, with Trevor's help, was trafficking drugs that Fourth of July weekend."

Raising his eyebrows and looking directly at Charlie, Ames said, "We think you know who that eyewitness is, or know who can identify that eyewitness."

"You know the attorney's code of ethics prevents me from doing that," Charlie replied somewhat apologetically. "As much as I want you to nail Hopkins and his partner in crime, my hands are tied. I could be disbarred in a nanosecond."

"Your client could waive the privilege. It would seem to be a civic duty for your client to do so in light of the gravity of the drug problem in the community, particularly where we have the opportunity to bag the big fish," Wynne responded.

"It's too bad you flunked the Kansas bar," Charlie told Wynne. "You would have been a credit to the profession."

"We know subpoenaing you before a grand jury would be futile because of the absolute privilege afforded an attorney," Wynne said. "By the way, thank you for the kind compliment. Maybe someday I will be able to put the Esquire behind my name. For now, however, I must help the department cut off the head of the monster that is responsible for much of the drug trade in Coronado County."

"You mentioned a grand jury," Charlie said. "Being an election year and Horace Henderson being a political animal, I assume it's just a matter of time before one is impaneled. That's the best way I know to shake the coconuts from the trees."

"That is one way to force potential witnesses out of hiding," Wynne said. "However, the DA says he doesn't want to embark on a witch hunt and end up with egg on his face. That's why we're out beating the bushes and seeking the name of the *Daily Mirror's* confidential informant so that we can make him or her ours. Not to beat around the bush anymore, Charlie, we think a high-profile reporter such as Nadine Siena has information the grand jury would be interested in. Call it a hunch or rumor or whatever, Noah and I think Nadine is the key to blowing this whole thing wide open. We would like to interview her. What say you?"

"For the sake of argument," Charlie replied, "if she or another reporter from the *Daily Mirror* had information from a source, and had pledged confidentiality, he or she would be unable either legally or ethically to reveal the identity of that source. Legally, he or she would be in breach of contract in revealing the source. Ethically, he or she would be compelled to keep the promise."

"Charlie," Wynne interrupted, "Kansas does not have a shield law. If Nadine is our gal and she is called by Henderson to testify before the grand jury, she has no choice."

"You don't know most reporters," Charlie replied. "You certainly don't know Nadine. If she is 'the gal,' as you put it, I would wager she would go to jail rather than burn her source. And don't read between the lines. I am in no way validating your hunch. Besides, maybe by the time Nadine or whoever is called, the Kansas legislature will have passed a state reporter's shield law. Nadine and the Kansas Press Association have been pushing for such a bill."

"Nadine won the Pulitzer Prize for her investigative reporting and championing the cause of the mentally challenged," Wynne countered. "I know she and her newspaper have also been waging a war on drugs. She has interviewed a number of us in the past and we don't need to be rocket scientists to know she is determined to expose the brothers-in-law conspiracy and will ultimately do so. I'm betting that the information she has access to would be key in obtaining an indictment and that she will balance the equities in favor of the public good. And don't count on the Kansas legislature passing a reporter's shield law anytime soon, or at least not in time to rescue Nadine or whomever."

"Suppose I arrange a meeting with you and Nadine and she proves to be the one with the source but refuses to divulge the sources identity. Will you still call her before the grand jury, knowing that her refusal will result in her incarceration? Remember, she is a principled individual and takes her commitments seriously. She wouldn't have received the Pulitzer had she been otherwise."

"That call is not ours," Wynne said while his partner nodded agreement. "Henderson is the quarterback. I don't know how Noah feels, but I would not want to burn her any more than she would want to burn her anonymous source. You have my word on that."

"Mine, too," Ames said. "Unfortunately, Jessie and I have no authority to make any promises. We will do everything in our power, if Nadine will help us put some pieces together, to persuade the powers that be that she should not be punished for honoring any pledge of confidentiality she might have made with her source."

"Who knows?" Wynne said, "Maybe Nadine or whoever has not made an absolute promise of confidentiality and can divulge the source's name or maybe the source can be persuaded to come forward and cooperate in this investigation and provide the missing pieces of the puzzle. Can Nadine or whoever provide information that can be corroborated by non-confidential sources or provide us with information that won't blow the source's cover?"

"Assuming one of the reporters at the *Daily Mirror* can provide the information you seek, what assurance does the reporter have that he or she will not be required to reveal the source's identity?"

"If you are seeking immunity, that will have to come from the DA," Wynne said.

"If the tradeoff is receiving information that would otherwise be unobtainable in exchange for immunity, Henderson might be predisposed to do so," Charlie suggested.

"You don't know Henderson," Ames quipped.

"Well, raise the flag and see if he salutes," Charlie said. "Then get back with me."

Less than an hour after Wynne and Ames had left his office, Charlie fielded a call from Wynne. In a subdued tone, Wynne said, "Bad news. Henderson says he can get the information we seek through a grand jury subpoena. Therefore, he is unwilling to make any concessions."

"Get Thornton on the phone, please," Charlie instructed Sandy.

"Thornton."

"Hopefully, you received the message indicating that I honored Pembrooke Police Department's request for a copy of Dr. Hopkins' deposition."

"You said if we didn't provide it they could get it by way of subpoena."

"Anyway, they reviewed it and sent two detectives to interview me."

"Which ones?"

"Noah Ames and Jessie Wynne."

"What did they want?"

"Appears they suspect it is Nadine who has the confidential source."

"Nadine's the one who provided you with the ammunition you used to drub Dr. Hopkins," Thornton said, "and instructed you to use it even though it might leave her exposed."

"As long as it didn't unveil the identity of her source," Charlie quickly added.

"That was done to bail the newspaper out of its predicament," Thornton said. "Obviously, we all were aware of the risk."

"She told me I was not required to dodge that line of questioning at the deposition and, of course, I didn't. Now, with the newspaper out of the line of fire, it is Nadine who is in the hot seat." Charlie sighed.

"What's next?" Thornton asked.

"The inevitable subpoenas to appear before the grand jury," Charlie replied.

"Did you say subpoena or subpoenas?"

"I used the plural. Both you and Nadine will be subpoenaed. Fortunately for you, Nadine never revealed the name or identity of her source."

"I'm sure Henderson is counting on Nadine revealing the name of her source in lieu of a term in the slammer."

"It will take more than the threat of incarceration to cause Nadine to break her promise to her source."

"Right you are. Henderson has grossly underestimated Nadine's resolve."

# CHAPTER 11

## REVEALING THE SOURCE

I t was an unseasonably cold April day. The wind drove sheets of rain against the buildings and pelted the windows. Nadine returned from lunch shivering and wet. She folded her umbrella and shook beads of moisture from her dampened hair when she looked up and saw the pumpkin-like face of Deputy Richland Covington of the Coronado Sheriff's Department. He was waiting for her.

"Nasty weather," Nadine said.

"I called the Chamber of Commerce complaining," Covington replied.

"Apparently it didn't do any good. Look, it ruined my hairdo."

"Send the chamber the bill," Covington playfully advised as he removed an official-looking document from a dampened manila folder and handed it to Nadine.

"Rich, did I just win the lottery? Do I need to produce a stub?" Nadine asked in obvious jest as she peered at the document.

"Looks like your presence is being requested by the Coronado Grand Jury," Deputy Covington said, grinning.

As Nadine examined the CGJ special invite, she quipped, "I don't see an RSVP and I doubt they would be satisfied with my regrets."

"The only excuses your host would accept if you're unable to attend would be if you were comatose or they had a note from your mortician. Otherwise, I will be serving you meals through a slit in the iron door at the county hotel."

"Very funny," Nadine groaned. "I think I'm going to be sick."

Nadine was not alone in her sentiments. Thornton had also received the specially engraved invitation, compliments of the CGJ. They were now sitting outside the large courtroom at the Coronado Courthouse, which had been commandeered for evening use. Their subpoenas said 8:00 p.m. While sitting on the hard oak benches pondering their fate, they spotted Charlie ambling down the long corridor, carrying his monogrammed valise. Charlie sat between them and pulled out a yellow legal tablet. On it, he hastily scribbled the battle plan. Then, licking his finger and turning the pages, he gave last-minute instructions.

"Thornton will probably be called first," he began, "since he doesn't know much more than me. Fortunately, since he doesn't know the identity of the anonymous source, his testimony will be short. All he will testify to is hearsay, what Nadine told him that she was told by her informant." He turned to Nadine. "Fortunately, you told him very little."

"You'll be in the grand jury room with me while I testify, right, Charlie?" Thornton asked. He was visibly nervous and not masking it well. Reporting on a court proceeding was one thing, but participating in one was not something he particularly relished, especially not this night.

"I will be in with each of you. Remember you will both be sworn in by the foreman of the grand jury. Both of you, of course, will be required to give your full names and residence addresses. Thornton, you will be required to answer all of the DA's questions. I don't anticipate you will be asked anything that might tend to incriminate you or anything that is privileged. If you are unsure, ask that you be allowed to confer with me. I will also motion to you if I think we need to confer. Remember the oath is twofold, to tell the truth and to keep your testimony secret. When you leave, you're not to discuss your testimony with Nadine or with anyone other than me."

Looking at his watch, Charlie said, "We still have ten minutes." He turned to Nadine.

"You are required to answer all questions with the exception of those that might elicit evidence that could be used against you. Since you are not personally involved in any wrongdoing and won't be accused of such, you can't invoke your Fifth Amendment Rights against self-incrimination. And, you will be taking the same twofold oath as Thornton."

"I understand," Nadine said.

"With regard to protecting your source, you haven't changed your mind have you?" Charlie queried.

"Absolutely not! The game plan is for me not only to refuse to identify the source but to refuse to give any information that might lead to his or her identification."

"Horace Henderson will be asking a series of questions to which you will respond 'My absolute promise of confidentiality to my source precludes me from revealing information that will identify him or her either directly or indirectly. To do so would be unethical and subject me to civil liability in a breach of contract action.'"

"That's my response the first time," Nadine said. "Then I decline to answer for the reasons previously given. Isn't that the easiest and best way to handle it?"

"Yes, and at some point Henderson will be advising you of your legal duty to respond and the penalty if you refuse to do so. Don't be bullied by him. It is the District Court Judge who must issue the contempt citation upon application of the grand jury and the judge must conduct a hearing before any sentence can be imposed."

"So," Nadine responded, "I will have time to pack my bags and arrange for a dog-sitter?"

The door of the courtroom swung open and the grand jury's special investigator ushered Thornton inside with Charlie at his heels. Nadine sat alone in contemplative anticipation.

Within a few minutes, Thornton left the court room. He nodded to Nadine and she stood, smoothing her skirt. She took a deep breath and followed the bailiff through the courtroom door. Nadine felt a rush of excitement as she was led into the courtroom. Seated in the jury box normally occupied by trial jurors were the six men and six women who had been selected by the DA and Chief District Court Judge, Fenton F. Mays, to investigate *inter alia* prescription fraud and drug trafficking within the county's territorial boundaries. The foreperson, who was a retired schoolteacher and someone who hadn't missed too many meals, administered the oath. With her right arm raised, Nadine promised to tell the truth, the whole truth and nothing but the truth, and to maintain secrecy. She sat down and folded her hands in her lap.

Outwardly, Nadine appeared self-assured; internally, her stomach churned like a cement mixer. Sitting on the witness stand, Nadine wondered if there wasn't some symbolism in the ornate oak balusters that resembled cell bars. Before she had time to assess the situation, Henderson was already at the podium, positioning a stack of legal pads in just the right configuration. The special investigator, who was also an investigator for the DA's office, Silas Reynolds, was seated at the prosecution's table poised to take notes. Henderson adjusted his gold-rimmed glasses on the bridge of his nose. The inquisition then began.

After soliciting the obligatory identification and background information, Henderson asked, "What do you know about the drug trafficking problem in Coronado County?"

Nadine wasn't prepared to answer such a broad and generic question and looked to Charlie, seated at the defense table, for help. Charlie just shrugged his shoulders.

"All I know is what others have told me. I have no personal knowledge." Nadine then related basic public information. She readily revealed the source of that information when asked by Henderson.

When she related the information regarding the

Hopkins-Simms investigation and was asked by Henderson to identify the source, however, she declined to do so. "My absolute promise of confidentiality to my source precludes me from revealing information that will identify him or her either directly or indirectly. To do so would be unethical and subject me to civil liability in a breach of contract action."

Henderson glared at Nadine as if he had no inkling she would invoke her First Amendment right in refusing to reveal her source's identity. It was obvious to Nadine that Henderson was playing to the grand jury and it had its intended effect, as Nadine observed by the facial expressions of the grand jurors.

With his face flushed and being brazen by his ability to evoke the ire of the grand jurors, Henderson bellowed, "It is the obligation and duty of every citizen to provide relevant testimony when it comes to criminal activity. You won a Pulitzer Prize for exposing criminal activity involving the abuse of the mentally challenged and now you are refusing to testify as to something as bad or maybe worse–drug abuse."

Nadine took a deep breath. "With all due respect, I have provided information to local authorities and now to you and the grand jury concerning the Hopkins-Simms investigation and how it bears upon the investigation into the death of Trevor

Watts. That information must have some importance, judging by your reaction. That information would not have been available to me and thus to you, and the grand jury, had it not been for my absolute promise of anonymity to my confidential source. It's what one would call the 'but for not' rule. *But* for the promise, there would *not* be such evidence."

"Hearsay, Ms. Siena, is inadmissible in court. Eyewitness testimony is not. If you identify the source, you provide my office with the ability to present admissible evidence and the key to unlock the door to possibly other admissible evidence."

"You're upset with me because I have come into contact with an eyewitness that law enforcement has failed to discover. Where in the law does it say it is the media's responsibility to investigate criminal cases? Take no offense, but I have never been deputized or commissioned to perform the functions assigned to your office, the Pembrooke Police Department or the Coronado County Sheriff's Department. With the leads I have provided through the testimony given, your compass should point you in the right direction."

"Ms. Siena, what you're asking is that special treatment be afforded to members of the press—treatment that is not afforded to other citizens. That's plain and simple discrimination. Where in the law does it say members of the press, or the media generally, should receive special treatment?"

"The Constitution of the United States, as you know only too well, is not a *shallow* document but a *hallowed* document," Nadine responded. "The First Amendment affords protection for a free press. Key to a free press is the ability to gather information. The ability to gather information would be stymied if the reporter's pipeline was cut off and there was no longer the free flow of information. Without a source of information, there would be no information—no information to relate to the public. Sometimes, that source, for one reason or other, desires to remain anonymous. If the reporter could not promise and keep the promise of confidentiality, less information would be available. You have been asking me all the questions. I think you should be asking yourself 'Has the Hopkins-Simms investigation been enhanced as a result of information that would otherwise not have come before the grand jury but for the expectation of confidentiality on the part of the source?'"

"Freedom of the press is not an unqualified or an absolute right," Henderson replied. "There are countervailing rights that have to be considered here, Ms. Siena. You emphasize the protections afforded the press. What about the protections afforded the public? What about the public's interest in effective law enforcement? In balancing these conflicting rights, which one should prevail? You're talking about the rights of your source—perhaps only one person. What about the thousands of citizens out there who would benefit from knowing who your source is and having him or her step forward and perform his or her civic duty? What happened to the concept 'the greatest good for the greatest number'?"

"The only way I can answer that is to say that if you start whittling away some rights, you eventually end up whittling away all rights. My point earlier was that by betraying a source, you risk drying up all potential future sources. If a journalist can't be trusted, he or she is no longer valuable and might just as well turn in her pad and pencil and enroll in law school."

Everyone laughed except for Henderson. Resigned, he stood with his arms tightly folded across his chest, his face flushed. He was livid and unable to regain composure.

"No further questions," he muttered as he stalked back to the prosecution's table. His voice crackled as he said, "Ms. Siena, you may step down."

# CHAPTER 12

## THE COURT-ISSUED RSVP

N adine didn't have to wait long to be served with the inevitable contempt citation. Nor did she have to wait long to appear in court to advance cogent reasons, if she had any, why she should not be held in contempt. The *Candela Daily Mirror* was served with a contempt citation as well. Since Nadine was acting within the course and scope of her employment, Charlie told her that the newspaper was vicariously liable for her actions.

Somehow the media caught wind of the hearing and were there in force. Nadine had been an officer in the state press association and was well respected as a journalist. Winning the Pulitzer Prize had catapulted her to the top of her profession, both in the eyes of the community and in the eyes of her peers.

"The courtroom is packed by your supporters," Charlie commented. "They regard you as a martyr and hero of sorts."

Nadine managed a smile.

"Fighting for the media's First Amendment

rights, especially in Chief Judge Fenton F. Mays' court is like David taking on Goliath," Charlie said. "Judge Mays has had disdain for the press ever since the press was critical of one of his decisions and publicized the reversal when it was taken before the Kansas Supreme Court. To say that Judge Mays is not media friendly is a gross understatement."

Nadine's heart stopped when she spotted a reporter from the *Globe*. Gwendolyn Cardinello had been a reporter with the *Daily Mirror* at the time Nadine was hired. Gwendolyn's tenure with the paper had not been a positive one. Though she had been hired to work on big and breaking stories, she was eventually relegated to reporting on local events and fluff pieces. When Nadine was hired, Gwendolyn's position was eliminated. In reality, she had been terminated to make room for Nadine and she had held a grudge ever since.

Gwendolyn had the tact of an army drill sergeant and the presence to go along with it. Her overpowering personality would make Genghis Khan look like a timid child. No one dared get in her path. Although it couldn't be verified, there was talk that her husband, Maurice, had been hospitalized as a result of a run-in with his wife after one of his late-night poker games with the boys. Apparently, he had missed curfew, lost his week's allowance gambling and had drunk too much fire water. He blamed the broken nose, the two black eyes and multiple contusions, abrasions and lacerations on having fallen down the basement steps. The authorities were skeptical, however, because the Cardinello residence didn't have a basement.

In appearance, Gwendolyn and Nadine were opposites. Even to the casual observer, it was clear that Gwendolyn would win no beauty contest. If someone said she had played linebacker for one of the NFL teams, it would seem quite plausible. People who had worked with her at the paper joked that Gwendolyn might benefit from the assistance of an exorcist. Because of her vicious tendency with the pen and her accusations that could neither be proven nor refuted, Gwendolyn's victims referred to her as the devil's scribe.

Condescending and derisive, Gwendolyn approached her adversaries with equal abandon. No disparity there. The editor of the *Globe*, though a bulk of a man, cowered in her presence. Several of Gwendolyn's male co-workers had been fired at her insistence because of their alleged inappropriate sexual advances towards her. Despite their adamant denials and disavowal of sexual interest or attraction, they were banished from the newspaper feeling fortunate they were not sued for sexual harassment—not as much for fear of an adverse judgment but fear of being labeled that hard up.

When Nadine won the Pulitzer, the *Globe* didn't

carry so much as a blurb. Every chance she got, Gwendolyn printed disparaging statements about the *Daily Mirror* and its coverage of the news. Her vigorous public ridicule and denunciation of the reporters at the *Daily Mirror* and, especially Nadine upon returning with the Pulitzer, greatly exceeded the bounds of propriety or fair and accurate criticism and comment. Bordering upon libel, the *Daily Mirror* on occasion considered legal action, but opted not to dignify the remarks but ignore them. The *Daily Mirror* didn't have the time or energy to waste on Gwendolyn.

Unfortunately, Nadine had to walk past Gwendolyn, who no doubt had positioned herself so as to be obtrusive. With disdain written across her cruel face, Gwendolyn snarled loud enough for Nadine to hear, "Don't think you're going to be able to finesse out of this one, sister!"

Nadine strode by without reacting and positioned herself next to Thornton, who was seated next to Charlie at the defense table. "We've got to quit meeting like this," Charlie whispered to Thornton and Nadine.

Henderson, who was seated in his usual spot with the grand jury foreperson, Estelle Friar, peered at Nadine with a Cheshire cat smile. Nadine responded with a disapproving glance.

"Please rise," the bailiff, a small, frail man in his

early sixties, barked as the black-robed figure emerged from the doorway. He took his place behind the large hand-hewn bench on which sat a nameplate bearing the name Hon. Fenton F. Mays.

"The Honorable Fenton F. Mays presiding," the bailiff announced as his honor maneuvered his bulky frame into a stubborn executive chair that was long in need of replacement.

"You all may be seated," the judge said brusquely. Banging his gavel, he announced, "This court is now in session."

Shuffling through the file folder placed on the bench by his clerk, and after what to Nadine seemed like an eternity, Judge Mays said, "The court calls the case involving Bernadine Catherine Siena also known as Nadine Siena."

Peering over his black horn-rimmed glasses at Nadine, he asked, "Are you Nadine Siena?"

Prompted by Charlie to stand, Nadine replied, "Yes, Your Honor."

Removing his glasses and still peering at Nadine, who had remained standing, he said, "Ms. Siena, you're here on a show cause order. You are here to show cause why you should not be held in contempt for refusal to disclose the identity of a confidential source before the Pembrooke County Grand Jury. Do you understand that?"

Again, Nadine replied, "Yes, Your Honor."

"Very well, then, Ms. Siena, you may be seated."

Directing his attention to the district attorney, Judge Mays said, "Since this is not a jury trial and the rules of evidence are relaxed, I will now ask you, Mr. Henderson, to make an offer of proof as to what the prosecution's evidence will show."

"Your Honor," Henderson began, "Ms. Siena appeared before the grand jury pursuant to a subpoena. She related information she obtained as a reporter for the *Candela Daily Mirror* relevant to the grand jury's probe. Unfortunately, the information was not based on firsthand knowledge but upon information obtained from a confidential source. She refused to reveal the source because, as she explained, she had made an absolute promise of anonymity. Without the source, the evidence presented by Ms. Siena would be hearsay and, therefore, inadmissible in a court of law because it doesn't fit under any of the exceptions. The prosecution is unable to obtain the source's name or the evidence by any other means. The name of the source, needless to say, is critical to the grand jury investigation."

Judge Mays, directing his remarks to Charlie, asked, "Mr. Atkins, would you advise the court as to what facts your client would stipulate to?"

"Your Honor, we are prepared to stipulate to the following facts. Ms. Siena, acting in her capacity as a reporter for the *Candela Daily Mirror,* was contacted by a confidential source with information that later apparently became relevant to the grand jury probe. In order to obtain the information, she was forced to enter into a verbal agreement whereby, in exchange for the information, she would not divulge the informant's name or identity. The promise of anonymity was a strict condition precedent. *But* for the promise, the informant would *not* have released the information. Ms. Siena did reveal that information to the grand jury but, in keeping her agreement with the source, declined to reveal his or her name or identity. Mr. Henderson will have to prove his other assertions, as we have no evidence to either confirm or refute the same."

"Since Mr. Henderson is an officer of the court," Judge Mays ruled, "the Court is inclined to accept his offer of proof without the necessity of him having to provide evidence in support thereof. To require otherwise would compromise and thus jeopardize the matter being investigated by the grand jury. It is a secret proceeding and for good cause. The Court intends to keep it that way."

Addressing his comments to Nadine, Judge Mays said, "Ms. Siena, the State of Kansas has no shield law that protects you from having to reveal the name or identity of your source. This is true particularly where the name or identity is sought by a grand jury. Refusal to provide that information is civil or indirect contempt because it didn't happen in the direct presence of a judge such as myself. If you persist in your refusal to reveal your source to the grand jury, I will have no choice but to find you in contempt and by law will be required to impose a sentence of imprisonment and/or a fine. I can also impose a fine on the *Candela Daily Mirror*. Do you understand what I have just stated?"

Rising to her feet, Nadine answered, "Yes, Your Honor, I understand."

"Because of what I am about to ask you affects the outcome of this proceeding and both you and your newspaper," Judge Mays continued, "I ask that you consider it carefully. Do you still persist in your refusal to reveal the identity of your source or are you willing to reconsider and provide the grand jury with the information they seek?"

"Your Honor," Nadine responded, "balancing the public's interest in obtaining the name of my source with my legal and moral obligation to the source has been one of the most difficult decisions I have been called upon to make as a journalist. As an investigative reporter, I am committed to exposing corruption, criminal activity and injustice. That has always been and will always be my goal. In achieving my goal, however, I can't break the law along the way or act in an unethical manner. Otherwise, I am just as bad as those whom I expose.

"I am in a no-win situation and apparently the system is not designed to cut me any slack. If I go back on my word and expose the source, I expose the source to the dangers my source feared when he or she chose not to go public. The agreement I have with the source is an enforceable contract. By breaking that contract, I subject both the newspaper and myself to the consequences that flow from that breach. Perhaps more important are the ethical considerations. Not keeping a promise is an anathema both under the code of the journalist and my own personal code.

"On the other hand," Nadine continued, "if I honor my agreement and keep my promise I will be at Your Honor's mercy. My ticket to freedom would be to expose my source. That certainly would be the easy way out and, to some, the most expedient. Then all of us, with the exception of my source, would live happily ever after. That happens in fairy tales. Unfortunately, this is not a fairy tale and even though it is balancing the interest of my source against the whole world, I still have to do the right thing. It can't be a numbers game. Otherwise it would be an easy choice.

"I am claustrophobic and have, since childhood, recurring nightmares of being locked in a closet. I remember deliberately leaving the door of a bird cage open in front of an open window when I was twelve and freeing the only pet I ever had growing up, a canary by the name of Feebie. I was saddened to let loose of my most trusted friend but felt exhilarated when I saw Feebie, haltingly at first, soar into the endless expanse of open sky, a free bird."

In concluding, Nadine confessed, "I'm fearful of being locked up in a human-sized cage with people I don't know and being away from my circle of comfort, but if I compromise my ideals and lose my own self-respect I will be imprisoned within myself forever. I have to do the right thing and so do you, and I do not fault you for it. I can't go back on my word."

There was an eerie silence in the courtroom. You could have heard a cotton ball drop. Even the usually rigid Fenton F. Mays was visibly moved although unfortunately not for very long.

"The court will hear arguments," he announced.

Henderson rose and argued first. "Society is constrained to consider the greatest good for the greatest number. If the good citizens of Kansas had wanted a shield law, the legislature would have enacted one. If such a law is so desirable, then why haven't all of the states enacted one? And, why isn't there a federal shield law? Knowing what the law was, Nadine had a choice when she promised anonymity. She assumed the risk. Solving crime is a compelling justification for requiring a journalist to disclose relevant information to a grand jury. Where there are conflicting interests to be reconciled, the court should favor the one having the greatest impact and the one with the broadest societal value. The judicial system would cease to function effectively if certain segments of society, such as journalists, were allowed to disregard the law with impunity. The tail would be wagging the dog. We know Your Honor will not allow that to happen here."

It was now Charlie's turn. Nadine wasn't sure Charlie could change Judge Mays' mind. Charlie had warned her beforehand that Judge Mays was unyielding and disliked the media. With the judge having been involved in the impaneling of the grand jury along with the district attorney as well as the appointment of Mrs. Friar as chairperson, both of whom were present in court opposing her, Nadine knew the odds were stacked against her.

"May it please the Court," Charlie began. "I was intrigued by Mr. Henderson's statement that the judicial system would cease to function effectively if certain segments of society were allowed to disregard the law with impunity. The more I think about that statement, the more I agree with him.

"That may also be the basis of my argument, Your Honor. The last I read the law, lawful interference with a contractual relationship was a tort, a civil wrong.

187

The elements to make out a cause of action are the existence of an enforceable contract, such as between Ms. Siena and her source, awareness by the wrongdoer that the contract exists, and intentional inducement to get Ms. Siena to breach that contract. And if Ms. Siena is convinced to break her contract with the source, the wrongdoer is liable for the resulting damages. And guess who the wrongdoer is. It is the man who took an oath to uphold the law, Mr. Henderson. Mr. Henderson better hope Ms. Siena keeps her promise. She should be commended, not condemned, for doing so.

"Being compelled by Your Honor, under penalty of a fine and/or imprisonment, to breach an agreement and break a promise somehow flies in the face of the First Amendment of the United States Constitution, which guarantees freedom of the press. In this case, Ms. Siena is required to waive her journalistic freedom in exchange for her personal freedom.

"To evade punishment for contempt of court, Ms. Siena is required to commit a tort. To avoid tort liability, she will be found guilty of civil contempt. Therefore, she is damned if she does and damned if she doesn't. That dichotomy violates Ms. Siena's due process rights under both the Fifth and Fourteen amendments.

"By finding Ms. Siena guilty of contempt and imposing a sentence, the free flow of information will be stymied in two respects. The source and future sources will be dissuaded from providing information to the press and thus less information will be made available to the public and law enforcement. The chilling effect of the Court's threatened action will benefit no one.

"Ms. Siena and the *Candela Daily Mirror* are asking Your Honor to use the contempt power at your disposal in a manner that promotes justice, not stifles it. Justice here would not be served by punishing a journalist who insists on keeping the promise of confidentiality, not because she benefits from it, but because it is both the legal and the right thing to do. And now, we're asking you to do the right thing. And, the right thing in this proceeding is not to hold Ms. Siena in contempt of court."

Judge Mays took a minute or two before announcing his sentence. It was not a question whether Nadine would be held in contempt, only what the consequences would be in not revealing the name or identity of her source to the grand jury.

Removing his glasses and fixing his gaze directly on Nadine, Judge Mays began, "The law does not carve out an exception for journalists when it comes to testifying before the grand jury. The law in Kansas is clear on that. Journalists do not have absolute First Amendment rights to refuse to reveal their sources, even in states that have shield laws. Kansas has no shield law. Therefore, in light of the facts in this case, the only issue for the court to decide is what penalty should be imposed for willful failure to disclose your confidential source.

"The court was initially prepared to impose an indeterminate sentence of incarceration in the county jail meaning, Ms. Siena, that you would be released only after you divulged the name of your confidential informant. In light of the circumstances, I am going to impose a hybrid—a mix between a determinate and indeterminate sentence. Accordingly, I am imposing a jail sentence of ninety days. However, if you or your source reveals his or her identity within that time period, you will immediately be released. In addition, during the period of your incarceration, Ms. Siena, your newspaper will pay a fine of one hundred dollars per day under the same conditions. You will check in at the Coronado County Jail tomorrow at 8:00 a.m. and your time will begin to run from that date. Good luck."

Nadine had no intent to appeal the decision or stay the sentence, nor did the newspaper. Despite Charlie's recommendations to the contrary, Nadine stood firm. She did not want to unnecessarily prolong the inevitable.

The story of a local reporter winning the Pulitzer didn't make the front page or even the back page of the *Globe*. But *LOCAL REPORTER JAILED FOR CONTEMPT* was emblazoned across the front page of that evening's edition, with a photograph of Nadine Siena below it.

*In a hearing this morning, Chief District Court Judge Fenton F. Mays declared    Ms. Nadine Siena guilty of contempt of court for willfully failing to reveal the name of   the source necessary in an investigation before the grand jury.*

*Commencing tomorrow at 8:00 a.m., Ms. Siena will begin serving a ninety-day jail sentence in the Coronado County Jail in Pembrooke. In addition, the* Candela Daily Mirror, *for whom she was employed, was assessed a fine of one hundred dollars per day.*

*Reporters in the state of Kansas are not shielded from providing information requested by the grand jury. Surprisingly, Ms. Siena, a pundit on various political issues and public controversies, was not aware of the laws of this state or, if aware, was unwilling to conform to the clear mandate of the Kansas legislature. Standing resolute on her refusal to testify, Ms. Siena sought First Amendment protection. In ruling against Ms. Siena, Judge Mays held society's interest in obtaining full disclosure of information concerning criminal conduct was paramount and clearly superseded her superficial and contrived claim of a reporter's privilege.*

*In a brief interview with Judge Mays immediately following his decision, Judge Mays unequivocally reiterated that in the state of Kansas, a reporter does not have either an absolute or qualified privilege to refuse to answer questions before a grand jury. In response to a question asked by the media following the hearing, Judge Mays agreed that it was the duty of every citizen, including members of the press, to provide information to solve and prevent criminal conduct.*

# CHAPTER 13

## THE PRICE OF VIRTUE

E xcept for a slight breeze and the trill of a western meadowlark high in the branches of a nearby cottonwood, the air was still and quiet. As Charlie's SUV pulled into the parking lot of the courthouse where the county jail was housed, a black cat darted out from under an adjacent Ford pickup and barely escaped being hit. Charlie slammed on the brakes, tossing his passengers against their seat belts.

"That was a black cat!" Thornton, who was riding in the front seat with Charlie, exclaimed.

Nadine shuddered and said, "Not a good omen."

Mother Catherine, seated in the backseat with Nadine, replied, "Nonsense, child. That black cat curse is mere superstition. In some cultures it is thought to bring good luck if a black cat crosses your path."

Looking in the rearview mirror in Nadine's direction, Charlie said, "Didn't the first multimillion dollar winner of the lottery claim that it was as a result of a black cat running in front of her as she entered the convenience store that prompted her to buy the ticket?"

"Maybe we should stop at a convenience store and buy lottery tickets after we drop Nadine off," Thornton suggested.

"Buy a ticket for me and, if it is a winner, maybe I can use it to buy my way out of jail," Nadine said, crossing her fingers.

"You played way too much Monopoly as a child," Mother Catherine said. "Unfortunately, it doesn't work like that in real life."

"Besides, if you tried to buy your way out," Charlie added, "I'd be defending you on a bribery charge."

"Don't want that to happen, Charlie," Nadine said. "Don't you dare buy me a lottery ticket."

As they entered the double doors of the lobby of the Coronado County Jail and stood in front of the information counter, the four embraced. Soon, they were greeted by a short, stout jail matron. As Nadine was being led away, she turned, and with tears in her eyes, said, "I will miss all of you."

"We will miss you, too," each of them said in turn.

"Remember," Mother Catherine said as tears swelled, "you're not lost or forgotten, just on a sabbatical."

"You are on paid leave," Thornton said.

"I will come to see you first thing tomorrow," Charlie promised.

"Keep me in your prayers," Nadine hollered as the door was locked behind her.

Once inside, Nadine was booked, fingerprinted and her mug shot taken.

"It is now official," the matron said without smiling, "you now have a record and a rap sheet."

Nadine was led to a small dressing room where she traded civilian garb for the famous hunter orange jumpsuit and slip-on tennis shoes. With her pallid face dominating her appearance, she looked less like a jail bird and more like a snow bunny, albeit with questionable fashion taste. Nadine bristled when the matron did the body search. Deputy Ellie Crawford was brusque and not at all gentle in searching all the private places that could be used to smuggle in contraband. With all the monitoring devices installed in and around the cells, privacy would be no more, at least not for the anticipated ninety days.

The court order issued by Judge Mays and directed to the Sheriff, Ignacio Rovera, authorized reading and writing materials for Nadine during the period of her incarceration. So that she could continue with some of her journalistic chores at the *Daily* Mirror, she was permitted free use of her cell phone. Otherwise, she was to receive no greater or lesser treatment than other prisoners.

Nadine preceded the matron to a cell in one of the female pods. Both bunk beds were unmade. She sat on the bottom bunk, chewing her lip and fighting back tears.

In the orphanage, she had had little privacy. When she left, she swore she'd never share a bedroom again. So far, the only exception had been when she was in college. Since then she'd cherished her privacy. With the cell's stainless steel privy and wash basin in the open, Nadine would have to improvise in the least obtrusive way to utilize each. The Coronado County Jail, obviously, was not designed for the bashful.

Nadine was committed to making the best out of the situation. She would stay to herself and not become embroiled in any discussions that could evolve into any arguments. The jail personnel were civil and she would avoid confrontation at all costs. Being a model prisoner was key to jail house survival. She imagined being in boot camp was much like her current situation. She would do as she was told and be courteous and conciliatory until she was released.

There had been a big drug bust before the end of her first week of incarceration, resulting in scores of arrests. The jail population more than doubled and her pod filled to capacity. Nadine now had a cell mate.

"Wow! You have this cell looking like an ad in a style magazine. I used to be like that."

"Here, let me help you with that," Nadine said as she assisted her new cellmate with the jail bedding.

"Thanks," the teenager said as she rubbed her arms now relieved of the burden.

"By the way, my name is Nadine Siena." Nadine then extended her right hand in a welcoming gesture.

"I'm Trudy Snowden, I've never been in jail before." Trudy's hand was clammy. Nadine didn't hold it long.

"What're you in for?" Trudy asked.

"I was held in contempt for willfully disobeying a court order. I received a ninety-day sentence."

When Trudy didn't respond, Nadine asked, "I take it you're one of the drug arrests, correct?"

"Both my boyfriend and I were busted in a raid by the DEA. We were caught with meth and charged with possession and possession with intent to distribute. We befriended a couple who turned out to be undercover cops. Guess we shouldn't have trusted them."

"Guess not," Nadine replied. "Are you from around here?"

"My father is a minister in a small town near Wichita called Hawthorne. I was born and lived there through my freshman year in high school. I moved with my mother to Pembrooke when my parents divorced, and I finished high school here."

"I'm familiar with Hawthorne. With what denomination is your father affiliated?"

Tears filled Trudy's eyes. "Do I have to tell you? I've embarrassed my father enough."

Nadine placed her arms around Trudy's shoulders and tried to console her. "It's not important. What is important is that you not embarrass him further."

"I'm worried about Chris. He's my boyfriend and, like me, has never been in jail before. I'm not sure they'll let us see each other." More tears flowed from Trudy's eyes.

"Drugs have been my downfall," Trudy confided. "I was introduced to meth the summer between my junior and senior years in high school."

"Have you tried to give up meth?" Nadine asked.

"It's not as easy as it sounds. Once you're hooked on it, it's almost too late. Fact is, I've never been serious about giving them up." Trudy looked down and picked at her nails. "Even though the counselor I saw for a while told me I should give up drugs and Chris, I couldn't do either."

"Maybe you'll dry out here," Nadine offered.

"Can't wait that long," Trudy sobbed. "I don't want to be here."

"If you haven't already, you should contact your father or mother."

"Can't. Both my father and mother told me if I ever ended up in the slammer, I could stay there and rot. I can't count on either one for help."

Nadine's heart leapt for Trudy. Just a teenager, Trudy's face already bore the signs of uncontrolled drug use. Trudy, she thought, was the poster child of a member of the favored class hitting rock bottom on a fast track.

Trudy attached herself to Nadine like a day-old pup who couldn't find its mother. She had no one else she could trust to turn to. Nadine appeared to be her lifeline.

Nadine always wondered what kind of mother she would make and had always been skeptical because of having been abandoned by her own mother. Pondering the probability of inherited traits was something that had not dissipated over the years and naturally was cause for grave concern. Nadine avoided any romantic entanglements for fear that would lead to motherhood and a test of her physical, mental and emotional constitution. She did not want to foist on her child what her mother had foisted on her. Yet, Nadine felt a maternal instinct towards this child who had been dropped off on her doorstep, so to speak.

What would transpire over the next several days would change the whole complexion of the investigation of the prescription fraud scandal in Pembrooke.

It was in the middle of the night when Nadine was awakened by Trudy's sobs.

"Bad dream?" Nadine asked as she stood on the lower rung of the ladder that led to the upper bunk.

"Just feeling sorry for myself," Trudy replied. "I don't know how I ended up in this mess."

Trudy climbed down from the top bunk and the two sat on the edge of Nadine's bed. "How did you get hooked on meth to begin with?" Nadine asked.

"Was introduced to it at a girlfriend's birthday party," Trudy sobbed. "Everyone else was trying it so I tried it, too. I found that I liked it and have been using it ever since."

"Is that the only drug you've tried?"

"The only illegal drug," she answered as she wiped her nose with her sleeve. "Beginning my sophomore year in high school, I took prescription drugs. Some were prescribed for me, some were not. My mother was an antidepressant junkie and her bathroom cabinet was always filled with various prescription drugs."

"I take it you just graduated high school?"

"In June."

"So you've only lived in Pembrooke for about three years?"

"Just during my sophomore, junior and senior years. Actually, it was during that time that I began taking prescription drugs."

"Were all of those prescribed for your mother or were some also prescribed for you?"

"I lettered in track all three of those years. One of my teammates was taking some performance-enhancing drugs and recommended I do the same. So, she gave me the name of her doctor and I obtained the first of many such prescriptions. That was when I was a sophomore."

"Did they work?"

"Like a charm. My performance improved to the point that I qualified for state. At state, I finished second in both distance events. My junior and senior years, I placed first."

"What was the name of your doctor?"

"Dr. Edmund Simms."

Nadine's jaw dropped. "Dr. Edmund Simms

prescribed the drugs?"

"Yes," Trudy replied.

"Those wouldn't by chance have been filled at Hopkins Pharmacy, were they?" Nadine held her breath.

"Dr. Simms directed me there."

*Oh, my God!* Nadine mouthed.

"For relaxation and to prevent anxiety and fatigue, Dr. Simms prescribed other types of medications."

"Were those prescriptions also filled at Hopkins Pharmacy?"

"I could always count on Dr. Maynard Hopkins. He was my guardian angel. Even when I didn't have a renewal, he would refill my prescriptions."

As if things could get any better, Trudy revealed some very damaging information about both Drs. Simms and Hopkins. "For the past three months, Chris has been employed by Hopkins Pharmacy as a delivery boy. One of the fringe benefits is that he can purchase prescription drugs at a discount and without a formal prescription."

"Heck of a deal. Who supplied your meth?"

"We supplied our own."

"How so?"

"Chris learned how to manufacture meth from Dr. Hopkins. Dr. Hopkins sold him most of the supplies to make it."

"How do you know?"

"Chris and I had run track together since our sophomore year. We were both the same age and were in the same grade. We started dating at the beginning of our junior year. There is nothing that we keep from each other. We tell each other everything." Trudy paused. "Actually, that's not totally true."

"What do you mean?"

"Around Christmas break of our junior year, I found out that I was pregnant. I panicked. I was afraid to tell my mother, so I went to Dr. Simms. At first he refused to perform an abortion but I threatened to expose his drug practices, so he finally agreed. I told Chris I had had a miscarriage.

"About midyear our senior year, we got high. I told him about the abortion. That was a huge mistake because Chris, whose father was a lab technician for the Pembrooke Police Department, used that information to blackmail Dr. Simms. Then he could force Dr. Simms to write as many prescriptions as he wanted. Hopkins Pharmacy filled them without any questions."

"I assume it was blackmail that landed Chris his job at Hopkins Pharmacy?"

"Yes, and it was by blackmailing Dr. Hopkins that Chris was able to get other concessions that he would tell me about when he was high."

"Wasn't Chris at all fearful of Dr. Hopkins and concerned that pushing the blackmail envelope too far might backfire?"

"Actually, Chris told me that, on one occasion, Dr. Hopkins reminded him that life was fragile and that what happened to Trevor Watts could easily happen to him."

Nadine could scarcely believe her ears. "Dr. Hopkins apparently trusted Chris."

"Not completely. Chris told me that Dr. Hopkins searched him several times, accusing him of having a body mike. Sometimes he had to empty his pockets."

"Your boyfriend's last name wouldn't be Campbell by chance?"

"How did you know?"

"I know a Casey Campbell who is a PPD lab tech."

"That's Chris' father!"

Nadine couldn't believe the coincidences. The incriminating information Trudy related brought with it, however, frustration for Nadine. It was like having a million dollars in her pocket and having nowhere to spend it. She would have to find a way to convey the information to Charlie. For now, the information that could seal the fate of the two doctors would have to sit in limbo.

Nadine pondered Trudy's motives. Nadine speculated that Trudy was spilling her guts to soothe her soul, not to save souls like her father and, being a minister's daughter, no doubt knew that confession, contrition and a firm purpose of amendment were conditions precedent to absolution. Whatever her motive, Trudy had taken the first step. Whether she would take the remaining two steps, Nadine could only hope.

When Charlie came to visit Nadine, she slipped him a note containing the gospel according to St. Trudy. She was afraid to say anything for fear their conversations were being monitored or recorded. The postscript on the note begged for guidance and a roadmap for a discreet method to handle the matter.

Before Charlie could get back with Nadine, Trudy had bonded out. Not surprisingly, Trudy's minister father had posted the bond and had also hired an attorney to represent her.

Trudy was back on the outside. However, the love of her life would have to remain behind bars because Christopher Campbell's parents had become disenchanted with their son's lifestyle and were no longer willing to be unwitting enablers. In the interim, Christopher would have to be content with a court appointed attorney and being locked away.

Although Nadine's circumstances were unique and being an inmate with a cell phone was an aberration, Nadine did not want to abuse the privilege. Nonetheless, just prior to Trudy's release, Nadine gave Trudy her cell phone number.

The day after her release, Trudy contacted Nadine. "It's me, Trudy," she said.

"Hey, how are things on the outside?"

"They're going great. Dad hired me an attorney. His name is Duncan Macklin. Do you know him?"

"You picked a good one. Have you met with him yet?"

"Actually, I have and that's one of the reasons I'm calling. He made me promise not to discuss my case with anyone but him. He told me anything I admitted to could be used against me and anyone I spoke with about my case could be called as a witness against me."

"Identifying those with whom you spoke would not be easy. The authorities can't call witnesses whose identities are unknown."

"Well, they would know you were my cellmate and would probably know I talked to you about my case. When Mr. Macklin asked me if I had spoken to anyone about my case, I admitted I had talked to you."

"So far, no one has requested an interview with

me. Mr. Macklin's advice is good advice. You have to be careful who you talk to and what you say."

"What I told you was a lie," Trudy blurted. "Very little of what I said was true. I made the whole thing up. Anyway, everything I told you was in strict confidence."

"I . . . I don't know what to say," Nadine said. "I believed what you told me to be true."

"Well, it wasn't," Trudy persisted. "Anyway, I have some great news. I now have a job and a way to raise money to get Chris out of jail."

"Where are you working?" Nadine asked.

"Hopkins Pharmacy," Trudy proudly replied.

Nadine's heart stopped and she felt as if she had just been stabbed in the heart with a dull serrated bolo knife. As far as Nadine was concerned, Trudy had signed her own death warrant.

It was now mid-July and Nadine had served half her time on the contempt charge. Her newspaper had already paid half their fines. It was now countdown to departure day. There was no anticipation that her source would come to her rescue by revealing his true identity and that wasn't even a blip on her radar screen when Charlie called.

"I will be in court all afternoon and am not sure what time I will be stopping by the jail. I didn't want you holding your breath until I got there."

"I'm sure our discussion will be breathtaking. In the interim, I will be taking deep breaths."

"The main reason I called concerns a call I received from Thornton who knows I plan to see you today. Apparently, Marci received a call earlier from a person by the name of Cordell Samuelson who was calling from San Mateo, California. Appears the caller is desperate to reach you. Do you want his number?"

"I have it," Nadine responded. "I'll call him right now."

When Nadine placed the call to Corey, she was hoping that the information that she had communicated to the authorities hadn't pointed in his direction. Corey hadn't wanted to blow the whistle on his fiancé's father for fear it would result in the end of his and Megan's relationship. The position in which he was placed had some rather serious implications, especially if Dr. Hopkins were to discover that his future son-in-law was a snitch. She didn't want to burn her source either directly or indirectly and hoped she hadn't.

After a number of rings, Corey answered. "Corey speaking."

"Corey, this is Nadine Siena. Sorry I missed your call."

"Hope I'm not bothering you. It is important that we talk."

"Shoot!"

"Megan and I have broken off our engagement."

"What prompted that?"

"With the pressure at home following the murder of Trevor Watts, Megan has become a basket case. Her father, according to her, has become paranoid following his deposition in the libel suit. He has accused everyone in the family, including her, of being an informant. Apparently, his accusations have also been directed at me."

"How about Megan? Has she been accusatory as well?"

"I'm not sure she thinks I informed on her father but she has asked the pointblank question. I, of course, have had to lie by denying my involvement."

"I imagine you have been conflicted by the charade."

"That is the reason for our breakup. I am in love with Megan but can't continue to live a lie. Megan also agrees that it is in everyone's best interest that we sever the tie and go our separate ways."

"Are the two of you still communicating with each other?"

"We are no longer on speaking terms. I just

hope someday Megan will be understanding and, when she becomes aware of my perceived betrayal, will forgive me."

"Have you confided in your father yet?"

"Believe it or not, I have. In fact, it is as a result of his coaxing that I've decided to go to the authorities with this thing. But first, I wanted to talk to you."

For the second time in less than a month, her heart stopped. She couldn't believe she heard him right. This was truly an admirable gesture on Corey's part, certainly an answer to a prayer.

"Are you still there?" Corey asked.

"I'm just trying to catch my breath," Nadine replied.

"By the way," Corey said, "I don't recognize the telephone number."

"I'm in the county jail. I'm calling you on my cell phone."

The pause now was caused by Corey. "Wh . . . what are you doing in jail?"

"I'm serving a ninety-day sentence after being held in contempt for refusing to reveal you as my source."

"You . . . you chose jail over breaking your promise to me? I . . . I don't know what to say except thank you. I knew all along you were the right person to contact. Who do you suggest I get in touch with?"

"I will be meeting with the newspaper's attorney later in the day. His name is Charles Atkins. I'll see who he suggests. In fact, I'll have him contact you directly if that would be agreeable."

"I'll have him speak with my father. Since they're both attorneys, they'll be able to understand each other."

"Lawyers do have a language of their own."

"I hope my coming forward will get you off the hook."

"Something tells me it will. Thank you."

"No, thank you!"

After the two hung up, each wondered where his or her new alliance would lead.

"Ms. Siena, I see we meet again. Gentlemen, my clerk tells me you have a joint motion."

"We do, Your Honor," Charlie and Horace Henderson said in unison.

"May I approach the bench?" Henderson requested.

"You may do so," Judge Mays said in a conciliatory tone.

*From a ferocious tiger to a pussycat,* Nadine thought as she watched the Honorable Fenton F. Mays review the document placed before him.

"Um-m-m," Judge Mays murmured as he set down the document and removed his glasses. Then looking at Nadine, he said, "I've been handed a document entitled Modified Mittimus authorizing your release, Ms. Siena. The court spoke with both attorneys in chambers before calling this proceeding to order and was made aware of the request in the motion that accompanies this order. It says that your attorney, in your behalf, has divulged the name of the source you previously refused to reveal. It also says the source has requested that his identity be made known to the district attorney. The court received by fax earlier today the authorization from your source. Do you know what that means?"

Standing, Nadine said, "In my case justice delayed is not justice denied."

In all the years that Judge Mays had been on the bench, no one had ever seen or heard him laugh in open court. History was being made as the courtroom erupted into laughter.

"Ms. Siena, it is good to know that forty-five days in jail has not dimmed your sense of humor."

"Nor yours," Nadine replied as she watched Judge Mays sign the modified mittimus commanding her release.

"If there is nothing further, this court will stand

adjourned," Judge Mays said as he smiled at Nadine and handed the original to his clerk. "Here, make copies and give one to each attorney." Pausing and peering at Nadine he said, "No, make that three. Give one to Ms. Siena for her scrapbook."

"Trade you these for what you're wearing," the matron said in a more kindly tone than when the two had first met. Handing Nadine the clothing she was wearing when she was first admitted, the matron said, "You can go into this private room and change." She then held the door open to the small changing room. "When you finish, I'll have all your personal belongings waiting."

After putting on her civilian clothes and picking up her personal belongings from the matron, Nadine was ushered into the lobby where she was met by Thornton.

As the two walked to the car, Thornton put his arm around Nadine's shoulder and said, "Welcome back to civilization. You don't look any worse for wear."

"Looks are deceiving," Nadine replied. "Remember, you can't judge a book by its cover."

Nadine rode to a now closed newspaper office with Thornton to break out a bottle of bubbly encased in ice that had been purchased awaiting this hallowed event. Soon they were joined by Charlie and Mother Catherine. With the nightmare swiftly fading, Nadine could now dare to dream.

# CHAPTER 14

## MOMENT OF REDEMPTION

T he word on the street was that detectives Noah
Ames and Jessie Wynne had flown to San Mateo,
California, to interview a key witness in the death
of Trevor Watts. Nadine knew that information hadn't
come from her and worried about its source. Was there
a leak in the police department or perhaps the sheriff's
department? In the back of her mind she was concerned
for Trudy's safety. If the investigation zeroed in on Drs.
Hopkins and Simms, they might need to get rid of
others who knew too much.

She had only been back at work a couple of
days when the call came into the office about a hostage
situation at the Coronado County Jail. Barely had the
call come in when Nadine had an urgent call from
Sheriff Ignacio Rovera. A prisoner who was
accompanied by a deputy sheriff from the exercise pen
to his cell overpowered the deputy and took the deputy's
service revolver. The prisoner had taken the deputy's
keys and liberated the other prisoners in the pod. The
now weaponless deputy was being held hostage at

gunpoint within the pod. All were trapped in the pod by armed jailers. The prisoner was threatening to execute the deputy if the prisoner and his confederates were not released.

"What has this to do with me?" Nadine asked.

"The prisoner has refused to negotiate or even talk to any of us. He has asked specifically for you. I assume he envisions you would serve as the intermediary or go-between between the prisoners and the jailers."

When Nadine hesitated, Sheriff Rovera added, "The situation is critical and the longer the standoff the more likely the violence."

"I don't know, Sheriff, I . . . ."

"The call is yours. If you decline, I will fully understand."

"By the way, what is the prisoner's name?"

"Christopher Campbell."

Nadine was stunned. "I'm not saying no. I need to discuss this with my boss. He's in today. I'll call you right back."

A lot of things were going through Nadine's mind when she headed for Thornton's office.

*Negotiating the release of a hostage is not in my job description. The newspaper does not provide hazard pay. That is outside the course and scope of my employment and excluded from the newspaper's insurance coverage. There is no policy against moonlighting as long as it is noncompetitive in nature and doesn't involve a rival publication. The only thing that would prevent me from taking on this special assignment would be my better judgment.*

Sheriff Rovera wants you to do what?" Thornton stammered. "Let me get Charlie on the phone."

"She wants to do what?" Charlie yelled over the speaker phone.

When the dust settled and Nadine related her conversation with Sheriff Rovera, Charlie cleared his throat and said, "Haven't you had enough of jails to last you a lifetime?"

"If it weren't for what Trudy told me about Chris, I wouldn't even consider it," Nadine replied.

"Isn't there someone else they can get, someone who is trained in hostage negotiation," Charlie asked. "Christopher Campbell is Casey Campbell's son and Casey is a crime scene investigator for the Pembrooke Police Department. Why wouldn't he be the likely choice?"

"Chris' parents have disowned him and his father is the last person he would probably want to face in a situation like this," Nadine speculated. "Knowing what little I know about him, I think I can convince him to surrender the weapon and release the hostage."

"Being a hero carries a certain amount of risk,"

Charlie warned.

"I have no desire to be a hero and certainly don't need the notoriety," Nadine replied.

"I would advise against it," Charlie offered.

"I echo the same sentiments," Thornton said.

"Why don't you call Mother Catherine?" Charlie suggested. "Maybe she can offer some insight."

When she spoke with Mother Catherine, she was told, "Maybe the Good Lord placed you in jail previously for this purpose – to prepare you for this very moment."

For Nadine, maybe she was wrong but she was not in doubt. "When do you want me?" she asked Sheriff Rovera.

"As fast as you can get over here," he responded.

When Nadine was escorted to Chris' pod, she was met by Sheriff Rovera. Soon she was introduced to Chris' father, Casey Campbell.

"We've been trying to persuade Chris to surrender the weapon before anyone gets hurt," Sheriff Rovera said.

"Which one is your son?" Nadine asked Casey.

"The tall one with the weapon in his hand,"

Casey replied as he pointed to Chris.

Nadine stared at the eighteen-year-old boy who looked more like a choir boy than a druggie jail bird leading a prison riot.

"He doesn't fit at all the image I had," Nadine said to the two.

"He's had time to dry out," Sheriff Rovera replied.

Nadine noticed Chris' hand was shaking as he held the service revolver. His eyes were pleading and, to her, he didn't appear at all intimidating or threatening. She also noticed that the other prisoners were not engaged in any actions that she would consider menacing. She could see that a uniformed individual was sitting on the edge of a lower bunk in one of the cells. There was no yelling or shouting and, if it weren't for what she was told, she wouldn't have known there was a riot or attempted jailbreak in progress.

"I don't mind at all going in there," Nadine told Sheriff Rovera.

"We can't let you go in there while they are still armed," Sheriff Rovera said.

"Then let me talk to Chris through the bars. Maybe I can get him to give up the weapon."

"First, let me convince him to leave the weapon behind," Casey pleaded.

"Chris," his father said, "you asked to speak

with Nadine Siena. She is the lady standing next to Sheriff Rovera. If you will leave the weapon behind and come to the bars on this door, I will move and you can speak to Ms. Siena in private."

Without any hesitation, Chris handed the service revolver to a fellow prisoner and stepped to the door.

Reaching through the bars to shake hands with Nadine, Chris said in a low tone, "Trudy spoke highly of you and said you had helped pull her through her jail ordeal."

"She's a fine young lady. She helped me as well."

"Trudy needed your help. Now I need help."

Chris then looked around and, in a barely audible voice, said, "The jailbreak was not my idea. It was Damon Rodden's idea. He's the guy you see locked up in my cell. He's one of the jailers and was one of my coworkers at Hopkins Pharmacy—before my arrest, that is. Anyway, we know each other and I have as much dirt on him as he has on me. When I was arrested and locked up here, Rodden began harassing me."

"What did he do to harass you?"

"Mostly threaten me. He told me that Dr. Hopkins was upset about my arrest and that I no longer had a job there. He warned me about making up stories about Dr. Hopkins. He said he could make life hell for me here if I got out of line. He told me that he is the only one I should talk to because of our having worked together at the pharmacy. He said he is the only one I should trust."

Glancing over his shoulder, Chris began speaking in a whisper. His hand had been clammy when he shook hands with Nadine. Now, he was alternating rubbing the palms of his hands with the thumbs of the other. He appeared apprehensive and desperate.

"Right after Trudy bonded out, Rodden became very friendly, more like he had been when we had worked together. He said that he didn't want to see me spend the rest of my life in jail and that the jail rumor was that one of the prisoners in the pod on the next floor, who was arrested at the same time as me, had labeled me a snitch. He said I was a marked man and that he didn't want anything bad to happen to me."

"Do you know the name of the prisoner Rodden was talking about?"

"Yeah. Talmad Sisman, a known drug dealer. On the street, he is known as The Enforcer for a small band of local thugs. He is from somewhere on the east coast and I have been told he has a row of cross tattoos lining his belly that represent the number of people he has killed. I have never dealt with him personally, but I know he is not someone I would ever want to mess with."

"How did you get Rodden's service revolver?"

"Rodden said he would help me escape. I told him no. When I ran into him this morning in the exercise pen, he said he would escort me back to my cell while the backup jailer was on break and give me his service revolver and the cell keys. I would pretend to hold him hostage and using the vehicle he had placed in the employee parking lot, I would make my escape. When he brought me back to the pod, he took out his Smith & Wesson and handed it to me. While I held it, he unlocked the other nine cells. That was when the backup jailer, Arreola Barrios, arrived from break. None of us knew what to do. We just winged it."

"Are you saying Rodden set all of this up?"

"I will take a polygraph on it right now. None of this was planned. You can ask the other inmates. They will tell you the same thing."

"Why would Rodden do this? What does he stand to gain?"

"It's obvious. To get rid of the supposed snitch. I knew too much. He was hoping I would try to escape so he could shoot me or let me escape. Either way, I would no longer be a threat to Dr. Hopkins and his operation."

"The first thing you need to do," Nadine said, "is retrieve the weapon and bring it to me pronto. I will then meet with your father and Sheriff Rovera so that order can be restored. Leave Rodden where he is and, after you bring me the revolver, instruct the other prisoners to go back to their cells. You stay close to this door until I come back. Now, go bravely and retrieve the revolver and bring it to me."

Nadine watched as Chris walked over to the prisoner holding the .357 Smith & Wesson and, though she didn't hear what was said, saw the prisoner hold the weapon by the barrel and hand it to Chris. Handing it to Nadine, Chris said, "Be careful. It's loaded."

As Nadine, in turn, handed it to Sheriff Rovera, she said, "Do not unlock the pod door until I explain the situation."

Sheriff Rovera arched his eyebrows and led Nadine to a quiet corner.

"Can I join the two of you?" Casey Campbell asked. When Sheriff Rovera looked inquisitively at Nadine, she nodded.

"Seems Damon Rodden orchestrated this whole thing and set Chris up in an effort to stage an escape and perhaps shoot Chris in the process," Nadine explained.

"To make himself appear as a hero?" Casey asked.

"No, something a lot more sinister than that," Nadine replied.

"I knew I shouldn't have hired the scamp,"

Sheriff Rovera mumbled. He then ordered the backup jailer, Arreola Barrios, not to let anyone in or out of the pod until otherwise notified. Sheriff Rovera thanked Nadine and shook her hand with both of his. "We'll let Rodden sit in the locked cell until after I've spoken with the DA. Come, tell me how Rodden fits into the escape attempt."

After Nadine related what she had learned from Chris, Sheriff Rovera just shook his head.

"If I may be so bold," Nadine said, "I think it would be wise for you to preserve Rodden's service revolver and do a ballistic analysis to determine if it was the weapon that killed Trevor Watts."

"Good suggestion, young lady," Sheriff Rovera said as he escorted Nadine to the jail lobby. "We can't thank you enough."

Nadine had been back at her office but a short time when Marci announced Charlie was there to see her.

"What have I done now?" Nadine asked as she greeted Charlie.

"I just finished a hearing with Henderson and he asked that I bring you by the DA's office. He wants to talk to you."

"It's almost 5:00 p.m. His office will be closed."

"He said he would leave the outside door to the DA's office open and for us to just let ourselves in."

"After hours on a Friday? He must desperately want to see me."

"He's probably tortured by the way he treated you and wants to make amends."

"A little late, don't you think?"

"Is it ever too late?"

Henderson was all smiles when he greeted Nadine and Charlie. "No hard feelings," Henderson said as he shook Nadine's hand with both of his.

"You were just doing your job in having me do the time," Nadine replied. "Hopefully, you felt the pain every time I stuck a pin in your voodoo look-alike."

"I do now," Henderson said remorsefully while hanging his head. "That was quite a thing you did today at the Coronado County Jail. Your bravery shall not go unnoticed or unrewarded."

Directing his attention to Charlie, Henderson said, "Your helping set up the contact with Corey Samuelson proved very productive. Thanks to both you and Nadine for your efforts in that regard. Corey will be in town on Monday to meet with us and will be testifying before the grand jury later that evening. I'm sure he'll want to meet with the two of you while he is here. He's scheduled to arrive on Sunday night and we have made arrangements for a safe place to hide him out."

"I think we have found one of the leaks and security breaches," Nadine said referring to Damon Rodden.

"Sheriff Rovera has already filled me in," Henderson replied. "He said he would have an incident report ready for me first thing Monday so that we can file criminal charges. In the interim, Rodden is being held without bail."

"I'm told Rodden's service revolver is of the same caliber as the weapon used in the execution of Trevor Watts," Nadine said.

"The ballistics report that is expected to accompany the incident report will tell us whether Rodden's service revolver is the weapon responsible for Trevor Watts' death." Looking at Nadine, Henderson said, "Off the record, I would not be surprised in the least if Rodden's service revolver turns out to be *the* murder weapon."

"Nor would I," Charlie said.

Looking at Nadine, Henderson said, "Charlie has filled me in on your discussions with Trudy Snowden and Christopher Campbell. I will arrange with

Charlie to have our lead investigator interview you. Because of your safety concerns for Trudy and Christopher, I will obtain Christopher's release and, at government expense, will provide housing for the two at an undisclosed location."

"That is wise, in light of all the strange things that are happening to key witnesses in the prescription drug investigation," Nadine said.

"Not to mention the Damon Rodden connection," Henderson added.

"I imagine the grand jury will be more than eager to hear what Christopher and Trudy have to say," Charlie said.

"I know they will be interested in what Corey has to say," Nadine said.

Henderson smiled. "That is the evidence they've been waiting for."

"For at least forty-five days," Nadine said as she put her hand to her forehead and thought of her time in jail. "Offering anonymity is not something I'll do again anytime soon and maybe never."

"Smart thinking," Henderson said. "At least you won't frustrate me or the grand jurors."

"Does that mean I'll have to get rid of your voodoo look-alike?" Nadine asked in jest.

"Think of all the money I will save by not having to purchase Band-Aids," Henderson chided.

Turning to Nadine, Charlie said, "Now you can get rid of your thimble and straight pins."

As Nadine and Charlie walked to the door, Henderson commented, "Even though I don't deserve a special favor, I'm asking for one. We don't need anything to appear in the newspaper that would compromise either the prescription drug investigation or the safety of the informants or would otherwise tip off the targets of the investigation. I assume that's not something you would do anyway."

"This is one of the times the public good trumps the right to free speech," Nadine said as she chuckled at the thought of how the roles had switched and that Henderson was now wearing the beggar's shoes.

"We owe you," Henderson said as Nadine and Charlie were leaving his office. "We owe you big time!"

The following morning's edition of the *Daily Mirror* ran a front page story of the previous day's jail crisis and the arrest of jailer Damon Rodden. Nadine's role in the negotiation process was duly noted along with quotes from Sheriff Ignacio Rovera and District Attorney Horace Henderson. The two praised Nadine's bravery and success. The story was authored by *Daily Mirror* reporter Hannah Sherman. Nadine had to chuckle when she thought of the *Rule for Journalists* that hung in her office. *Do not become part of the story!*

Although the *Globe* covered the story as well, under the authorship of Gwendolyn Cardinello, Nadine's name was not mentioned. The only hint was a reference to a former inmate who participated in the negotiation process.

"Have a good weekend?" Charlie asked as Nadine answered her extension.

"Miss the powdered eggs and watered-down orange juice, but other than that, my lungs are getting used to fresh air again."

"Just received a call from Henderson's office. The ballistics report confirmed that the slugs recovered from Trevor Watts' body were indeed fired from Deputy Damon Rodden's service revolver."

"No surprise there," Nadine replied.

When Nadine reported the findings to Thornton, he said, "If I were Damon Rodden, I'd be shivering in my boots."

"How so?" Nadine asked.

"Think about it," Thornton replied. "Damon Rodden and Trevor Watts had something in common other than having worked together at Hopkins Pharmacy. They also shared another significant trait."

"Which was?"

"Both knew too much."

"What's your point?"

"Rodden had found a way to silence Watts but had failed in his novel scheme to silence Campbell. Rodden's bosses can't be very happy. He's no doubt fallen out of favor and is considered a liability. He's the only witness alive who can corroborate the anticipated testimony of Campbell. The authorities have placed Campbell in protective custody for good reason. There is still a price on his head. I wonder what bounty has been placed on Rodden."

"I see your point," Nadine said. "I'm glad I don't possess personal knowledge. Being exposed to hearsay was bad enough. And, being incarcerated is not necessarily a safe harbor for anyone. It is probably only a matter of time before we print Rodden's name in the obits."

The authorities doubted Rodden blew the whistle that resulted in the large drug bust involving Trudy and Christopher. However, it was possible for a number of reasons. Talmad Sisman and his band of thugs were cutting in on the drug trade in Coronado County through fear and intimidation. Since Sisman's arrival on the scene, the share of the market by his competitors was shrinking rapidly. His network was operating with uncharacteristic precision and he was recruiting distributors and dealers from unlikely sources. Through strong-arm tactics, he was able to infiltrate his competitors, learn their trade secrets and use confidential information to blackmail them. In other words, until he eliminated his competition completely, he could be content in receiving a portion of their profits.

Icing Trevor Watts had generated too much law enforcement attention. With the FBI now assisting in the investigation, a lot of heat was being exerted on drug trafficking in the once tranquil outreaches of Coronado County. The trail in the investigation into the death of Trevor Watts was leading to Drs. Hopkins and Simms. But also, unbeknownst to the general public, a fairly well-defined trail was leading in the direction of Talmad Sisman. Only a special few, such as Deputy Damon Rodden, would have been privy to that information.

To ice Christopher Campbell in the same or similar style as Trevor Watts would point the compass back in the direction of the two doctors. To divert attention away from their direction and in that other direction, his executioner had to be more enterprising. When Rodden was arrested, he had a .380 Beretta tucked in his boot. Killing a fleeing felon or an escapee in the line of duty would result in a commendation rather than condemnation. The byproduct would be the perpetual silencing of a potential informant particularly one that had become a liability.

In the drug trade, being well informed may either be an asset or a liability. One needs to be informed to be effective and that can be an asset. There can come a time, however, when one knows more than one should. Once that someone is busted, the code of silence is no longer as sacred to him or her as it once was. The grant of immunity and witness protection in exchange for testimony (and freedom) is a lure. That's when the well-informed becomes a liability. Christopher Campbell had become a liability.

Damon Rodden had reached the end of the line. There comes a time when even the executioner has to be eliminated. He was now a target of the criminal justice system as well as a target of his two employers. The sheriff's department would mete out its own form of justice and so would the two doctors for whom he moonlighted. And, if he were lucky, he would not be playing one on one in the exercise pen with Talmad Sisman, or one of his band of thugs. He had sold his soul for a little more than thirty pieces of silver. Now, he would fashion a noose from his blanket, hang his head in disgrace and avoid all the nasty retribution—at least in this life.

# CHAPTER 15

## ALL'S WELL THAT ENDS WELL

The indictments handed down by the grand jury listed multiple counts of drug violations containing a litany of various drugs classified under various statutory schedules and schemes. The illegal distribution and dispensing of controlled substances and the conspiracy to do so were the main themes that permeated the various counts. Some of the counts with which Dr. Hopkins was charged were pharmacy specific. Likewise, some of the counts with which Dr. Simms was charged were physician specific. The prosecution of Dr. Simms for Trudy Snowden's illegal abortion would be a separate action.

The brothers-in-law were not charged in the death of Trevor Watts. Since dead men don't speak and Trevor Watts and Damon Rodden were indisposed, the weak circumstantial evidence otherwise available was insufficient to obtain an indictment. At least for now, the brothers-in-law were not charged with any capital offenses.

While Corey Samuelson was in town, Nadine and Thornton had a brief visit with him at the home of the Pembrooke chief of police where Corey and his attorney father were secreted. After visiting with Corey's father, a civil litigator in San Mateo, Nadine and Thornton understood from whence Corey's core values had emanated. With all the pre-trial and constitutional issues the indictments would spawn, Corey and his father would become frequent visitors to Pembrooke and indispensible to the success of the subsequent prosecutions.

The pomp and pageantry that accompanied receiving the Governor's Award of Valor was something Nadine had not expected. She had already been presented with awards of merit from both the state and local press associations. With the mayor of Pembrooke proclaiming August second officially Nadine Siena Day in Pembrooke and the governor appearing personally to present the award, Nadine was once again the front page story.

The fanfare had sparked much resentment on the part of Gwendolyn Cardinello. She had done everything she could to undermine Nadine. As she sat in the Pembrooke Civic Auditorium, she was unsure as to how she would exact her perceived pound of flesh, but just knew she would.

While Governor Millner Whitaker extolled Nadine's virtues in choosing jail over betraying a source, in negotiating the release of a hostage, in thwarting a jail escape and in lobbying for a Kansas reporter's shield law, Gwendolyn bristled and left abruptly through a side door of the Pembrooke Civic Auditorium. While leaving the parking lot and being fraught with anger, she used her Ford F-350 as a battering ram and demolished Nadine's hapless Saturn Sky. Unfortunately for her, Gwendolyn was observed by a Pembrooke traffic cop who gave chase. In an attempt to elude, Gwendolyn hit a light pole, disabling her Ford F-350 and herself and ended up in the now famous Coronado County Jail. It was there her sinister plot to even the score was hatched.

During Gwendolyn's denunciation of Nadine and resulting tantrum, Nadine was presented with the Governor's Award of Valor followed by the city's Award of Heroism and the district attorney's Award of Merit. Mayor Brandon Masterson presented the heroism award and District Attorney Horace Henderson presented the prestigious award of merit for her role in helping curb the drug problem in the district. *What a difference a few months make*, Nadine said to herself in quiet reflection.

At the reception following the ceremony and while talking with Mother Catherine and Governor Whitaker and his aid, Mayor Masterson directed his attention to Nadine. Twelve years Nadine's senior and recently widowed, the mayor caught Nadine's attention as well. Nadine had interviewed the mayor on a number of occasions and had been at various events where the mayor and his wife had been present. Nadine had sized him up as being somewhat pompous and aloof. Him having come from a prominent family with wealth, she could understand why a reporter didn't tweak his interest. This night, however, he appeared different.

Mayor Masterson was ignoring the governor and focusing his attention on Nadine. As the dialogue unfolded, Nadine found herself captivated by his dark eyes and the broad smile that dominated his chiseled, tanned face. There was a familiarity that was indefinable about him and although she felt apprehensive, she could not turn away. She was not anxious for this moment to end and it didn't appear that the mayor did either.

Although Nadine was tempted to return the

favor, she convinced Thornton not to print the story about the runaway Ford F-350. Gwendolyn was charged with reckless driving, leaving the scene of an accident and eluding police. She had claimed her accelerator had stuck but couldn't explain how it happened in such quick succession as several portions of the Saturn Sky had been damaged. Maurice had dutifully bonded her out and while she was driving his four-wheel Hyundai, Maurice was riding Gwendolyn's Schwinn.

It was 11:00 a.m. on a cool September Friday when Nadine received a telephone call from Mayor Masterson wanting to meet her for lunch. Even though she had planned to have lunch with Mother Catherine, she cancelled and she and the mayor had lunch in the General Hawthorne Room at the Haverford Palace Hotel. He had arrived first and the maître d' ushered Nadine to his table without inquiry or delay. The mayor rose and greeted Nadine with a warm smile and double handshake. He seated her in the chair across from him. She was barely seated when the waiter arrived to take their drink order. The waiter looked at the mayor quizzically when he ordered the same drink as Nadine, ice tea with a lime wedge. With Nadine dressed in black slacks and a stylish knit sweater and the mayor in tan slacks and a midnight blue dress shirt, Nadine did not feel out of place. She was relieved that she had chosen the outfit she was wearing instead of the usual drab office attire.

"Why are you looking at me like that?" Nadine asked self-consciously. "Did I smear my eye shadow?"

"On the contrary," the mayor replied, "you look stunning."

Nadine could feel her face flush. "Why thank you, Mr. Mayor. I was thinking how handsome you look."

"Why so formal?" the mayor asked with a smile.

"I didn't intend to be," Nadine replied as the waiter set the drinks in front of them. "Telling the mayor that he is handsome may be bold but certainly is not formal."

The mayor laughed. He then lifted his glass in a toast. As Nadine followed suit, he said, "Here's to familiarity and to no more formality."

"I'll drink to that," Nadine said as they clinked their glasses together and took a sip.

As the two set their glasses down, they looked into each other's eyes far longer than either expected. Finally the mayor broke the silence. "My formal name is Brandon, but please call me by my nickname, Bat. Our family has traced our linage back a number of generations to the famous western lawman, Bat

Masterson. He is thought to have been a distant cousin of my great-grandfather. At least, that's what the family has claimed. I have been called Bat for as long as I can remember."

"Impressive," Nadine replied. "The Masterson tradition of accomplishment and public service apparently is in the genes."

"Not really all that impressive," Bat said. "It only appears that way."

"I see humility also runs in the family," Nadine said as the waiter stood ready to take their order.

After they ordered, Nadine said, "Everyone in Coronado County is familiar with the Masterson name."

"That goes back to my grandfather, Cornwall Masterson, who founded Masterson Sunflower Flour Mills and endowed Masterson College. When he died, my father and his two brothers ended up with the business. Eventually, my father bought out his two brothers and is the sole stockholder. I assume you grew up in Pembrooke," Bat said.

"I was born here, although I can't prove it," Nadine replied.

When Bat arched his eyebrows, Nadine responded, "I'm told I was literally left on the steps of St. Vincent de Paul Orphanage. I stayed in the orphanage until I graduated from high school. I have no clue as to where I was born or who my parents were."

"Looks like you weathered it well," Bat said as he gestured toward Nadine.

"I owe it all to Mother Catherine and the caring sisters at SVPO."

"I notice you're not wearing a ring," Bat said as Nadine held onto her drink with her left hand exposed.

Nadine peered at her ring finger. "I've never been married."

"Have a significant other?" he blurted.

Nadine observed his face turn crimson as she said, "That's rather personal, isn't it?" Sensing his embarrassment, she quickly added, "Not yet!"

Folding his arms and leaning on them while fixing his gaze on Nadine, Bat said in obvious approval, "I want to again commend you for putting Pembrooke on the map and especially for your recent exploits in freeing a hostage and preventing a jailbreak. We are all waiting to see what you do next!"

Nadine blushed and, looking down, managed to say something incoherent that sounded vaguely like, "You're pretty amazing yourself." She then added, "And what about you?"

"My wife, Sonya, to whom I was married for twenty-seven years, passed away three years ago. She was only forty-eight at the time.

"That's awfully young."

"Four months after she was diagnosed with cancer, she died."

"Must have been quite a shock."

"It was. Fortunately, we didn't have children – even though we wanted them."

"Both your parents, of course, are still living."

"Yes. Both are now in their eighties and in remarkably good health."

"I hear that your father has turned the mill over to you."

"I have been the CEO of Masterson Sunflower Flour Mills now for almost two years. My father still serves on the board and makes an appearance nearly every day. He says staying involved keeps him young."

"And, your mother?"

"Has some hip problems. But, for the most part, still stays active."

"Any brothers or sisters?"

"One brother and two sisters. Bancroft is eighteen months younger than me and is a stockbroker in New York. My two sisters live in California. Corinne just turned fifty and Colleen will be forty-eight in two months."

"That doesn't tell me how old you are."

"Is that a question?"

Nadine blushed.

"Actually, I am fifty-four. And, you?"

"You know it's not polite to ask a woman her age. Let's just say you're my senior by over a dozen years."

Bat arched his eyebrows.

In an effort to change the subject, Nadine commented on the winter scape hanging on the far wall. "Are you a skier?"

"Funny you would ask that question. Just this morning my mother called to make sure I was still planning to attend a family reunion with them in Steamboat Springs at the start of the ski season."

"I take it you are a skier. I've never been on a pair of skis and never been to Colorado."

"Thanksgiving is when Mount Werner cranks up its ski lifts. That's where my mother grew up and where I learned to ski. My mother actually made the U.S. Olympic Ski Team but had to back out because of a hip injury, one that accounts for her problem today."

"Did you father also grow up in Steamboat Springs?"

"No, but that's where my parents met. My father was spending his Christmas break skiing with his fraternity buddies from Oklahoma State and, at least according to my mother's version, it was while skiing in a snow storm at the top that they literally ran into each other."

"I'll bet it's beautiful there in the winter."

"All year around. Some years ago, my parents and uncle and aunt remodeled the old family homestead, an old stone two-story rambling structure that sits on eighty acres of pine near Rabbit Ears Pass. That's where we stay because of its proximity to the ski hill."

"Sounds like a dream castle."

"It is. You'll have to go with me sometime."

"I'm not much of a skier."

"I'll teach you."

"Promise?"

"I promise."

The two sealed the deal with a handshake–a touch neither would forget.

# CHAPTER 16

## MY FAIR LADY

N adine had never been fond of costume parties and all her life had shied away from the conspicuous. Even as a child she avoided pretend or dress-up.

When invited by Bat to attend the Pembrooke Chamber of Commerce Masquerade Ball, Nadine was hesitant. Her trepidation was caused as much from her lack of dancing experience as her costume quandary. Nadine didn't want Bat to misconstrue her hesitancy and managed the courage to confide in him. Although the two had been having lunches together and coffee several times a week, their relationship was casual. Mother Catherine characterized it as cautious expectation and Nadine was careful not to characterize it at all—especially during the third-degree from Thornton.

It was while at coffee one brisk October day that Nadine's resolve would be seriously challenged. Bat knew of a band that was playing at the Cherub Club in East Pembrooke that coming Friday night. There

Nadine would be called upon to dance. If Nadine needed tutoring, Bat would provide it. Even though Nadine was not sure that she was coachable, Bat was. And so, carrying the banner of Practice Makes Perfect, the two embarked on a training session that, over time, they hoped would make even Arthur Murray envious.

The rehearsals sputtered at first and there was even a time when Bat doubted. The rhythm of the music and the harmony of their closeness, however, were making their dancing superfluous. Each was becoming acutely aware of the other and when the two were apart each was preoccupied with a yearning for togetherness. Dancing was becoming a means to an end and an excuse to be together.

It was fitting in light of Nadine's rise to prominence that she be cast as Cinderella. And, for Bat, what else but a prince? Maybe for them, it was not a masquerade after all.

The PCC Masquerade Ball was *the* social event of the year. It was an assemblage of W*ho's Wh*o in the political, scientific, literary, artistic, business, educational and social communities, not only local and statewide but national as well.

Nadine and Bat soon found themselves in a circle of notables that included United States Senator Morford Medena and his wife, Dorena, Congressman Merrill Doran and his wife, Alicia, Governor Millner Whitaker and his wife, Cerena, Kansas State Representative Dana Cortez and her husband, Alejandro and Pembrooke City Councilwoman Rosalyn Sewell and her husband, Amand. The aforementioned, together with Pembrooke Chamber President Maxwell Parker and his wife, Rosella, comprised the head table.

Not surprisingly, Nadine was the center of attention. Not only was she the focus of the gentlemen but the ladies as well. Her celebrity status had been established when she won the Pulitzer and had become deeply entrenched as a result of the recent bestowal of the Award of Valor, the Award of Merit and, of no lesser note, the Award of Heroism. The presenter of the award last mentioned stood beaming as he held tightly the hand of his fair lady.

Nadine was nervous and tentative at first as Bat led her onto the dance floor. Nadine now had more appreciation and empathy for the contestants on *Dancing with the Stars*. Gliding across the dance floor in the arms of her Prince Charming and despite feeling the constant gaze of the onlookers, Nadine did not feel the least bit inhibited. The dance steps had become natural and suddenly she was almost hoping she and Bat would be noticed.

"I hope I'm not embarrassing you." Nadine whispered into Bat's ear as the two held each other close.

"Are you kidding?" Bat whispered back. "I'd like to take the credit but I think you sand-bagged me. You're a natural. You must have been a professional dancer in your past life."

"How can I miss with you as my coach and with you at my side?"

"I like it too," Bat whispered as he kissed Nadine softly on the cheek.

The two stopped momentarily, even though the music hadn't, and gazed into each other's eyes. "I feel like I've known you a lifetime," Bat said, his voice husky.

"I feel the same way," Nadine replied.

It was a wintery afternoon in November, and Nadine was frantically putting the finishing touches on a feature column that was to appear in the Sunday edition of the *Daily Mirror*. She had skipped lunch because of the press for time and an unrealistic deadline for which the newspaper business was famous. She was not in a panic mode yet but would be if she didn't have divine inspiration and a lot of it–now!

Nadine was not a person to put things off to the last minute and, if anything, was always ahead of the curve. All her life, she tackled the difficult first and left the easy for last. She had few anxiety attacks as a result. In the present situation, it was not she who caused the last minute rush but circumstances beyond even her errant colleague's control. Hannah Sherman had unexpectedly gone into labor.

It was at the worst possible time, therefore, that the newspaper's longtime receptionist buzzed Nadine with the news that she had a visitor.

"Marci, I told you I was not to be disturbed," Nadine snapped. "Who is it?"

"Mayor Masterson."

"Oh, my God!" Nadine blurted. "Tell . . . tell him I will . . . ah . . . be right there."

*Frantic* probably would have been the word Nadine would have used to describe her true state of mind. *Delirious* was the word Marci later used to describe Nadine's reaction to the announcement. *Maniacal* was Thornton's description of Nadine's rush past his office door on her way to the lady's room.

As Nadine administered damage control to the image that peered back at her from the mirror, she just shook her head in disgust and disbelief and muttered several times in quick succession "The timing couldn't be worse. The timing couldn't be worse."

Regaining her composure and concerned more about her appearance than her deadline, she greeted Bat.

In contrived composure and extending her hand, she said, "What a pleasant surprise!"

It was then that Nadine noticed the three adults who accompanied Bat.

"I want to introduce my brother and sisters," Bat said, "I hope we're not interrupting anything."

"Not at all," Nadine said as she was introduced to and shook the hands of Bancroft, Corinne and Colleen.

As Nadine looked at Bat and then at his three siblings, she thought they looked little alike.

There was a moment when the five just stared at each other. Nadine broke the silence by inviting them into the conference room and asking if they all would like a cup of coffee. Marci then brought in five steamy cups of java and a tray of assorted cookies.

It was Bat who spoke first. "We only have a minute. It is mother's birthday tomorrow and the family is surprising her with a celebration at the Haverford Palace Hotel. She has no idea that the whole clan will be there."

"We would very much like for you to join us," Colleen added.

Before Nadine could respond, Corinne chimed in, "We'd all be very disappointed if you didn't."

"Don't say no," Bat pleaded. Bat's look told her that he wanted her to be there.

Searching for the right words to decline gracefully so as not to offend or convey the wrong meaning, Nadine managed to say, "I'm honored to be invited. Unfortunately, I'm up against a deadline. My frazzled look is as a result of the panic that is setting in."

"You don't look frazzled to me," Bancroft said and quickly added, "I mean, I can see why our brother wanted us to meet you and why he thought you should be invited."

"I think he just wants me to make him look good on the dance floor," Nadine said as she smiled at Bat.

"Absolutely," Bat acknowledged. "Having you beside me enhances my image and you know how important public perception is to a politician."

Nadine was momentarily tempted to put her assignment on hold, but she knew only too well what had priority.

As Nadine and his sisters said their goodbyes, Bat commented on how much the three women resembled each other. Even Nadine was taken aback by the similarities.

After they left, Nadine could not erase from her mind the images of Bancroft, Corinne and Colleen. It was as if she had known them in another lifetime. She felt comfortable and secure in their presence and troubled by having to decline their most gracious invitation. She hoped there would be a return engagement.

# CHAPTER 17

## THE FRAME-UP

Police sirens wailed as three black and whites screeched into the paved parking lot on the west end of St. Michael the Archangel Episcopal Church. Nadine had parked in front of the west entrance of the church as she had been instructed. With guns drawn, six uniformed Pembrooke police officers surrounded her new Chevy Corvette.

"Get your hands up and get out of the car now!" she heard an officer bark.

*What the . . . ?* she thought. *What have I got myself into this time?*

"Turn around with your face towards the car and put your hands behind you," the burly uniformed cop ordered as she opened her door and stepped onto the pavement. He immediately placed handcuffs on her. She could hear the clicking sounds as the cuffs inched tighter and tighter.

"Ouch! That hurts," she heard herself say as she could feel the metal cut into her wrists.

"It's supposed to," the same cop said as a

female cop began frisking her.

"Stand still," the female cop ordered as she spread Nadine's legs roughly with her gloved hands.

"Have any weapons?" the female officer asked gruffly.

Nadine shook her head.

"I asked, do you have any weapons?"

As Nadine teetered and struggled to maintain her balance, she mumbled, "No."

"Can't hear you!" the female cop yelled in her ear.

"I said no!" Nadine yelled back as she turned her head and watched as blood started to drip from her left wrist.

Nadine was then ordered to turn around.

Now faced in the direction of the restaurant on the other side of the street, she could see Thornton's car in the parking lot and Thornton racing towards her. She watched as one of the officers extended his hand and prevented Thornton from advancing further.

"I'll call Charlie," Thornton yelled as he was being restrained.

Nadine wasn't sure Thornton heard her "Gottcha!"

Almost immediately, the Pembrooke police chief, Duncan Corrigan, arrived at the scene, followed by Gwendolyn Cardinello and *Globe* photographer,

Milton Hobson. Chief Corrigan appeared to recognize Nadine and ordered that her cuffs be removed. In the interim, Gwendolyn and Milton were busy producing their press credentials to one of the uniformed officers.

By the time Milton unleashed his camera, Nadine's cuffs had been removed. Before long, Milton was taking repetitive angle shots of Nadine surrounded by uniformed police officers.

*Plenty of photographs for Gwendolyn to choose from for the night's edition of the Globe,* Nadine surmised. She was too worried to be embarrassed.

It was at that moment, Nadine noticed Charlie's arrival. "He's Ms. Siena's attorney," Chief Corrigan yelled. "Let him pass."

As Charlie approached, Chief Corrigan said, "Appears we have a misunderstanding here. Your client just walked into the middle of a police trap. She'll have some explaining to do."

"I'm sure she'll have a plausible explanation," Charlie responded.

"Blake," Chief Corrigan said to the uniformed officer, "give Ms. Siena's attorney her purse and car keys."

Turning to Charlie, Chief Corrigan said, "You and Ms. Siena are directed to remove your vehicles from the scene and follow me to the Pembrooke Police Department. You'll probably want to be present when we interview Ms. Siena."

Charlie pulled a clean handkerchief from his pocket and wrapped it around Nadine's bleeding wrist. "Hold still," he said as Nadine trembled. "Everything is going to be all right. Follow me to police headquarters. Chief Corrigan wants a statement."

"Do you know what is going on?" a shaking Nadine asked.

"No, but we'll find out soon enough," Charlie replied. "Are you able to drive? If not, you can ride with me. In either case, we need to move your car."

"It's not far," Nadine muttered. "I'm . . . I'm okay."

Chief Corrigan arrived at the police station first. Already out of his vehicle, he motioned to parking spaces reserved for police personnel. One by one, Charlie, Nadine and Thornton parked their vehicles.

As Chief Corrigan escorted the three through the lobby, they passed Dr. Hopkins and his wife seated on a leather sofa in front of a large rectangular coffee table. A tape recorder sitting on it. Although Dr. Hopkins and his wife looked up, they quickly turned back to their magazines without uttering a greeting.

"It looks like you unwittingly walked into the middle of our police trap," the chief said to Nadine.

Masking her apprehension, Nadine asked, "I take it Dr. Hopkins has something to do with this. No?"

"First, I need to know why you were parked in front of the west entrance of St. Michael the Archangel Episcopal Church at 11:00 a.m. on a weekday. I know that's not your regular church."

"At the end of last week," Nadine began tentatively, "I received a telephone call from someone who was obviously disguising her voice. I knew it was a female voice but I didn't recognize who it was. The caller said she had some confidential information about a local pharmacist who was involved in illegal drug trafficking. She said she was afraid to go to the police for fear she might be implicated. When I tried to set up an appointment to have her come in and speak with me, she said she would not come in for fear of being recognized by others and would only meet me at a neutral location such as a restaurant that was out of the beaten path. She then suggested the Spires Café across from St. Michael the Archangel Episcopal Church and asked if that would be okay. I told her it would. She then said she would call me today and schedule the time. At 8:00 a.m. this morning, she called and said she would meet me not at the Spires Café but across the street in the church parking lot in front of the west entrance of SMAEC at 11:00 a. m. sharp."

"Did you record the conversations?"

"The second one, but not the first. I have the tape in the top drawer of my desk."

"I have heard the tape," Thornton volunteered. "Nadine came into my office right after the first call and told me all about it. It was I who suggested she start taping the calls, as the first one sounded a little suspect."

"I would like to have that tape, if I may. I want to compare it with a tape I already have and two tapes Dr. Hopkins has promised to provide. But, Nadine, continue with your story. After you received the second call and recorded it, what did you next do?"

"I took the tape into Thornton's office and played it for him. He said it sounded like a set-up and he feared for my safety. Since we were familiar with the area, it was decided that we would drive to the meeting place. I would drive to the west entrance of the church. Thornton would go into the Spires Café and sit at a table close to the windows overlooking the church parking lot. He would observe and make sure I was not in harm's way. In addition, we each had our cell phones at the ready."

"Did you see anyone else in the church parking lot or near the church?" the chief asked.

"It was completely empty until I was swarmed by police cars and uniformed policemen with guns drawn."

"Sorry about that. We were told last week by Dr. Hopkins' attorney that his client had received two extortion calls on Friday and had only taped the second call, much like yourself. Dr. Hopkins was told the extortionist had some incriminating and disturbing information that would hang him but he could purchase silence for twenty-five thousand dollars. The extortionist would call back this morning to schedule the closing of the transaction if he was interested. He had received two more calls this morning, one at approximately 7:45 a.m. and the other at approximately 8:15 a.m. Dr. Hopkins said he advised the extortionist during the first call this morning that he had the money and was interested in the deal. During the second call, he said he was given instructions to meet in front of the west entrance of St. Michael the Archangel Episcopal Church at 11:00 a.m. He was informed he would be met by a female driving a late model Chevy Corvette."

"Of course! I have a Chevy Corvette!"

"When we ran IDs thru DMV and called the dealership, we found a number of you who owned Chevy Corvettes."

"So, I was identified and marked before I even drove into the parking lot?"

"Again, unfortunately, yes. And, in addition to the information we received from Dr. Hopkins and his attorney, the PPD received an anonymous tip by telephone that an extortion plot was in progress and that the payoff was to take place at 11:00 a. m. in the parking lot at St. Michael the Archangel Episcopal Church."

"What time did your call come in?" Charlie asked.

Looking at the sheet of paper clipped to the top of his investigative file, Chief Corrigan answered, "8:19 a.m."

"Were you able to trace the call?" Charlie again inquired.

"By the time the information was filtered to me, it was too late."

"I was actually ten minutes early when I drove into the church parking lot," Nadine said. "I wasn't there five minutes when the police arrived. That means when Gwendolyn and her cameraman arrived, it was exactly 11:00 a. m. How did she get the advanced notice? The *Globe* is clear across town."

Before the chief could respond, Thornton interjected, "I meant to mention this sooner because it seemed odd to me that when I arrived at the Spires Café, Gwendolyn and Milton Hobson were sitting at a front table also overlooking the church parking lot. They must have been sitting there for quite some time because they were just finishing what looked like a late breakfast."

"We didn't notify anyone of what was going on," the chief said. "We only advised Dr. Hopkins and his attorney to stay clear and let us handle it. We didn't want to tip off the extortionist and certainly wouldn't have wanted the press to know about it."

Nadine, on the verge of tears, blurted, "I knew it. The minute I saw her, I was certain Gwendolyn was framing me. She has been gunning for me ever since I replaced her at the *Daily Mirror*."

"It is obvious it was a prearranged scheme and that Gwendolyn must have had something to do with it," the chief said as he stroked his chin. "I was wondering myself how Gwendolyn and her cameraman almost beat me to the scene. It is not often that the media has an inside track on our stakeouts."

"Maybe you should pull her in and see what she knows," Charlie suggested. "It would be interesting to check her cell phone and see if she is the one who has been placing all the calls."

"Before we do that, I would like our lab people to analyze those tapes and see if they compare. I will call Gwendolyn and see if she will come in and tell us what she knows without tipping our hand or hinting that she is a suspect. I will have the technician record Gwendolyn's voice while I talk to her on the phone and we can use the recording to see if it matches the voice on the tapes we already have and the ones you and Dr. Hopkins are to provide."

"It is common knowledge that telephone toll records can be incriminating, and knowing how devious and underhanded Gwendolyn is," Charlie said, "I doubt Gwendolyn would use her own telephone or one that could be traced to her to make the calls."

"You never know," the chief said. "Some very smart people leave some very damaging clues."

An enlarged colored photograph of Nadine Siena graced the front page of the next day's edition of the *Globe*. The bold headlines across the width of the newspaper read: *REPORTER ARRESTED IN POLICE STAKEOUT*. The caption under the photograph read *Pulitzer Prize investigative reporter from the* Candela Daily Mirror, *Nadine Siena, is pictured here after her arrest on Wednesday.*

The front page story read:

*The stakeout by the Pembrooke Police Department came to an abrupt end on Wednesday with the arrest of Nadine Siena, a high profile investigative reporter for the Candela Daily Mirror. Ms. Siena is best known for having exposed the purported abuse of the mentally challenged at a care center in Pembrooke some years ago, for which she had been awarded a Pulitzer Prize.*

*According to sources close to the Globe, the Pembrooke Police Department acted on a tip of an extortionist plot against a local pharmacist who was charged with illegal drug distribution. Reportedly, Dr. Maynard Hopkins was the victim of a plot to extort twenty-five thousand dollars in exchange for the extortionist's pledge of silence.*

*The police first learned of the blackmail scheme on Friday of last week and with the assistance of Dr. Hopkins lay in wait as the extortionist was to retrieve the cash at a prearranged drop site near the west entrance of St. Michael the Archangel Episcopal Church. Advance intelligence revealed that the extortionist would be driving a late model Chevy Corvette.*

*At precisely 11:00 a. m., the prearranged time for the pick-up, a Chevy Corvette driven by Ms. Siena arrived in the church's parking lot and parked in front of the west entrance. Ms. Siena and her vehicle were immediately surrounded by four police cruisers blocking her exit. With guns drawn, approximately eight uniformed police officers ordered Ms. Siena from her vehicle, handcuffed her and placed her under arrest.*

*Although the Pembrooke Police Department refused to issue any official statement, it was learned that Ms. Siena was taken to the police station, questioned and later released. Ms. Siena was observed by a reporter from the Globe leaving the police station in the company of her newspaper's editor, Thornton Marimon, and her attorney, Charles Atkins. Also observed leaving the station shortly thereafter were Dr. Hopkins and his wife, Katherine.*

*The reader might recall that Ms. Siena was the subject of a libel suit filed against her by Drs. Hopkins and Simms that was later dropped. For failure to provide the name of a so-called confidential source to the Paraiso County Grand Jury, Ms. Siena was also jailed and served the better part of a ninety-day jail sentence. Her newspaper was also fined because of her refusal to cooperate with authorities. As of the time this story went to press, Pembrooke Police Chief, Duncan Corrigan, had not returned the Globe's telephone call.*

The editorial in the *Globe* was just as unbalanced and inaccurate. The heading read: *YELLOW JOURNALIST.* The editorial itself read:

*With the arrest of a rival investigative reporter, the Globe must hang its head in journalistic shame. The disgraceful attempt of a member of the media to cash in on the misfortunes of a pharmacist charged with illegal drug distribution defies the bounds of all decency and tarnishes the image of one of the oldest and noblest of all the professions.*

*For a reporter to attempt to obtain a story at all costs is one thing. But to attempt to blackmail a subject of a story in exchange for suppressing a story is to plunder not only the subject thereof but the public, who have a right to be informed, as well. To despoil by duress and greed is to undermine the very foundation upon which the First Amendment is based.*

*To whom much has been given, much is expected. To say we are disappointed in you, Ms. Siena, is an understatement. We are also disappointed in the* Candela Daily Mirror, *not necessarily by what they did, but by what they didn't do in regard to the whole despicable incident. By your acts and omissions, you have shamed us all.*

"Thank you for coming in," Chief Corrigan said.

"What can I do for you?" Gwendolyn asked as she fidgeted in her chair.

"We have some questions as to how it was that you had advance knowledge of our stakeout at St. Michael the Archangel Episcopal Church on Wednesday."

"Why is that a matter of concern?"

"We are wondering if we have a security breach in our ranks and whether we have a leak that needs to be plugged."

"I received a tip from an anonymous source and I can't say whether or not it came from one of your personnel."

"You won't say or you don't know."

"I don't know."

"What did the tipster tell you?"

"The disguised voice on the telephone said that if the *Globe* wanted a breaking story, we should have a reporter and a cameraman present at the parking lot at the west end of St. Michael the Archangel Episcopal Church at 11:00 a.m. on Wednesday."

"Is that all you were told?"

"I was also told that it involved an investigation of a local pharmacist."

"Anything else?"

"No."

"Did you recognize the voice?"

"No, as I said, the voice was disguised. I can't even say whether it was a man or a woman."

"I'm told you were seen in the Spires Café with your cameraman sometime before 10:00 a.m. on that day having breakfast."

"Melton and I wanted to make sure we had a front row seat. So, we arrived early. Since neither of us had had breakfast, we arrived earlier than we previously planned."

"When did you receive the anonymous call?"

"About 4:00 p.m. on the previous Friday."

"In your newspaper article you claim that the amount being extorted was twenty-five thousand dollars. How did you come up with that figure?"

"I believe the anonymous caller mentioned that or perhaps one of the officers at the scene."

"Ms. Seina claims that someone was trying to set her up."

"I'm not surprised. Nothing is ever her doing. I guess I would claim I was framed, too, if I was her."

"There seems to be hostility between the two of you."

"That was a war she started when she schemed to replace me at the *Daily Mirror*.

"I'm sorry, but I have to ask you this question. Did you stage the event at the church so you could embarrass Ms. Siena?"

"She doesn't need my help to make her look bad."

"Please, just tell me. Did you try to frame her?"

"No. I'm told you have recovered some of the extortion tapes and have had them analyzed. Surely, that would be the best evidence as to whether or not I was involved."

"Unfortunately, the voice on the extortion tapes was sufficiently distorted to prevent identification."

"So I surmised."

"You seem smug."

"Chief, you would make a poor poker player. If you had the goods, you would already have found some crime to charge me with."

"I don't imagine you'd be willing to take a polygraph?"

"For what purpose?"

"To clear the record."

"The record's already cleared. I wasn't involved in the unfortunate circumstances that led to Nadine Siena's arrest."

"She wasn't arrested."

"Call it what you want, Chief. It was still an arrest."

"Charlie," Chief Corrigan said, "the results of the comparison of the known voice of Gwendolyn Cardinello with the voice on the extortion tapes are inclusive."

"I assume that means that criminal charges won't be filed against Gwendolyn."

"Correct. At least, not for the present. My interview with her produced nothing incriminating. I, of course, discount everything she told me. She did not hide her dislike for Nadine. It was obvious Gwendolyn had found a treasure trove in the events at the church and was delighting in the havoc it was causing Nadine."

"I take it you're not terminating the investigation."

"Not until we solve it."

Feeling compelled to set the record straight, Chief Corrigan issued the following press release:

*As a result of misinformation, the Pembrooke Police Department detained the wrong suspect in an extortion attempt involving a local pharmacist. Investigation disclosed that both local newspapers, the* Candela Daily Mirror *and the* Coronado Globe Telegraph *were notified of the extortion attempt in advance and had reporters present at the purported drop sight. Unfortunately, Nadine Siena, an investigative reporter for the* Candela Daily Mirror, *entered the bull's-eye of the extortion target. She incorrectly was thought to be the extortionist. However, at no time was Ms. Siena ever placed under arrest.*

*Gwendolyn Cardinello, an investigative reporter for the* Coronado Globe Telegraph, *along with newspaper photographer, Milton Hobson, were also on the scene, having been stationed beforehand at the Spires Café across the street from the drop site.*

*It appears from the police investigation that the so-called extortion plot was, in all likelihood, a hoax. The investigation, however, is continuing and voice recordings of the purported extortionist are being analyzed by the FBI lab in an effort to ascertain the identity of the voice on the tapes. Whether a true extortion attempt or a prank, the culprit will be subjected to felony prosecution to the fullest extent of the law. If anyone has any information regarding this matter they are asked to contact the Pembrooke Police Department. All contacts will be held in strictest confidence.*

In true Gwendolyn fashion, the chief's press release was not published in the *Globe*. Also, Charlie's demand for a retraction and apology fell on deaf ears. A libel suit against Gwendolyn and the *Globe* was now ripe. In this libel action, unlike the previous, Nadine and the *Candela* would be the plaintiffs.

# CHAPTER 18

## LEX TALIONIS

S eated in Chief Judge Fenton F. Mays' crowded courtroom in the press section on the prosecutor's side of the courtroom, Nadine and Thornton were poised to record the proceedings. Seated only a few seats away was the devil's scribe, Gwendolyn Cardinello, along with her editor, Richland Covington. Although cameras were not allowed in the courtroom, members of the electronic media were there in force along with other members of the print media from around the state. It was referred to in the press as the county's case of the century and it was also receiving national attention.

The maligned doctor of pharmacology and the maligned doctor of osteopathy were conservatively but smartly dressed. Their cases had been joined for trial and the brothers-in-law were seated with their respective attorneys. Dr. Hopkins was seated next to Rebecca Lindsay, Dr. Simms next to Courtland Wiggins. These were the same attorneys who represented them in the libel case and both had criminal trial experience as prosecutors and, of late, defense counsel.

Seated at the prosecution's table was District Attorney Horace Henderson, along with his investigator, Percy Armine. Behind the railing separating the aforementioned section of participants sat the press corps and, in a specially designated section, the panel of prospective jurors from which the twelve-person jury would be selected. Spectators, who were seated on a first-come basis, were crowded into the remaining seats. Some of those who had been turned away huddled outside the partially glassed doors hoping to catch a glimpse of the proceedings.

The bailiff ordered all to stand as the Honorable Fenton F. Mays, entered the courtroom. Seating himself behind the imposing bulk of oak, Judge Mays proclaimed the court to be in session. After inquiring as to whether the defendants were present and both sides ready to proceed and, after having had both questions answered in the affirmative, the case of *State of Kansas, Plaintiff, v. Maynard R. Hopkins and Edmund P. Simms, Defendants*, was underway.

After the prospective jurors were called to the box, they were questioned by first the judge, then the prosecutor and then the defense. In theory, the inquiry was aimed at ascertaining who could be fair and impartial jurors, not just to one side or the other, but as to both. In reality, the prosecuting and defense attorneys were trying to ascertain and select jurors who were most sympathetic to their cause and who would ultimately find in their behalf. In other words, Horace Henderson was trying to select twelve jurors who were prosecution-minded. Rebecca Lindsay's and Courtland Wiggins' quest was the seating of twelve tried and true souls who were defense-minded and predisposed to vote in their respective client's favor.

By the luck of the draw, the make-up of the jury consisted mainly of older rural males native of Coronado County. Comedian Foxworthy would likely label them *rednecks*. Especially, on a drug case such as this, the defense knew they were not playing on an even field. The cards they were dealt were mostly discards. Having used up all their peremptory challenges, all they could do now was pray.

Horace Henderson gave the opening statement for the prosecution. Therein he outlined the evidence the prosecution would produce to prove the elements of the crimes of illegal distribution and dispensing of controlled substances and conspiracy to distribute and dispense controlled substances. Rebecca Lindsay and Courtland Wiggins immediately followed with opening statements proclaiming each of their client's innocence.

"Ladies and gentlemen of the jury," Lindsay began, "opening statements by the prosecution and now by the defense are not evidence. They are only outlines of the evidence each side expects will be presented during the course of the trial.

"Keep in mind that the prosecution has to prove the charges to your satisfaction beyond a reasonable doubt. Neither Drs. Hopkins or Simms is required to present any evidence. They are both presumed innocent of the charges and that presumption prevails throughout the whole trial.

"Since the burden is on the prosecution, they are required to present their evidence first. Depending on the evidence, the defendants may not have to present any evidence and can rely on the presumption of innocence. We ask that you keep an open mind and not draw any conclusions until you've heard all the evidence."

Courtland Wiggins was a seasoned trial attorney and he had a trial plan. His strategy was to divert the wrongdoing, if any there be, from his client to co-defendant Dr. Hopkins.

"Ladies and gentlemen," Wiggins said in a deep voice, "I represent Dr. Edmund Simms. I don't speak for Dr. Hopkins, only Dr. Simms." Clearing his throat and setting his notes aside, he continued, "Even though Dr. Simms does not have to testify, he plans to do so. He feels you should hear his side of the story. Why? Because the prosecution will be unable to prove any wrongdoing on his part and because he is innocent.

"What will the evidence show? Dr. Simms is a second-generation physician in Pembrooke. He is well respected and can justify every prescription he ever written. He didn't illegally distribute or dispense any controlled substances nor did he conspire with Dr. Hopkins or anyone else to do so. If he directed any of his patients to fill their prescriptions at Hopkins Pharmacy, it was for the purpose of the patient's convenience and for absolutely no ulterior motive. He does not have nor has he ever had a business interest in Hopkins Pharmacy or any other pharmacy and it is immaterial to him where his patients fill their prescriptions.

"Remember, the burden is on the prosecution of proving Dr. Simms' guilt and it is not Dr. Simms' burden to prove his innocence. That means if the prosecution fails to prove each and every element of a crime charged, you are required to return a not guilty verdict to each such charge. If you conclude that Dr. Hopkins is guilty of some crime, that doesn't mean that Dr. Simms is also guilty. In fact, though the prosecutions against the doctors are joined for trial, the prosecution against each doctor is separate and the guilt of each must be determined separately and on its own merits."

Over the next four days, some two dozen witnesses were called by the prosecution. Many testified as to having been a patient of Dr. Simms and having been directed by him to fill their prescriptions at Hopkins Pharmacy. Wiggins, during cross-examination, defused the sting by getting most of the witnesses to admit that they had asked Dr. Simms for a referral or didn't remember whether or not they had asked for a referral.

The most damaging testimony was against Dr. Hopkins. The prosecution called witness after witness who established that Dr. Hopkins filled or refilled orders for drugs where prescriptions were required but none were produced. That prescription bottle labels oftentimes did not contain the name of the prescribing physician nor did the records seized from Hopkins Pharmacy reflect that the drugs had been prescribed by a physician. That some labels that bore a physician's name had, in fact, not been prescribed by the named physician. That bogus physician names were listed on some of the labels.

Nadine covered much of the trial and was intrigued by the effectiveness of Corey Samuelson's testimony and was disappointed by the testimony of Christopher Campbell. It appeared to Nadine that Chris was fearful of retaliation against Trudy, who was still employed at Hopkins Pharmacy. Whereas, he had been certain of events and incidents initially, at trial he was tentative and uncertain.

CARROLL MULTZ

The prosecution was dealt a blow when Judge Mays held certain evidence inadmissible. Critical to the conspiracy charge, for example, was Corey's anticipated testimony concerning the conversation he had overheard between Drs. Hopkins and Simms while staying at the Hopkins' residence and the exchange of money he had observed take place between the two. Judge Mays ruled that such evidence was speculative and, therefore, inadmissible.

Judge Mays excluded all of the evidence that had any reference to Trevor Watts and Damon Rodden. He reasoned that such evidence had little probative value and what probative value it did have was outweighed by the prejudicial effect it would have on the jury. Not wanting to risk a reversal in the event of a conviction, the prosecution did not press the issue.

By Judge Mays having excluded key evidence needed for a conviction of Dr. Simms and Wiggins' effective cross-examination of key witnesses, the prosecution felt that they would probably not survive a motion for judgment of acquittal as far as Dr. Simms was concerned.

When the prosecution announced they had rested their case-in-chief, both Wiggins and Lindsay asked Judge Mays to dismiss the case against their respective clients. Wiggins' argument that there wasn't sufficient evidence to allow the case to go to the jury

276

was echoed by Lindsay.

"As far as the quantity and quality of evidence presented in this case is concerned," Judge Mays said removing his glasses and peering at Henderson, "the court finds ample evidence has been presented in the prosecution of Dr. Hopkins. In the prosecution of Dr. Simms, however, the court is inclined to agree with Mr. Wiggins in his characterization of the prosecution's evidence as it applies to his client. The court, therefore, grants his motion. All pending charges against Dr. Simms are hereby dismissed."

There was wild celebration by Dr. Simms' supporters and loud grumbling by his detractors. Banging his gavel hard enough to crack it, Judge Mays thundered, "Any further outbursts, I'll clear the courtroom!"

When order was restored, Judge Mays said, "Dr. Simms, your bond is exonerated and you are free to leave."

"Looks like we came in just in the nick of time!" Thornton said to Nadine as they found a seat in the crowded courtroom. "I guess we saw that one coming."

"The prosecution was prevented from presenting everything in its arsenal," Nadine said. "He's not out of the woods yet."

"Are you referring to the abortion case involving Trudy Snowden?"

Nadine nodded her head as she watched Dr. Simms shake the hands of several spectators as he and his attorney found their way to the door.

The prosecution having rested its case and the charges against Dr. Simms having been dismissed, it was now time for Dr. Hopkins to present his case-in-chief.

"Ms. Lindsay, you may call your first witness," Judge Mays said as he nodded in her direction.

Rising but not moving towards the podium, Lindsay announced, "Your Honor, Dr. Hopkins has opted not to present evidence since the prosecution has not met their burden of proof. Instead, he will be relying on the presumption of innocence which is his constitutional right." She then sat down, leaned back in her chair and looked at the ceiling.

"Where you been?" Thornton whispered as Charlie sat next to him. "You missed all the fun."

"Just finished a hearing in Judge Beacom's courtroom," Charlie whispered back. Noticing that Dr. Simms and his attorney were not in the courtroom, he whispered, "Did Judge Mays grant Wiggins' motion for judgment of acquittal?"

Thornton nodded and whispered, "Lindsay just announced that she rested her case without putting on any evidence."

"What a surprise," Charlie responded. "She must know what she's doing."

"You'd think so," Thornton said as Judge Mays announced the court would be taking a brief recess.

As the court emptied, Thornton, Charlie and Nadine stayed behind.

"Two shockers in a row," Nadine said to Charlie.

"I'm not surprised by the dismissal of Dr. Simms' case," Charlie said. "I am by Lindsay's decision not to put on any evidence. From the jury's perspective, innocent defendants take the oath and testify. Guilty defendants do not."

"What's Lindsay's strategy in not putting on a case?" Thornton asked as some of the spectators started filtering back into the courtroom.

Before Charlie could respond, Nadine said, "She didn't dare put Dr. Hopkins on the stand. Henderson would have torn him to shreds on cross. Much like what Charlie did at the deposition."

"That might have been part of the reason," Charlie responded. "By the defense not putting on any evidence, the prosecution is prevented from presenting rebuttal evidence. She probably considers the evidence to be pretty weak at this point, especially in light of Dr. Simms' dismissal, and knows that Henderson oftentimes holds back some of the prosecutor's most damaging evidence for rebuttal."

"If that be the case, Henderson's plot was

foiled and, in the future, he may want to rethink his strategy," Thornton offered.

With everyone back in the courtroom, Judge Mays announced that he and the attorneys would be working on jury instructions. "The trial is adjourned until 8:00 a.m. tomorrow at which time the attorneys will be making their final arguments," Judge Mays said. "This court is adjourned until then."

"The jury has now been instructed on the law," Judge Mays said in a raspy voice. "It is now time for final arguments." He then nodded in the direction of the prosecution's table.

Henderson thanked the jury for their service and reminded them what he said the prosecution would prove, what the prosecution did prove and his slant on how the law should apply. He then said, "The role played by a jury in our criminal justice system is just as important as the role played by the judge, the prosecutor, and the defense attorney. In fact, at this juncture, the role the jury plays is the most important of all. By your verdict, you send a message to the community. You can either condemn a pharmacist who, instead of helping the sick, creates addicts by abusive practices in order to line his pockets. Or, you can condone such practices and tell pharmacists and others, by your verdict, that they can flout the law without any consequences.

"Pharmacists occupy a position of trust. We literally place our lives in their hands. You might say they have power over life and death, much like a physician. In light of the evidence, do you think Dr. Hopkins is someone in whose hands you would place your life or the life of a loved one? If so, then you should probably acquit him. If you say no, then you need to look to the evidence to see why you feel that way. And, if you find that Dr. Hopkins engaged in the criminal conduct with which he is charged, and you are convinced beyond a reasonable doubt, you should return guilty verdicts as to all such charges. And, as the case is turned over to you, ladies and gentlemen, that's what we are asking you to do."

"Short and sweet," Thornton whispered to Nadine.

"And most effective," Nadine whispered back.

It was now Lindsay's turn to try to convince the jury that they should rule in favor of the side that she represented. Lindsay took a glass of water with her to the podium and took her time in arranging her notes in the right configuration. Looking at the judge, she said, "May it please the Court." Directing her attention towards the jury, she said, "Ladies and gentlemen of the jury. I, too, want to thank you for your service." Several of the jurors strained to hear.

"Speak up," Judge Mays admonished. "It appears some of the jurors are unable to hear you."

"Sorry, Your Honor," Lindsay replied as she took a sip of water. "I seem to have lost my voice."

"She's nervous," Charlie whispered to Thornton. "I've never seen her like this."

"She knows she doesn't have a case and obviously doesn't relish the role of being the underdog," Thornton whispered back.

"Defense attorneys take it personally when they lose," Thornton responded, "even when their client is guilty."

"You may proceed, Ms. Lindsay," Judge Mays said impatiently as Lindsay shuffled her notes.

Looking at the jury, Lindsay said, "I must not have heard the same evidence as Mr. Henderson. Although Dr. Hopkins may have been careless with his record keeping, I didn't hear any testimony that Dr. Hopkins did anything that was criminal in nature. The evidence may have hinted that Dr. Hopkins did something criminal, but there was no real proof beyond a reasonable doubt that he did, in fact, commit any criminal act. All we have is speculation and Mr. Henderson saying that he did. Remember, Mr. Henderson saying Dr. Hopkins is guilty, doesn't make it so. Otherwise, all of Mr. Henderson's prosecutions would end up in a conviction and we wouldn't need any jurors.

"Judge Mays instructed you on the law that you are to follow. One of the instructions he gave you says that you must not convict if you entertain reasonable doubt. Reasonable doubt is created when you are hesitant to act because you do not have enough information to make a valid decision. For example, what evidence did Mr. Henderson present to prove the conspiracy charge? Because Hopkins Pharmacy filled prescriptions written by Dr. Simms apparently is a conspiracy by the prosecution's assessment. What about the prescriptions Hopkins Pharmacy filled that were written by other physicians? Was there a conspiracy with them as well? Should they have been prosecuted along with Dr. Simms?

"Notice I said Hopkins Pharmacy. Notice also that, although Mr. Henderson equated Dr. Hopkins with Hopkins Pharmacy, the evidence, if it inferred criminality, pointed almost exclusively to Hopkins Pharmacy and not to Dr. Hopkins personally. The evidence presented was muddled. Dr. Hopkins was the owner but only one of many who was involved in the day-to-day operations of the business."

"Objection, Your Honor," Henderson interposed. "Ms. Lindsay's arguments misstate the evidence and assume facts not in evidence."

"Overruled, Mr. Henderson," Judge Mays said emphatically. "The jury can evaluate Ms. Lindsay's reiteration of the facts based on their own recollection."

Lindsay then continued, "If a determination of Dr. Hopkins' guilt is based on conjecture, then you probably have enough to support guilty verdicts. But, if Dr. Hopkins' guilt is to be determined on the basis of proof beyond a reasonable doubt, which the law requires, then you must return verdicts of not guilty not only to the conspiracy count but all the other counts as well. And, that is what I'm asking you to do."

"Wow!" Nadine whispered to Charlie. "She made a lot out of nothing."

"She didn't get the nickname TNT for nothing," Charlie whispered back.

The jury was out almost three hours. When they returned, the foreman gave the verdict forms to the bailiff who in turn gave them to Judge Mays.

After Judge Mays studied the verdict forms, he read aloud, "We the jury find the defendant, Maynard R. Hopkins, not guilty on the conspiracy charge. As to the remaining charges, we find the defendant, Maynard R. Hopkins, guilty."

"Was and is this your verdict?" Judge Mays asked each juror, to which each responded, "Yes."

"Very well," Judge Mays said, "judgment is hereby entered on the guilty verdicts. Sentencing is continued to two weeks from today at 9:00 a.m. Your bond, Dr. Hopkins, will continue to that date."

"Did you notice Dr. Hopkins didn't even flinch when the guilty verdicts were being read?" Thornton asked Charlie.

"The back of his neck turned red," Nadine interjected.

"I could see his hands shake when he handed a note to his attorney after the verdicts had been read," Charlie added.

"I noticed none of his family was here for the verdicts," Thornton said.

"They were pretty scarce throughout most of the trial, at least during the time I was here," Charlie said.

"The only one I ever saw attend was his wife," Nadine said, "and that was just during the jury selection phase."

"I don't suppose Dr. Hopkins wanted them here," Thornton said.

Neither Nadine nor Thornton was able to be

present for the sentencing. After the sentencing, however, Charlie stopped by the *Daily Mirror* and left a joint message for Nadine and Thornton. It read:

> *Dr. Hopkins didn't ingratiate himself with Judge Mays. He took no responsibility for his actions and blamed the press for his conviction.*
>
> *Judge Mays gave him two years on each of the fourteen counts to run consecutively. He was denied probation. He was very upset with his combined twenty-eight-year prison sentence. Lindsay was able to obtain a stay of execution pending an appeal. She also convinced Judge Mays to allow Dr. Hopkins to remain on bond pending the outcome of the appeal.*

> *Charlie*

"Writing a book?" Marci asked Charlie.
"Get paid by the word," Charlie replied.

The Kansas Supreme Court ultimately affirmed Dr. Hopkins' fourteen convictions and his prison sentence was reinstated. By the time he served out his sentence and returned to Pembrooke, he would be qualified to receive Social Security benefits. Shortly after arriving at the Kansas State Penitentiary, Dr. Hopkins was advised that his license as a pharmacist had been permanently revoked and not subject to reinstatement. In but a short period of time, Hopkins Pharmacy would become just another name in the discarded telephone directory.

Much braver than her now husband, Trudy Snowden-Campbell testified in the abortion prosecution of Dr. Edmund P. Simms. He was found guilty and after his conviction ran the appellate process, he joined his brother-in-law at the Kansas State Penitentiary. He would be paroled after serving only three years. However, his license to practice medicine would never be reinstated. As a convicted felon, his inability to obtain a professional license would be the least of his problems.

# CHAPTER 19

## AIR OF FAMILIARITY

"Hey, you don't get paid to look out the window," Thornton said as he stuck his head in the door of Nadine's office.

"I was just marveling at nature's adaptation to the passing of the seasons," Nadine replied. "So the snow doesn't burden the trees by falling on the leaves, the tree just sheds its leaves."

"Isn't that what all living things do?" Thornton asked as he watched the golden castoffs flutter past the window from a cluster of nearby silver maples.

"You mean when our career gets burdensome, we can just discard it?" Nadine asked.

"Not if you're a Pulitzer Prize winner and the best journalist in the nation," Thornton replied.

"It's been a rollercoaster ride since winning the Pulitzer, Thornton," Nadine said as she sat down and motioned for Thornton to take a seat. Slumping in her executive chair, she took a deep breath and exhaled as if she were blowing a smoke ring.

"That bad, huh?" Thornton commented. "Let me go get a couple sodas from the fridge."

"Mind drinking out of the can?" Thornton asked as he returned with a diet soda.

"No," she replied as she straightened herself in her chair.

"Think you need to get away for a few days. Sitting in court all day and writing all night tends to make a person weary. You know you have vacation time coming."

"I thought I used up all of my vacation time for the next three years sitting in the Coronado County Detention Facility."

"Oh, did they change the name?"

"No, I just thought detention facility sounded better than jail."

Both were laughing as Marci tapped on the doorframe. "Mayor Masterson is here to see you," Marci said to Nadine. "Said he didn't have an appointment."

"Show him in," Nadine said raising her eyebrows.

"Guess I better leave," Thornton said as he scurried out the door. Turning, he said, "You better be careful what you pray for."

"I heard that," Bat said as he and Thornton shook hands on the run.

"You were supposed to," Nadine said as the two embraced.

"What is it exactly you are praying for?" Bat asked still holding both of Nadine's hands in his.

"A knight in shining armor or a prince on a white horse," Nadine answered smugly.

"How about both?" Bat asked.

"Can I get both?"

"Two for the price of one."

"Come in and sit down," Nadine coaxed. "I was just thinking about you."

As Bat sat down in the chair just vacated by Thornton, Nadine asked, "Can I get you a soda?"

"That would be great," Bat said as Nadine left and returned with a root beer.

"All we have that's cold," Nadine said as she handed it to Bat.

The two sat looking at each other for a long moment.

"To what do I owe this unexpected pleasure?" Nadine said as she fluttered her eyelashes.

"I figured it would be more difficult for you to turn down my invitation if I asked you in person."

Now it was Nadine's heart that fluttered. Gazing into his dark inviting eyes, Nadine said, "It's not fair."

"What's not fair?"

"Using your physical presence to overwhelm me."

"Last time I was here, you declined my invitation."

"Maybe this time, I won't."

"Remember me telling you about our family usually spending Thanksgivings in Steamboat Springs, Colorado?" Bat asked as he pulled his chair closer to Nadine's desk.

"Yes . . . ."

"And, my promise to teach you how to ski."

"Yes . . . ."

"Well, my parents are excited about the prospect of having you spend Thanksgiving with us. The ski slopes are usually groomed by then. It would be a great opportunity for you to learn to ski."

*Be careful what you pray for!* Nadine thought. *What do I do now?*

"Are you all right?"

"I was just thinking about what Thornton said just before you walked in. He said I needed to get away for a few days."

"Is that a yes?"

"Ah . . . I'd love to spend Thanksgiving with you and your family."

From the Great Plains of Kansas to the great Rocky Mountains of Colorado, Nadine and Bat talked non-stop and seemed to relish in the company of each other. Both of their earlier lives were a fog but both had fond memories to recall about their formative years, emancipation and how they got to where they were today. The close quarters and the readiness to confide were conducive to the establishment of an intimate and comfortable relationship. Nadine was somewhat shocked at the ease with which Bat was able to dismantle the barriers she had been erecting for the past forty years. She had always avoided exposing herself to vulnerability. Now she was readily relegating caution to the wind.

Nadine was fascinated by the view from her window seat. Bat was relishing in his role as tour guide. Almost all the sights he was pointing out from the air he had been to at some time in his life mainly as a preteen and teen. West of Denver, Bat pointed out some of the well-known ski areas where he had skied: Loveland, Vail, Winter Park, Aspen in the distance, and ultimately the great slopes of Steamboat.

Obedient to the command of the flight attendant, Nadine and Bat placed their trays and seats in their full upright positions and made sure that their seatbelts were securely fastened. In doing so, Nadine couldn't help but think back to the masquerade ball, their lunches together and   to that moment minutes ago when Bat had leaned across her and placed his hand on her thigh while pointing out the sights on the ground below. She could still smell the pleasant freshness of his closeness and the sensation caused by his gentle touch. The tingling still lingered and Nadine hoped Bat could not hear the thumping of her heart. She fought to hide her excitement.

The plane actually touched down at the Yampa Valley Regional Airport approximately twenty minutes from Steamboat. There waiting for them behind the glass in the terminal were Bat's parents, Bingham, who went by the name Bing, and Clarice Masterson, along with Bat's aunt, Olivia.

There was an instant chemistry between them all, including Bat's aunt, who took an instant interest in Nadine. On the drive to Steamboat, Bat sat conversing with his father in the front seat. Nadine was sandwiched in the backseat between Bat's mother on the left and Bat's aunt on the right, trying to be attentive to both.

Olivia said, "Clarice tells me you're an award-winning investigative reporter with one of the Pembrooke newspapers. Your family must be most proud."

"My friends are. I'm not aware of who my family is or was. I was orphaned at a young age."

"Were you raised by foster parents?"

"No." Nadine swallowed hard. "I was raised at an orphanage by a nun who treated me as her own child. She was like a mother."

"That must have been a difficult time for you."

"Not really." Nadine shook her head. "St. Vincent de Paul Orphanage treated me well and we were all like one big happy family. I didn't know any different and thought for a long time that that was the way everyone was raised. I knew I had more brothers and sisters than most kids and missed not having a real father and mother but I never really felt deprived."

Up to that point, Clarice had sat silent, just listening. Turning to Nadine, she asked, "What is your astrological sign?"

Nadine replied, "Taurus."

Clarice trembled.

Looking in the rearview mirror, Bat's father asked, "Is this your first trip to Steamboat?"

"I've never been to Steamboat. In fact, as I told Bat, this is my first trip to Colorado."

"The snow on the ski slopes of Mount Werner

is the best in the world. Are you a skier?"

"I've never been on a pair of skis in my life."

"Good," Bing said. Turning to Bat, he remarked, "Looks like I've found someone to ski with."

"Even at your age, you're still a tiger on the slopes," Bat said.

Clarice added, "He's still got the moves!"

"I may be old but I'm not dead," Bing said. "I'll be skiing until I die and then I want you to place my coffin on skis and lead me down one of the Black Diamond slopes one more time!"

"Are you afraid to go down by yourself?" Olivia asked as all chuckled.

"Even in a coffin, Pops will be the first to reach the bottom," Bat said.

As they drove in the direction of Steamboat Springs, Nadine marveled at the amount of snow for that time of year. When she commented, Bing said, "You need to be here in December and January when there is no place to pile the snow."

"I assume they keep the streets fairly well plowed," Nadine said.

"There is a downside to that, too," Olivia said pursing her lips. "Once the streets are plowed, you have to tunnel your way through the drifts to go from the garage to the traveled portion. That can take some doing."

Turning around and facing Nadine, Bat added, "Sometimes the pile of snow is as high as the trees."

It was only 5:15 p.m. but the sun had already disappeared behind the mountains, filling the valley with dusk when they reached the Dickerson Mansion. A two-story stately stone structure with a steep pitch to the heavy metal roof, specially designed for the area because of the heavy snowfall, stood on a hillside facing the ski slopes. The roads had been plowed and sanded and, with the studded snow tread on the four-wheel drive vehicle, they were able to access the over-sized double car garage with relative ease.

"You're still shivering," Bat said as he pulled Nadine close. "Let me fuel the fire."

"You've fueled the fire enough," Nadine said as she snuggled in Bat's warmth.

Bat raised his eyebrows.

"No, don't even think about it," Nadine said.

"Hey, what are the two of you squabbling over?" Bat's mother asked as she and Bat's father carried in four steaming hot buttered rums. Olivia was close behind, carrying one of her own.

Now, there were five huddled under quilts sitting on the floor in front of the open fireplace.

"Feels good to sit on the floor, doesn't it?" Clarice said to Bing.

"Been a long time," Bing replied as he and Clarice cuddled together under their shared quilt.

"You doing okay?" Bat asked Olivia, who was wrapped alone in a quilt staring at the flames as they licked the burning pine.

"I was just thinking of your poor uncle, Leland, who is snowed in at home without me, Olivia replied. "I don't think he misses me as much as I miss him."

"Why don't you move over closer to Nadine and me? You'll keep us warm and we'll keep you company," Bat suggested.

"Good idea," Olivia said as she tucked in her quilt and waddled to a spot barely big enough to accommodate her in the middle of the floor.

"Good God, Olivia," Clarice exclaimed. "You don't have to sit on our laps."

*Good thing Bat didn't offer to share our quilt,* Nadine thought as Olivia scrunched up against her.

"We're a close-knit family," Olivia whispered to Nadine.

Smiling at Olivia, Nadine whispered back, "I can see that!"

After another round of buttered rums, Nadine started yawning.

"Tired?" Bat asked.

"Just relaxed," Nadine replied trying to stifle another yawn.

"Where do you want us to sleep?" Bat asked his mother.

"We'll put Nadine upstairs in the bedroom next to Olivia's," Clarice replied. "You can use the guest room adjacent to our room downstairs."

"Why so far away?" Nadine whispered to Bat. "What if I have a nightmare or can't sleep?"

"You'll just have to fend for yourself or crawl into Olivia's bed," Bat teased. "I know you'll not be crawling in with me."

"Damn straight!" Nadine replied loud enough for Olivia to hear.

"Sleeping accommodations not to your liking?" Olivia asked Nadine.

"No, they're perfect!" Nadine replied. "Just perfect!"

Olivia gave Nadine a quizzical look. "I'm headed for bed," Olivia announced. "I'll show Nadine her quarters."

Nadine was normally a light sleeper and her nights were usually accompanied by a lot of dreaming and waking up unable to fall back asleep. But not this night. She slept like a baby. When she awakened, she was surprised it was already 7:45 a.m. Wondering where the night had gone, she dozed off again only to be awakened by a knock at the door. It was 8:30 a.m.

"Who is it?" Nadine asked.

"It's me," Bat said. "Please open up, I have my hands full."

"Just a minute," she replied as she hopped out of bed and opened the door.

"What are you doing up at this ungodly hour?" she asked as she peered at Bat who was clad in cotton pajamas, a multi-colored robe and buckskin slippers.

Smiling at Nadine, Bat said, "Room service." He brought in a tray with two mugs of piping hot coffee and crystal creamer and sugar bowl which he set on top of a small table next to the bed. Bat then motioned to Nadine to return to bed where he propped up two queen-sized pillows behind her and helped tilt her in a sitting position. Doctoring the coffee to her liking, he handed her the mug and, picking up the other mug, joined her. The two then toasted in their first morning in Steamboat.

"We've got to quit meeting like this," Nadine said in a drowsy voice.

"You look like an angel in the white flannel nightgown," Bat said as he kissed Nadine on the lips.

Nadine blushed and pawed at her hair. "I

retrieved the cotton flannel from the closet. It was the warmest thing I could find. The night gown I brought was the warmest I had but obviously unsuitable for the Steamboat temperature."

"Mom apologized for not warming your room sooner. As you can tell, we turned up the heat. Hopefully, you won't need that extra comforter tonight."

Bat had left the door to Nadine's guestroom open, inviting a fully dressed Olivia to make her presence known. "Is your birthday in April or May?" she asked.

"May twentieth," Nadine responded. "If you're asking what my age is, forget it. I've quit having birthdays."

"Me too," Olivia said somewhat pensively. "Well, I'm off to help with breakfast."

After she left, Bat apologized to Nadine, "Sorry for the inquisition. Aunt Olivia has always been inquisitive but this rises to a whole new level. Is nosy a more obnoxious term that would apply?"

"I don't know," Nadine replied as she drained the last drops of the tasty brew. "But, I don't mind. I would be curious, too, if a strange woman, especially a journalist from Kansas, had accompanied my handsome and eligible nephew to Steamboat Springs to meet his parents and spend a week with the family."

It was Bat's turn to blush. "I hope you don't think I had ulterior motives."

"I would be disappointed if you didn't," Nadine said raising her eyebrows and fixing her deep penetrating eyes on his.

Bat seemed at a loss for words and Nadine was attracted by his shyness and boyish reaction. This was certainly not the Bat the public knew. It was a side she liked and sensed it was a side he revealed only to his intimate circle, which she now suspected included her.

"Care for another cup of brew?" Bat asked as the two heard Bat's father yell, "Breakfast is almost ready."

Nadine scurried to get ready and was the last to reach the kitchen. Upon her arrival, Clarice embraced her. "We are delighted to have you as our guest." Then taking both of Nadine's hands in hers she said, "You're always welcome."

"I'm delighted to be here," Nadine said as the two stood with their hands still joined.

Nadine could tell Clarice had been crying. Her eyes were puffy and red and her nose was runny.

When Nadine asked if she was all right, Clarice said she felt a cold coming on. So as not to embarrass Clarice, Nadine did not pursue the issue.

"Come sit by me," Bat urged as he ushered Nadine to a large ornate antique kitchen table and seated her.

"What a beautiful table!" Nadine commented as she lifted the corner edge of the scalloped lace table cloth and slid her hand across the polished table top.

"Was a wedding gift from my great grandparents to my maternal grandparents," Bat said.

"Was given to Bing and me by my mother on our wedding day," Clarice said as she continued to snuffle. "It is one of my most prized possessions."

Nadine could see that Clarice was having a difficult time controlling her emotions and marveled at how Clarice managed to display the semblance of a happy face.

Several times Nadine had caught Bat's parents staring at her. Feeling self-conscious and thinking gravy from the biscuits had missed their mark, Nadine dabbed nervously around her mouth with the cloth napkin, trying not to be too conspicuous.

Clarice had remained silent throughout much of the meal. By the time Bing and Bat had finished with their second helpings, Clarice had become much more talkative.

"Bat tells me the two of you would like to go downtown and perhaps visit the ski shops," Clarice said. "I'm pleased you waited to do your shopping so I could help with the selections. Bat has asked both Olivia and me to go along. His father is not much of a shopper and will probably stay close to home. I hope you don't mind if Olivia and I tag along."

"Bat tells me you and Olivia keep him current with the trends. He says he is like his father and would rather go to the dentist than go shopping."

As Clarice and Olivia cleared the breakfast dishes and Nadine rose to assist, Bing motioned for her to remain seated. Retrieving the coffee pot, he refilled the mugs. "I want to tell you how Clarice and I met."

Clarice rolled her eyes and collected the unused silverware. "Remember, this is Bing's version," she told Nadine.

"It was during Christmas break my senior year in college and me and some of my fellow Sigma Chis were partying in the Golden Goose Bar & Grill in downtown Steamboat."

"Golden Swan," Clarice corrected.

"Golden whatever," Bing replied. "I said Golden Goose because that's where I found the golden egg. Anyway, the women were outnumbered by the men and every time I or my buddies found someone to dance with, some cowboy would cut in."

"The next part of Bing's story is also pure fabrication," Clarice interrupted.

"We hadn't been there long when female reinforcements arrived. Everyone stared as the Dickerson sisters appeared. Leading the pack were

Clarice and her two sisters, Vivian and Olivia. Back then they were referred to as the Wild Bunch.

"While the band was playing *Don't Give Me Tomorrow*, Clarice came over to our table and begged me to dance."

Clarice coughed. "Bing has it all backwards."

"We danced together until the bar closed," Bing continued. "Vivian and Olivia had already left, as had my fraternity brothers. Clarice was worried because she missed curfew and blamed me. I had to find a way to get her home and into her room without awakening her father.

"As luck would have it, her father was standing in the doorway as we arrived, with his arms folded, scowling. He was a burly guy and someone you didn't want to mess with. I wasn't sure I could outrun him so I just stood my ground.

"I was snatched from the front stoop and soon found myself sitting in front of not only Clarice's father but her nightgown-clad mother as well. I had a lot of explaining to do."

"You usually refer to the conversation with my parents as an inquisition," Clarice said.

"That's really what it was," Bing replied. "However, I was merely trying to be diplomatic in front of our house guest."

"When you tell a story, you're prone to

exaggeration," Clarice said. Looking at Nadine, she confessed, "For a while I wasn't sure if I should call for an ambulance or wait and see how fast Bing could run."

Even Bing laughed.

"As it turned out," Clarice continued, "Bing finessed his way out of the situation and through sweet talk was welcomed back the next day with open arms. Less than six months later we were engaged and within the year were married."

"That was almost fifty-five years ago," Bing said as he smiled at Clarice.

"In some ways, it seems a lot longer ago than that," Clarice said and grinned.

Although Bing stayed behind to catch up on some paperwork, Clarice and Olivia accompanied Nadine and Bat on their shopping excursion. Bat's ski wardrobe and equipment had become dinosaurs. He and Nadine agreed they would purchase what they needed in the heartland of winter fashion. Otherwise, if they had made the purchases in Kansas, it would be like making lemonade without lemons.

Fearful they might not be able to find what they wanted, they discovered it was just the opposite. It was akin to going to Baskin-Robbins for ice cream; there were too many choices. Although it was impractical, but at Bat's insistence, Nadine selected a stylish white ski outfit with turquoise trim and accessories. Except for the striping, Bat's was navy blue. The skis, poles and boots were of the latest technology and of the best quality. Clarice and Olivia insisted on that. And, over the objection of both Nadine and Bat, Clarice picked up the tab. It was their early Christmas present.

It was the third day in Steamboat and decked out in authentic ski garb and looking every bit the part, Bing, Bat and Nadine ascended the ski slopes of Mount Werner, named after a local Olympic skier, Buddy Werner, who was killed by an avalanche while making a movie in the Swiss Alps.

Starting at the beginner's slope and learning the rudiments of skiing from Bat and his father, Nadine was introduced to Alpine skiing. Starting out with the snowplow, Nadine learned how to slow down and stop. It was not long, however, before Nadine was doing short swings utilizing a series of parallel turns and coming to a sliding stop. Bat began calling Nadine "Christie" because of her adeptness in keeping her skis parallel as she made her turns. She was soon able to steer her turns, stop on a dime and build up confidence. She was able to control her speed by traversing the slopes at an angle rather than the fall line. Schussing would come much later. She, however, was not brave enough yet to ski straight downhill without turning or stopping. Besides, she was not in that big a hurry. Although skiing the moguls intrigued her, she would save that for the last day.

It was obvious Bing and Bat were accomplished skiers. However, they were patient and were more interested in teaching Nadine to ski than extolling their prowess. Bing was remarkably agile and more daring than she thought he would or should be at his age. Nadine had trouble keeping up with the two but was determined to conquer the slopes. The wipeouts were numerous and there were times she doubted whether she was cut out to be a skier. Other than a few bruises to her body and her ego, she was enjoying the day with Bat and his father and, of course, the white powder and invigorating fresh air of Steamboat.

When they returned to the ski lodge for lunch, it felt good to shed the skis.

"Well," Bing asked Nadine, "now that you've had a taste of it, do you want to make skiing a career?"

"Do you think I'm ready yet?" Nadine asked already knowing the answer.

"With a little practice, you'll be ready for the Olympics," Bat teased.

"Is it possible to enjoy the glory without the pain?" Nadine asked, again knowing the answer.

"You know the drill," Bat replied. "No stress or pain, no gain."

"Just like everything in life," Bing interjected. "There don't appear to be any shortcuts."

"The skiing is the fun part," Nadine said. "Walking in these plaster casts you call boots is still a challenge."

"You wouldn't like cross country skiing then," Bat warned. "What goes down must come back up."

"I don't know," Nadine replied stretching her legs. "At least you wouldn't be risking your life mounting and disembarking from the moving chair lifts."

"If you have a problem moving on level ground," Bat persisted, "imagine what it's like going uphill in skis and ski boots. I always feel like a penguin when I cross country ski."

"I feel like a penguin now," Nadine confessed. "I can't imagine what it would be like to ski uphill."

"It's like working in a steel mill," Bing said. "It's a lot of hard work."

While they were finishing their lunch, Nadine

noticed a middle aged man at the table across from them leering at her. She guessed the well-built man to be a professional athlete of some sort. Although, with his black curly hair and gleaming teeth, Nadine figured he could be a movie star.

When the man got up to leave, he walked past Nadine and smiled broadly. Nadine smiled back. Bat, observing the exchange, showed his displeasure by saying, "You're making me feel insecure. Even the snow nymphs are looking green-eyed at you."

"Does that mean you're jealous?" Nadine asked coyly.

"You could say that," Bat replied. "I never consider myself possessive but I want you all to myself."

Nadine blushed. "You're the only one who turns my head and makes my heart flutter."

By the end of their week in Steamboat, the relationship between Nadine and Bat and Bat's parents and aunt had solidified.

*It's amazing what a difference a week makes!* Nadine thought as she lay awake reliving the events of the preceding few days. *It seems like we barely arrived and tomorrow we'll began our journey back to Pembrooke.*

Instead of flying back to Pembrooke, it was

decided that Bat and Nadine would drive back with Bat's parents.

"We're taking you away from this amazing corner of the world prematurely," Nadine protested.

"We insist," Clarice persisted. "Besides it will give all of us a chance to become better acquainted."

"Truthfully, I don't really want to leave. It's been like an answer to a prayer to be here with all of you," Nadine said as she placed her arms around Clarice and Bing and hugged them. Noticing Olivia, Nadine added, "And you, too, Olivia. Come join us. I want to hug you, too."

"It was a tearful goodbye as they left Olivia behind to await the arrival of her husband.

"Maybe you'll get to meet Bat's uncle at Christmas time," Olivia said to Nadine as she kissed her goodbye.

"I look forward to it," Nadine said as she rolled up the window and the four drove off leaving a waving and wondering Olivia.

# CHAPTER 20

## CONTEMPLATING A LIBEL SUIT

Bat's uncle had been delayed and Nadine didn't have a chance to meet Olivia's husband. Because of the late departure from Steamboat, Nadine, Bat and Bat's parents spent the night in Denver and drove virtually non-stop the next day to Pembrooke. It was a Thanksgiving the likes of which Nadine had never experienced. It felt like family the way she had always envisioned. Nadine thanked God for bringing Bat into her life and for filling her life to the brim.

Nadine, however, was baffled by Olivia's Thanksgiving prayer—at least the part that gave thanks to the almighty for having provided a new life and a new hope for a life and hope long lost but not forgotten. She was fairly certain it was not a reference to her, at least not as far as her being a substitute for Bat's deceased wife. Nadine probably wouldn't have thought much about the statement had it not been for Clarice squeezing Nadine's hand and holding it tight at that moment.

First thing Monday morning following Thanksgiving weekend, Charlie met with Nadine and Thornton regarding a possible libel action against Gwendolyn and the *Globe*.

"They're hanging out there," Charlie said as the three sat around the large conference table in Thornton's office drinking java and eating the fresh cinnamon rolls Charlie had provided.

Sitting in front of each of them was the back issue of the *Globe* with the offending article written by Gwendolyn Cardinello several months before. Staring at the headline, REPORTER ARRESTED IN POLICE STING, Charlie commented, "That is clearly defamatory and false."

"The picture of me surrounded by uniformed police officers still gives me the shivers," Nadine said. "And the caption under it describes the event as 'after her arrest.'"

"Since there was no arrest," Charlie said, "both the headline and the caption underneath your photo are false. They also mention the arrest again several times in that front page story."

"It's certainly wasn't a misprint or inadvertence," Thornton commented. In turning to the editorial page of the same issue, he pointed to the reference again of Nadine's arrest.

"Reading the story," Charlie continued, "you come away with the impression that there was an extortion plot against Dr. Hopkins, that it was foiled and that Nadine was the extortionist."

"That certainly was the impression that Gwendolyn intended to convey," Thornton said, flipping back to the front page.

"How do we prove that Gwendolyn orchestrated the whole event and set me up?" Nadine asked. Agitated, she pushed aside her partially eaten cinnamon roll.

"We don't have to," Charlie countered. "That's something we will leave up to the police. We really don't have to concern ourselves with the criminal action. For an actionable libel suit, all we have to prove is that Gwendolyn and Richland Covington and the newspaper published false and defamatory statements concerning you and your newspaper and that that harmed your reputation and that of the newspaper. Needless to say, we will also have to prove that Gwendolyn and Richland were at fault. The fault requirement, however, is what causes the problem.

"The fault requirement is dependent on how Nadine is classified. If she is deemed to be what is called an all-purpose public figure like a celebrity or sports star, then we have to prove that Gwendolyn and Richland deliberately lied or acted with such disregard for the truth that they are deemed to have deliberately lied.

"If she is classified as a private individual, all Nadine has to prove is simple negligence, that is, the failure to exercise that degree of care that a reasonable and prudent journalist would have exercised under the circumstances. At least, that is the law in most states."

"I take it," Thornton said, "that Nadine would be deemed to be a public figure because of her celebrity status as a Pulitzer winner or maybe because of her publicized involvement in the investigation of the drug trafficking cases."

"That would be my take as well," Charlie responded. "That is the way we would approach the case, and I assume the courts would as well. Regardless, however she is classified, she will be able to meet the fault requirement."

"What defenses do you envision Gwendolyn, Richland and the *Globe* would assert?" Thornton asked.

"Truthfulness is always a defense to a libel claim," Charlie replied. "However, everything they have printed that is defamatory is false. I guess they could claim qualified privilege. However, that is bogus as well, since their statements were not obtained from the government at an official proceeding or through official reports or statements."

"How about Richland's editorial?" Thornton asked. "Isn't fair comment and criticism exempt from libel?"

"Opinion statements normally are protected if they involve a matter of public interest and concern and are based on fact. In Richland's editorial there is no factual basis. In fact, his comments are grounded on false assumptions."

"What do we gain by bringing an action against Gwendolyn and Richland, other than to clear my name?" Nadine asked.

"We teach them a lesson and send a message to those considering doing the same thing," Thornton responded. "Ruining reputations is not something that should be trifled with. The offenders will only become more brazen in the future and damage other reputations if they think no one will do anything about it."

"You're entitled to actual damages," Charlie said to Nadine. "Your personal and professional reputation, your standing in the community and your credibility have all been damaged. This entitles you to be compensated for that as well as the mental pain and anguish you have experienced. And even though there is a limitation in our state on the amount of punitive damages you can collect, because of the egregious conduct on the part of Gwendolyn and Richland, you are entitled to additional damages to punish them and to serve as a deterrent to others. There have been some huge awards in cases such as yours. Besides, wouldn't you like to own another newspaper?"

"Only if we could *fire* Gwendolyn and Richland," Thornton said.

"You might have your chance," Charlie answered.

"How much time do we have to make up our minds?" Nadine asked.

"As I mentioned in connection with the Hopkins-Simms libel action, the statute of limitations for libel suits in Kansas is one year. That means you would have to file a libel suit no later than one year from the date of publication or you'd be forever barred from bringing the action."

"I think Chief Corrigan pretty much cleared up the matter and corrected the public's misconception," Nadine said.

"That doesn't matter much as far as the suit is concerned," Charlie said. "I call it the Humpty-Dumpty rule. Once a reputation has been damaged, you can't put all the pieces back where they were. It's impossible. The public will always have lingering doubts. It is not always easy to separate fact from fiction."

"Isn't the fact that the *Globe* has refused to apologize or print a retraction evidence of actual malice towards Nadine and our newspaper?" Thornton asked.

"Absolutely," Charlie said with enthusiasm in his voice. "The issue is not whether you will win, but how much you will be awarded."

"Can we sleep on it?" Nadine asked, rubbing her temples. "I'm not sure I want to fight Gwendolyn's vitriol with vindictiveness. I have neither the time nor the energy."

"Why don't I draw up a libel complaint just in case?" Charlie suggested. "I won't charge you for it unless we use it."

"We'd only use it if Gwendolyn pushes us into it," Nadine said.

"With Gwendolyn," Thornton said, "it's just a matter of time."

# CHAPTER 21

# MOMENT OF TRUTH

When the word got out that the mayor and Nadine had spent a week skiing together, Gwendolyn's vindictive spirit was aroused. It was like letting a wild animal out of her cage. With uncontrolled vituperation, Gwendolyn undertook the task she had vowed to complete—the complete annihilation of her long-time nemesis, Nadine Siena.

Gwendolyn knew Nadine's age and that her birthday was May twentieth. This information she had obtained through a cousin who worked at the Kansas Department of Motor Vehicles. She knew Nadine had grown up in an orphanage. She thought that Nadine's lineage might hold the key to the closet where Nadine's skeletons where locked. Motivated by hatred and contempt, she prevailed upon her husband, Maurice, to use his contacts in the medical care arena, where he spent all his adult years, to ferret out Nadine's origins.

Maurice didn't have far to go. Searching the records at his place of employment, Bethesda-Coronado Medical Center, for the year Nadine was born, Maurice found the records from Sylvia Lehman, a midwife who had been employed by the Center at the time. Although there was no record of a birth of a female on May twentieth, the month and day provided by Gwendolyn's cousin, he did find two births recorded the preceding week. The baby born on May fifteenth was a female born with a cleft palate. The parents' names were Bingham and Clarice Masterson.

It was the week before Christmas and Bat's parents had invited the two to spend Christmas Eve and Christmas Day with them. Since Thanksgiving, Bat and Nadine had been dinner guests on a regular basis at the Masterson mansion, ten thousand square feet of elegance with a carriage house, riding stable and more, situated on the rolling hills on the outskirts of Pembrooke. Nadine had been preoccupied with finding just the right gift for Bat as well as for his parents. Although she had found some small gifts, she was finding it virtually impossible to find the signature gift for each.

As Nadine prepared for a dinner engagement with Bat at their favorite restaurant and a movie afterwards, she glanced at the evening edition of the *Globe*. She subscribed to the *Globe* in order to keep abreast of the competition and to see how many stories the *Globe* pirated from the morning edition of the *Daily Mirror*. The front page heralded the unveiling of a column in *Section B* entitled "Stories with Happy Endings."

Out of curiosity she turned to *Section B* at the page indexed. December twentieth, it would turn out, would become a day that would live in infamy. Nadine felt faint and the next thing she remembered was Bat's quivering voice on the telephone asking if she had read the evening edition of the *Globe*. Even though he was not due to pick her up for another hour, he was on his way. Nadine rushed to get dressed, all the while in a tearful daze. When Bat arrived, they just held each other tightly while a flood of anguish, frustration, despair and disbelief rained down.

With pleading eyes, Nadine said, "Bat, please tell me none of this is true."

Bat's facial expression and especially his eyes said it *was* true.

"Can't be," Nadine sobbed as she slumped to her knees and buried her head in her hands.

Bat knelt beside her, held her close and didn't let go.

Pembrooke was all abuzz about the piece in the December edition of the *Globe*. Gwendolyn had given herself an early Christmas present—as she termed it, "the mother of all Christmas presents." Maurice's reward for his diligent detective work was being granted the privilege of spending the night in his wife's bed. History, however, didn't record whether Gwendolyn remained there with him.

The copy that would break Nadine's heart and Bat's as well and change the course of history in Coronado County read:

### *"Stories with Happy Endings"*

*In the early morning hours of May twentieth, forty-two years ago, a five-day-old baby girl born with a birth defect was dropped off by her parents at St. Vincent de Paul Orphanage. There she grew, thrived and overcame her birth defect. In a true Cinderella story, she blossomed into an attractive accomplished woman, much sought after and desired both personally and professionally.*

*By a twist of fate, the* Globe *was able to find the family and the baby girl to whom the glass slipper fit and solve the riddle as to the lineage of Cinderella. As it turns out her parents weren't lost after all, they were just misplaced. They are Clarice and Bingham Masterson of Pembrooke. And, that baby girl? Nadine*

*Siena.*

When Richland Covington, the editor of the Globe, was contacted by Charlie, Richland denied knowing anything about the column, let alone the piece that appeared in the column. He apologized and said he would have excised the piece had he known. The next edition of the *Globe* printed an apology. The damage, however, had been done and the newspaper knew it would be on the losing end of another lawsuit. It was not long before the *Globe* was advertising for a new reporter and shortly a new editor as well.

With a Christmas wreath in his hand, Bat rang Nadine's doorbell. He did this several more times. Just as he turned to leave, the door opened.

"Hi," Nadine said. "I was on the computer putting some finishing touches on a story for tomorrow. It is difficult to hear the doorbell in the backroom."

"I just happened to be out and about and thought I'd drop this off."

"It's beautiful," Nadine said as she bent and smelled the fragrance of the fresh sprigs.

"Had it custom made just for you."

"You shouldn't have," Nadine said and seeing

the hurt look in Bat's eyes, hastened to add, "I mean going to all the trouble, not coming by to see me."

Bat's eyes brightened and he smiled. "I had hoped you would not be upset by me stopping by."

"I have been thinking and praying," Nadine said. "The noncontact pact we entered into makes little sense. I still love you regardless of how you're classified."

"I was thinking the same thing," Bat replied as he brushed the freshly fallen snow from his hair.

Nadine shook her head in disgust. "How rude of me not inviting you in." She moved to the side so as to allow Bat to pass. She closed the door.

"I still feel I have been struck by lightning," Nadine said as Bat removed his coat and placed it over a chair.

"Do you want me to help you hang this?" Bat asked, retrieving the wreath.

"We can hang it on the outside of the door. I think I still have a hook from last year."

As Bat helped Nadine position the wreath, their eyes met. Nadine quickly looked away. She felt the same sorrow she had felt the day the earth stood still for her, Bat and the whole Masterson family.

"My mother says she has left messages for you. She is hopeful you will call her back. You can imagine the effect all of this has had on Mom and Dad."

"I can't bring myself to call," Nadine said shaking her head. "I've been trying to get up the courage to call ever since I received her first message."

Bat pulled out his cell phone. "Let's call her now," he suggested.

"Well . . . . I . . . ." Nadine could not find the right words. She knew the longer she waited the more difficult it would be. *Perhaps the spontaneous approach would be the best.* So, she nodded.

"I have her on the phone," Bat said as he handed it to Nadine.

"I don't know what to call you," Nadine said as she spoke into the phone.

"Just call me Mom," the voice on the other end replied.

Nadine could restrain herself no longer, nor could Bat or their mother. The three cried and laughed often at the same time. Nadine now knew who her parents were and her parents knew that Nadine was their daughter. The larger problem, nonetheless still loomed like a black cloud above them. Bat was her brother!

Nadine limped through her duties at the *Daily Mirror*. Thornton thought she was doing remarkably well, considering what Gwendolyn had put her through. Gwendolyn's latest caper was the straw that broke the camel's back. Nadine was no longer tentative about bringing a libel action against Gwendolyn, Richland and the *Globe*. Not only that, she would be adding other claims commensurate with Gwendolyn's recent outrageous conduct. The provocation warranted drastic action and swift justice and this time there would be no turning back.

"We'll be incorporating two additional claims in the libel suit," Charlie said, "giving publicity to private facts and intentional infliction of emotional distress."

"All I remember," Nadine confessed as she, Thornton and Charlie sat at the conference table in Thornton's office, "is that giving publicity to private facts is one of the privacy torts."

"It is," Charlie replied. "And, unlike libel, it involves truthful information. In your case, Gwendolyn and the *Globe* published information that was not newsworthy and that was published only to embarrass and humiliate you."

"It did do that," Nadine said, "and it didn't matter to Gwendolyn at all who else might be damaged in the process."

"The Mastersons have a cause of action as well," Charlie added. "They received underserved collateral damage and, I suspect, are considering legal action of their own."

Nadine left work early so she could drop off her Christmas gift for Mother Catherine.

"I wasn't sure I would catch you in, Mother," Nadine said using Mother Catherine's official title.

"I don't suppose I will any longer be the only person you call mother," Mother Catherine commented.

"As strange as it sounds," Nadine replied, "I'm having a difficult time getting used to the idea."

"You've been curious since your childhood about who your biological parents were," Mother Catherine said.

"I know, Mother," Nadine said as her eyes narrowed, "but since my early twenties, I have been comfortable in not knowing who they were."

"Did you have an inclination that Bat's parents were also yours? I remember you mentioned that when you were introduced to Bat's brother and two sisters, you had this feeling that maybe you knew them in another life. Even Bat had apparently told you how much you and his sisters looked alike."

"That did arouse my curiosity and, of course, my suspicions. My antennas, however, were really raised the Thanksgiving week I spent with Bat's parents and his Aunt Olivia."

"*Your* parents and *your* Aunt Olivia," Mother Catherine corrected.

"*My* parents and *my* Aunt Olivia," Nadine responded.

"Has a good ring to it, doesn't it, Nadine?"

"That's the only part that does," Nadine said as she pressed her lips together and her eyes moistened.

"When you met Bat, I'm of the opinion you did not sense the same familiarity as you did with the rest of the family."

"That's still the case, even with all the overwhelming evidence to the contrary. Bat doesn't look at all like the other members of the family."

"You're having a difficult time accepting the fact that Bat is your brother and I would, too, if I were in your situation."

"My mind has taken me in a thousand different directions and I still don't know what to think. There is something inside of me that says it will all work out."

"There is something inside of me telling me the same thing," Mother Catherine said as she put her arm around Nadine. "Continue to trust in the Lord!"

"It is that trust that is keeping my dreams alive," Nadine said as she straightened her shoulders and kissed Mother Catherine on the cheek. "Merry Christmas," she said.

"And to you also my child," Mother Catherine said and, with a twinkle in her eye, added, "you have overcome adversity before, and with God's help, you'll do it again."

Maurice and Gwendolyn's violation in the breach of privacy of personal medical information in violation of the Health Insurance Portability and Accountability Act had been turned over to the U.S. Department of Health and Human Services. Even though Maurice was just his wife's puppet, he would be exposed to the penalties provided under the act the same as his wife.

"I can't believe I let you talk me into it," Maurice said when he found out he could be fined and imprisoned for violating HIPAA.

Cowering over Maurice, Gwendolyn said, "You're trying to throw me under the bus for something you did, you poor pathetic excuse for a husband. It was *you* who did the deed, not me. Don't be a coward. Stand up and take the blame like a man!"

"But I . . . ." Maurice started to explain but, not wanting to risk certain death, said nothing.

Two days before Christmas, Gwendolyn, Richland and the *Globe* received a surprise Christmas present served by the Sheriffs' Department. It was in the form of a summons with an attached petition. This would be one Christmas greeting to which she would have to respond. Two days after Christmas, Gwendolyn and the *Globe* would receive their Christmas bonus—the summons and petition filed by Clarice and Bing.

Both petitions were turned over to the *Globe's* insurance carrier. Gaird Giles was general counsel for Tanner Insurance Company of Kansas and would be representing the three respondents.

In the Siena suit, the respondents admitted to the publication of the front page story as well as the editorial. However, they denied that the information was false or that they acted with malice or negligence.

With regard to the claim alleging the publication of private facts that invaded Nadine's privacy, they admitted they published the piece that appeared in the "Stories with Happy Endings" but denied that it was offensive or not a matter of public concern. They asserted that Nadine was a newsworthy person and that the piece was published in the good faith belief that it was a human interest story that deserved to be told and that it did not in any way portray either Nadine or the Mastersons in a bad light. It was indeed a story with a happy ending.

In response to the intentional infliction of emotional distress claim, the respondents admitted to the publication of the material but denied that it was extreme and outrageous. The respondents asserted that none of the material was published with intent to discredit, defame, humiliate, embarrass or mock Nadine or pry into her private life.

On all three claims, respondents asserted the following defenses: truthfulness, newsworthiness, fair comment and criticism, opinion, qualified privilege and lack of malice or intent to cause harm.

At trial, Gwendolyn's defense was predictable. On direct examination, she testified that the revelation about Nadine's biological parents was not instigated by her but was as a result of Maurice having stumbled on the information while organizing old records at his place of employment. She contended that, by his disclosure, she had come into contact with the information legally and, having obtained truthful information legally, she had a privilege to publish it.

Gwendolyn's cross-examination by Charlie was classic Charlie.

"Ms. Cardinello, you have been employed as a reporter for the *Coronado Globe Telegraph* going on a half dozen years. Is that correct?"

"Yes."

"And prior to that you worked for the *Candela Daily Mirror* for approximately a year. Is that also correct?"

"Yes."

"The truth of the matter is that you have been a reporter for various newspapers around the state for over twenty-five years."

"Is that a question?"

"Yes!"

"Yes, actually I have been a newspaper reporter or journalist overall for almost twenty-six years."

"I take it then that you're familiar with the Kansas libel laws as well as the laws dealing with invasion of privacy?"

"That's true. Although I don't claim to be a legal expert."

"When you are unsure of whether you are on solid legal footing, I assume you speak with someone in the know, such as the newspaper's attorney?"

"Yes, but I know my way around after having been a reporter for as long as I have."

"So, Ms. Cardinello, when you printed the story about Nadine Siena having been arrested at St. Michael the Archangel Episcopal Church, you knew that if the story were not true that that might be the basis of a libel action. Did you not?"

"Of course."

"That was no mystery to you, was it?"

"No."

"So, am I correct in assuming that when you wrote the story for the *Coronado Globe Telegraph* you did so with your eyes wide open, so to speak?"

"Of course."

"Did you by any chance ever receive and read the one and only press release from the chief of police of the Pembrooke Police Department relative to the incident in question?"

"You mean the press release issued by Chief Corrigan after my article appeared in the *Globe*?"

"Yes."

"Yes, I received and read that release."

"Let me hand you a copy of what purports to be Chief Corrigan's press release and ask if this is the one and the same."

Examining the exhibit, Gwendolyn answered, "Yes, this is the one and the same."

"Referring to that document, would you read aloud to the jury the fifth line of the very first paragraph."

"'However, at no time was Ms. Siena ever placed under arrest.' So?"

"So, don't you and didn't you consider that an

official press release from the Pembrooke Police Department?"

"Yes, but I was provided that *after* I wrote my article and after I was told that Nadine had been placed under arrest."

"Ms. Cardinello, just answer the question. Didn't you consider that document you are now holding an official statement?"

"Yes."

"Doesn't that statement indicate that Nadine Siena was detained and never placed under arrest?"

"Yes."

"The word arrest was used only once in that whole document and that was to proclaim that Nadine Siena had never been placed under arrest. Is that not true?"

"Correct."

"Now, even though it was not in response to my question, you stated here moments ago under oath that you had been told that Nadine Siena had been placed under arrest. Here is your opportunity to tell the jury the name of the person who told you that Nadine Siena had been placed under arrest. What was his or her name?"

"I don't know his name, but it was a uniformed police officer who was at the scene when I arrived at St. Michael the Archangel Episcopal Church."

"You quoted someone in your article whose name you didn't know and to this day still don't know?"

"That's true, although I was also told the same thing by a confidential source."

"And, who might that be? Or is his or her name also a secret?"

"You know I can't reveal the name of a confidential source. That would be unethical."

"Yet in your article that is the subject of this suit you made quite an issue out of the fact that Nadine Siena failed to provide the name of a so-called confidential source to the Coronado County Grand Jury and was jailed for having failed to do so."

"Is that a question?"

"Ms. Cardinello, you really don't like Nadine Siena and haven't since she replaced you at the *Candela Daily Mirror.* Isn't that true?"

"I've never kept that a secret. I think she is way overrated and is not much of a reporter."

"In fact, Ms. Cardinello, when Nadine Siena won the prestigious Pulitzer Prize some years ago no story to that effect appeared in the *Globe*, did it?"

"No."

"And, when Nadine Siena negotiated the release of the hostages in the Coronado County Jail and foiled the jail escape, you referred to Nadine Siena not by name but as a 'former inmate,' isn't that true?"

"Yes."

"And, when Nadine Siena was awarded the Governor's Award of Valor, The Pembrooke Award of Heroism and the District Attorney's Award of Merit, you reported on none of those, did you? None appeared in your paper?"

"No to both questions," Gwendolyn answered defiantly.

"That was despite the fact that you were present in the Pembrooke Civic Auditorium when Nadine Siena was presented with those awards. Isn't that true?"

"That's true."

"Your distain for Nadine Siena was so great that when you left the Pembrooke Civic Auditorium you used your Ford F-350 as a battering ram and demolished Nadine's Saturn Sky. Is that not a fact?"

"That was an accident."

"Running into her vehicle a half dozen times in succession you classify as an accident?"

"I only hit her car a couple times."

"Weren't you arrested for the incident?"

"That was politics."

"Now, Ms. Cardinello, it is important to the outcome in this case and to the jury to know whether it was you who staged the event that was the subject of the story that formed the basis of the article that is claimed to be libelous. Before I ask the question, however, I want to remind you of the oath you took to tell the truth and also advise you that perjury is a criminal offense under Kansas law. Now my question is this: Was it you, Ms. Cardinello, who staged the event that was the subject of the story that formed the basis of the article that we claim to be libelous?"

"A categorical no. As much as I dislike Nadine, I would never stoop to that level. She doesn't need my help to be discredited."

"If that be true, then how is it that you and your cameraman, Milton Hobson, just happened to be at St. Michael the Archangel Episcopal Church at the time everything went down?"

"Everyone was there before Milton and I arrived."

"Then how is it that you and your cameraman were seen stationed at the restaurant just across the street from the church long before Nadine Siena or the police ever arrived?"

"That was a mere coincidence. Milton and I were having breakfast at the Spires Café and were just finishing our breakfast when we saw the commotion across the street."

"Are you telling the jury that you and your cameraman were not staking out St. Michael the Archangel Episcopal Church in anticipation of the arrival of Nadine Siena and the police and just happened to be having breakfast with your newspaper's cameraman at a restaurant clear across town?"

"I eat at the Spires Café on occasion and besides I had a tip by an anonymous caller alerting me to the events that were about to unfold."

"Was that anonymous caller another one of your confidential sources, someone whose name you can't divulge, or someone whose identity was not disclosed?"

"The caller did not identify himself."

"So, you have no idea then who it was. Correct?"

"True."

"So, you grabbed your cameraman and the cameraman grabbed his camera and the two of you drove clear across town not knowing whether it was a crank call or not?"

"True."

"The last few questions deal with your column in the *Globe* entitled "Stories with Happy Endings." Specifically, I direct your attention to the revelation of Nadine Siena's birth and her having been placed in an orphanage and being the child of two prominent citizens of the community whose names you made public for the first time. The first question is this: How many stories have been reported in that column?"

"Just one. But, I intended it to be a series."

"Just so the jury knows, the only story that has appeared to date in the column is one exposing Nadine Siena's lineage, isn't that correct?"

"I didn't *expose* her lineage, I *disclosed* it. But, yes, it is the only story to appear in the column. However, I envisioned more."

"It was your sole intent, was it not, to embarrass Nadine Siena by including her in your column and thus subjecting her to public scorn and ridicule?"

"No, that wasn't my intent at all!"

"If that wasn't your intent, then what was your intent?"

"Every orphan is curious about his or her biological parents. If I was one, I know I would want to know who my parents were. I did it more as a surprise, or call it a public service."

"Even though you didn't like Nadine?"

"Yes, I don't hold a grudge forever."

"Did you think you were doing Nadine Siena a favor?"

"Not only her but her parents as well."

"Didn't you consider the disclosure of these private facts to the public to be offensive to Nadine Siena and her parents and maybe the public as well? Weren't these private facts that should have remained private facts?"

"What do you mean? You're asking me numerous questions."

"I mean, leaving a child on the doorsteps of an orphanage is not something to be commended but condemned, isn't it? And, pointing out that the abandoned child had a birth defect doesn't speak kindly of the parents, does it? Nor is it a fact that the child would particularly want revealed to the world? 'Solving the riddle as to the lineage of Cinderella,' as you describe it in your column, isn't that of such a private nature that it would shock the sensitivities of even the most insensitive? That's what I mean. Now, do you want me to rephrase the question?"

"No. I think the story is an uplifting one–one that is truly inspirational to the reader."

"Then, why didn't you run it by your editor or at the very least discuss it with Nadine Siena and the Mastersons before you printed it?"

"As I said earlier, I wanted it to be a surprise."

"To whom? The public?"

"No, to Nadine and her biological parents."

"Wouldn't it have been just as much a surprise if you had kept the private affair private and not have broadcast it to the world?"

Gwendolyn hung her head and did not respond, nor did Charlie push for an answer. A non-response spoke volumes and was even more effective from Charlie's point of view than even an affirmative answer.

This was not lost on the jury. Putting the pieces together made it clear for whom the surprise was intended. Gwendolyn's ulterior motives were exposed. It didn't take rocket scientists to figure it all out.

When Richland testified, he admitted that he was the author of the offending editorial and that the source of the information utilized therein was Gwendolyn. He also readily admitted that he had not attempted to verify the accuracy of the arrest assertion through any other source and was not aware of any official statement issued by law enforcement authorities to the effect that Nadine had been arrested.

With regard to the story that appeared in the December edition of the *Globe* in the "Stories with Happy Endings" column, Richland denied he had reviewed the piece prior to publication. He stated he was responsible for printing the apology and ultimately Gwendolyn's termination. He was unable to explain why the newspaper had not printed a retraction and apology relative to the article and editorial that formed the basis of the libel claim. In retrospect, he said he would have done so.

Nadine was the quintessential plaintiff-witness. She was a blend of all the qualities attorneys think of in their definition of the ideal witness. Unlike Gwendolyn, it was easy to identify with Nadine. She did a great job describing the emotional distress generated by the *Globe* through Gwendolyn and Richland without being ultra-dramatic. She established the falsity of the various assertions and innuendos and the malice-driven motives of the defendants, particularly the devil's scribe.

Charlie's summation was more emotional than even he intended. Starting with the heart-wrenching story of being dropped off at an orphanage, having endured the pain and anguish of rejection and a physical deformity, having overcome all the bad cards she had been dealt and rising to prominence as an award-winning journalist, it had all been for naught. She was reduced to a pile of rubble, at least in her own mind and in the minds of her family, friends, neighbors and acquaintances, thanks to the massive and pervasive campaign waged by her jealous competitor. What Gwendolyn did was unforgivable. "The willful, deliberate and malicious intensity with which Gwendolyn undertook to discredit, malign and humiliate Nadine shocks the sensitivities of even the most hardened," Charlie told the jury. "Gwendolyn became more brazen with each stroke of the pen."

Less than two hours after receiving the case, the

jury returned its verdict. On the first claim for relief, libel, they awarded actual damages of $1,000,000 and, at the bifurcated phase, punitive damages in the same amount as against each of the three defendants. On the second claim for relief, publication of private facts or invasion of privacy, they awarded actual damages again of $1,000,000 and, at the bifurcated phase, punitive damages in the same amount as against Gwendolyn and the *Globe*. On the third claim for relief, intentional infliction of emotional distress, they awarded damages of $2,000,000 against Gwendolyn and the *Globe* and $1,000,000 against Richland.

The jurors flocked around Nadine after the verdict was announced and judgment entered thereon, offering a mix of condolences and congratulations. Some were apologetic because the award hadn't been higher. Charlie thought $15,000,000 wasn't too shabby considering the insurance coverage was only $5,000,000. He asked Nadine what she was going to do with another newspaper, especially one she was probably going to own.

The amount of the award wasn't as important as the verdict in their favor. Nadine had pledged to donate her award to St. Vincent de Paul Orphanage the same as she had done with the Pulitzer Prize money. Charlie would be doing the same thing with his attorney's fees. He never thought he would ever earn a fee of $3.75 million, let alone donate such an amount to charity.

The law had not finished with Gwendolyn. Placing the blame on Maurice for the HIPAA violation didn't work. Gwendolyn was facing imprisonment and a fine and had finally reached the end of her demon-inspired journey. In Gwendolyn's case, no bad deed would go unpunished. In Nadine's case, she would rest in the comfort that good ultimately prevails over evil and that it pays to take the high road and stray not from the straight and the narrow.

The Mastersons prevailed in their lawsuit and received awards totaling $5.5 million. To pay off the judgments in the two cases, the newspaper would take out bankruptcy and ultimately their fixed assets would be sold to a printing company. What few personal assets the Cardinellos had, even with their statutory exemptions, would go toward the judgments and other costs. Penniless and without a job, Gwendolyn blamed Maurice for her woes and filed for divorce. Maurice did not contest it and moved to Emporia after his release from prison. His memory of Gwendolyn would be in the form of recurrent nightmares.

As for Gwendolyn, she, for all intents and purposes, had literally been cast into the fiery furnace of hell, no longer able to roam the earth with impunity. With her wings clipped, or more aptly, her pitchfork removed, Gwendolyn could no longer raise havoc on the world. Her wickedness and malevolence would follow her into eternity and they, together with excruciation and torment would be her constant companions. And, worst of all, she had no one but herself to blame.

# EPILOGUE

The intent little canine bustled about like a bumble bee in her self-absorbed snobbery, probing anything and everything that looked suspicious. With her button-like snout as her compass, she sniffed her way in a zigzag pattern across the cuts between two now snow-barren ski slopes. Unabashed, unafraid, and uninhibited she darted towards every sound the woods proffered. Undaunted, she flushed and chased everything, large or small, that walked, ran, crawled or flew. The size and color of an all-white cotton tail, the family Bichon Frise, who answered to the name of Maya—when she felt like it—completely ignored all commands, and was unruly at best. When she returned from her jaunt, her coat covered in dirt and burrs, she was not endearing herself with the Masterson clan.

Mount Werner was just as inviting in the summer as it was in the winter. Its stately pines and Colorado blue spruce flourished. Without the deep snow, however, the countryside looked somewhat exposed and exuded a whole new aura. Some liked its summer beauty more than even its winter wonder. Clarice had grown up liking both.

Now in their late eighties, Clarice and Bing were still hiking the trails of Mount Werner, always fascinated by its views and sights. They were never disappointed because there was always something breathtaking they had not observed before. Helping them enjoy mother nature and keeping them young, as they would boast, were three of their grandchildren, Kate, age seven, Emily, age five, and Kirstin, age three. The girls were spitting images of their mother and spent almost as much time with their grandparents as they spent with their own parents. The girls loved Steamboat Springs and were coaxing their parents to move there. Most of the summer and much of the winter already was being spent in Steamboat. Although the Masterson's daughter, the girls' mother, was in favor of the move, her husband, who was heading up the family business in the state of Kansas, was understandably unable to acquiesce—at least for the foreseeable future.

The girls' parents had taken a side excursion and would be meeting them at a prearranged spot near the top of the mountain. As the five, with Maya in the lead, neared the picnic area, an area that had been Clarice and Bing's favorite spot, they could see that lunch had been set out and was waiting for them. With Kate, Emily and Kirstin racing towards them and Maya yelping excitement, the girls' parents, who were embracing each other, embraced them. The circle of intimacy was soon expanded to accommodate the girls' grandparents.

With the sun resting high in the blue of the

Colorado July sky, all looked with wonder at the vast expanse of the lush Yampa Valley below.

"I feel like I'm sitting on top of the world," Nadine exclaimed. Turning and looking into the deep, dark, inviting eyes of Bat, she asked, "Darling, have I died and gone to heaven?"

"I never thought I would ever be ecstatic about learning that I was adopted," Bat said. "But, I wouldn't trade you for anything. Neither of us has died, but all of us have gone to heaven."

Clasping Nadine's hands tightly, Clarice whispered, "Amen. Now I can face my maker in peace"

The hurts of the past diminished with the passing of the seasons, and soon they were lost in obscurity. Only the good memories lingered, and they foretold of the things that were yet to come. Nadine would someday tell her children, grandchildren, and great-grandchildren: *Live with excited expectation. God has great things in store for you. Wisdom breeds tolerance and forgiveness, and tolerance and forgiveness breeds love and peace.*

On April 15, 2010, the governor of Kansas signed into law a state shield law for reporters. Kansas became the thirty-eighth state in the nation to do so, thanks in no small part to the efforts of the Kansas Press

Association, Nadine and others like her. As a result of
the new law, reporters in Kansas no longer are
compelled to disclose the identity of their confidential
source unless it is firmly established that the information
is relevant to the controversy, cannot be obtained by
other reasonable means and there is a compelling
justification for disclosure.

# About the Author

*Carroll Multz* has authored or co-authored twelve books and technical manuals. This is his fifth novel. A trial lawyer for over forty years, a former two-term district attorney, assistant attorney general, and judge, he has been involved in cases ranging from municipal courts to and including the United States Supreme Court. Multz's high profile cases have been reported in the *New York Times, Redbook Magazine* and various police magazines. He was one of the attorneys in the Columbine Copycat Case that occurred in Fort

Collins, Colorado in 2001 that was featured by Barbara Walters on ABC's *20/20*. Now retired, Multz is an Adjunct Professor at Colorado Mesa University in Grand Junction, Colorado, teaching law-related courses at both the graduate and undergraduate levels.